THE
SALUDA RIVER
SIGHTING

Glenn D. Parham

G. D. PARHAM

THE
SALUDA RIVER
SIGHTING

TATE PUBLISHING & Enterprises

Published by Tate Publishing & Enterprises, LLC
127 E. Trade Center Terrace | Mustang, Oklahoma 73064 USA
1.888.361.9473 | www.tatepublishing.com

Tate Publishing is committed to excellence in the publishing industry. The company reflects the philosophy established by the founders, based on Psalm 68:11,
"The Lord gave the word and great was the company of those who published it."

Book design copyright © 2011 by Tate Publishing, LLC. All rights reserved.
Cover design by Amber Gulilat
Interior design by Sarah Kirchen

Published in the United States of America

ISBN: 978-1-61777-197-2
Fiction / Science Fiction / Adventure
11.03.08

For Tara.

TABLE OF CONTENTS

CHAPTER 1

Dad is our cautious weatherman. He spends many winter nights on our front porch, watching for a winter front. He has years of experience that let him know when heavy snow will fall. It is late night. I can hear his footsteps as he nervously walks back and forth, watching the cold night sky.

He says, "Because an arctic cold front can bring about changes in nature, even bringing death, as much as possible it is always best to be prepared." Nevertheless, some changes cannot be avoided, such as when nature is forced to change. While listening to loose boards creak on the front porch, I stand next to the heater, warming myself. I want to ask him to come inside, but his stubborn persistence will cause him to shout, "In a little while, James. In a little while!"

I stay close to the heater but am never warm enough. Outside, wind blows hard against the cabin. It makes an eerie howling sound as grandmother's old clock strikes twelve times. It is now time for Dad to come inside and make sure fire is still crackling in the heater. Finally, he comes in nearly frozen like a Popsicle, stomping his cold feet against the floorboards. He passes by me and then speaks. However, cold air numbs his face, causing words to come out slowly.

"The clock's clanking sound reminds me of my knees knocking together. That icy wind blows hard tonight, James!" Dad shivers, pressing his hands against the sides of his face. "I can hardly speak!"

While he rubs his hands together briskly, Dad shakes like a leaf and makes his way to the heater. He stands with his backside against the hot stove, warming himself, close enough to scorch his pants. Dad spies his blue flannel pajamas draped across the back of his favorite chair. Mom leaves them there as an invitation every night. She is already in bed. Dad takes hold of the chair's armrest.

With little effort, he turns himself around toward their bedroom and shouts, "I am going to sit here for a while, Ina! My toes feel frostbitten!"

Before Dad sits down, his rough hand brushes a thin coat of dusty coal cinders off his chair, something else for Mom to sweep away. Finally, he plops his cold, tired body down into a soft cushion. He doesn't say much. He is just trying to thaw. While rubbing his hands together, he talks softly to me.

"Christmas Eve is passing away, James." He then leans forward over the heater. "This hot heater sure feels good. It is so windy and cold out there! Shouldn't you be in bed, Son?"

He stretches and yawns as he leans back in the chair. Soon Dad looks over to grandmother's old clock and realizes how late it is. Christmas morning is coming. Just the same, tonight is somewhat like any other cold winter night.

He must go out one more time into the winter to take care of things. Dad opens the front door, letting a cold burst of winter into the room before shutting the heavy, hinged door again. It is time to get more coal for the heater, close the hen house door, and draw water from the well. Mom cooks with it in the morning. Even though dressed warmly, the icy wind chills him to the bone, so he works quickly and hurries back to the warm cabin.

Once more, I watch Dad stomp the cold from his feet and body. Before he puts his blue flannel pajamas on, he needs to stoke our heater with black, nasty coal. Everyone hates to heat with the stuff. I have heard it from him a million times. He complains about black stains left on his hands and clothes. It doesn't matter. As hard as he tries, grimy grit always gets all over him.

Mom is snug in bed. Nevertheless, after hearing him stoke the fire, she shouts, "Make sure you get that nasty stuff off you before coming to bed, Jack. Don't want that black grime on me or my clean sheets!"

Mom's disappointment reflects in her voice. I know she hates the way we live. I hate to see her so unhappy. Without a doubt, tomorrow is another day, and good things can happen.

I like to end my day on the front porch, observing the stars. All I can do tonight is stare out the window into a dimly lit night. A full moon glows, dimly obscured by cloudy skies. It is quite late. Darkness falls fast this time of year, and I never stay up this late, but it is Christmas Eve. Now that Dad is inside, I had better get to bed. I leave him at the heater and then open the door to my room. Shut off from the rest of the cabin, the cold air in here prickles my skin with goose bumps. Jack Frost is already nipping at my heels. My room is the coldest room in the house. After climbing in bed, I pull my heavy quilts snugly around my neck, shaking under the still-frigid sheets. I grumble to myself with vapor rising from my mouth, "I should have opened my door earlier and let some warmth enter."

As I lie in bed, shivering under the heavy quilts, I stare at a small hole in the ceiling with tired, heavy eyes. I can see a mouse looking down at me. His dark brown eyes are wide open while whiskers twitch about. He too waits for Christmas morning. My furry companion will carry away any morsels left over from our meager meal. I know it is the coldest night yet. I can feel it in my bones. In bed, but not so cold now, I listen to soft footsteps as they approach. Mom is now out of bed. As she tucks my bedcovers tightly in around me, I feel Mom's warm hands.

"There now. That should keep you nice and toasty, James. You're as snug as a bug."

She kisses me on my head then walks away. After settling in, my body rests heavily in the warmth of my bed. I soon drift off to sleep. Not long after drifting off, I sense Dad open my door. The door's squeaky hinges slowly wake me. As he pokes his head in, he reminds me of a turtle coming out of its shell.

"There will be deep snow Christmas morning, Son!"

Why did he wake me? Before closing my eyes again, it occurs to me that for the past few days Dad has spent a lot of time pacing around the cabin. He always needs something to do, a kind of busybody. He gets in Mom's way a lot, so she barks at him. Mostly it happens when Mom is busy and Dad watches her prepare our bread.

Mom has a favorite saying when she is stumbling over Dad's feet in the small kitchen: "Jack, can you go find something to do?" She then mutters under her breath, "I declare, the man needs to get out and find something to do! He spends too much time in the kitchen around me."

After Dad leaves my room, I go back to sleep, dreaming of Mom making chocolate rolls for Christmas.

Soon, twilight breaks through my bedroom window. Still stretching and yawning, I manage to wake enough to sit at the edge of my bed. My warm feet are not yet touching the cold floor. To hold myself up in bed, I rest my hand on my headboard. Dad's skillful hand carved Hansel and Gretel leaving breadcrumbs in the forest. As I look at it, my fingers trace the rough designs his knife left in the soft pine.

This is a special day. Demanding my reverence, the morning sun spreads a rainbow of iridescent colors of pink and blue across my room. They proclaim this wonderful day. Today, I turn twelve, but his birthday is important too.

My feet, now cold, have slipped back under my warm covers. Finally, I push the heavy quilts off me. To see how cold the floor is, I slide my feet over the edge of the bed to the floor. Quickly, I rush by Mom and to the front door. In my mind, I am painting a picture of a snowy Christmas morning. Mom is standing beside the heater in her furry bedroom slippers. Hiding from view is Chester, my cat. Somewhere near the coal box, he crouches in his early morning, warm spot. He is patiently waiting for Mom to move. He likes to pounce on her feet. To him, her furry bedroom slippers look like rabbits.

"Merry Christmas, Mom."

She watches me run by her to the front door. "Stop that running through the house, James!"

I look back at her and then reach for the door. Cold as my bare feet feel, the heater always fails to warm the cabin when not stoked all night with coal. My toes hurt pressing into the wood, smooth and cold as marble. I unlock the front door and stand in the doorway.

"Look, Mom, at all the snow. It's so beautiful!" I hold the door open as long as I can before Dad says something.

Deep snowdrifts cover the ground. It is windy. As snow makes its way to the ground, it swirls about furiously. Suddenly, with a chilling blast of cold air, large flakes rush into the house. They slowly melt, leaving the floor wet.

"Close the door, James! You're freezing me to death."

Before closing the door, I look toward the heater where Dad sits. It is hot and glowing red. Again, Dad is close enough to scorch his pajamas. One of these days, he is going to do it again—catch his pant leg on fire.

He holds a cup firmly with both hands, sipping on a hot cup of cocoa. After sliding himself closer, he places his cup on top of the heater. There, his cocoa gets too hot for me to drink. First thing in the morning, Mom makes it for him.

He looks my way and then shouts, "When we go rabbit hunting this morning, James, make sure you bundle up good!" He says it so loud his voice echoes around the room.

He must have something wrong with his ears this morning, too much cold air from standing on the porch. He notices his loudness himself. He then looks over at me. I stand there quiet and watch

Dad to see if he says anything, but he just turns his head toward the kitchen, where Mom is cooking breakfast. Dad's right hand scratches his head as he curiously watches her. She is a better cook than he is. Nevertheless, he still reminds her not to burn the biscuits. She just looks back at him and then rolls her eyes in a noncompliant way. Before opening the oven, she lowers the stove's warmer and then reaches in for her mittens.

Soon, a tasty aroma of biscuits fills our small cabin. It makes my mouth water. Dad looks at me, saying something about Pavlov's dog.

At that moment, Mom says, "Never mind him, James."

"Hurry up, James, and get dressed for breakfast. Bundle up good. The cabin is still a little cold." He is standing at the table, getting in Mom's way. "Don't want you getting sick."

On Christmas morning, I am the first to look under our tree. It's easy to be distracted by its decorations. Mom says I take after Dad. I think she means I am always in a hurry, cannot wait, that sort of thing. Remembering what Mom said, I stand in front of the tree and then look around it, making sure to show my patience. I am a little disappointed. I see something for Mom and something for Dad.

"Where is mine?" I ask like the spoiled child I am.

"Look closer, James." Dad wants me to labor for it. He sits patiently in his chair, observing the formalities, but he really wants to get out of the house.

With little effort, he rises from his chair without saying anything. There is only a brief sigh. He then points to something hidden by our Christmas tree. I move forward toward the tree and see it leaning against the window. My wondering is put to rest. With my right hand, I reach out and grip it firmly. Then, with my left hand, I rip the wrapping paper from around a long, thin, but somewhat heavy box.

"It's a twenty-gage shotgun!"

I greatly admire my rise in stature. It's not every day Dad trusts me with such great power.

Shreds of colorful jolly Saint Nick wrapping paper lie in a heap at my feet as I firmly hold my present with amazement. Now holding it up with my left hand, I stare at Dad's big gun still fixed in its place over the mantel. I admire my first gun, running my hands along the smooth, cool metal. It's my first time having a weapon of my own.

"I have never fired a twenty-gage, Dad. The shell chamber looks huge."

Proudly holding it in my hands, I really want to be out on the trail. There, I can fire it, feel how hard it kicks against my shoulder, and hope it doesn't knock me down.

"Hurry, James. Bundle up, and let's get underway!" He says it firmly.

"Right, Dad. I'm right behind you!" I say it firmly back at him.

Not only does Dad want to bed a rabbit in the snow this morning, but Daisy, our milk cow, did not come to the barn last night. Mom and Dad are concerned. Most of the time, Daisy finds her way home; but winter is harsh, and deep snow did fall overnight.

Standing tall and erect, he is now in the front yard, shouldering his shotgun, waiting on me. I close the door and then follow behind him. Now we are off to the river bottom to fetch Daisy. Rabbit hunting, he calls it. Usually, when she doesn't come home, Daisy is there grazing on tall, yellow grass left over from summer, and going there is about a mile hike. While holding the big gun's barrels, Dad's strong hands grip the gun's cold, heavy, blue iron. He loves it more than most things. It is one of those old, long-barreled, rabbit-eared guns. When he fires it, it makes a horrible sound. I have to press my fingers into my ears to muffle its loud, scary noise.

Clouds moved back in this morning, but it's not snowing hard now. Nevertheless, big flakes are still falling. Beauty can be deceiving. It looks inviting, beckoning, come on out here and enjoy a good time. Out here, the weather is still freezing. Not far from the cabin, we make our way down a snow-covered dirt road toward the river.

"Look at the big flakes, James." He speaks without turning his head around, but I still hear him.

"Slow down!"

"Stay behind me, Son, so you don't get shot. Try to keep up."

"Dad, the snow is deep. Your long legs take two steps to my one!" If it weren't true, I would not have said so.

"How long have you been out of the army?"

He jerks his head around, looking at me with his piercing gaze as if to say, "Why did you ask that question, James?"

I look up at him, shrug my shoulders, and grin. I then quickly glance out through the snow-covered field. Quietly, I snuggle into my coat and then speak to myself in a quiet voice, "Dad is marching again!"

"Oh, about two years. I came out about two years ago. Why do you ask?"

"Mom said you still act like a soldier sometimes."

He stands silent for a moment and then speaks. "I will have to talk to your Mom about that, Son." He tries not to smile at me while I stand there, shivering, with snow nearly up to my knees.

So that he does not hear me, I whisper, "It is so cold this morning!" I manage to get the words out through my shivering lips.

"Button up your coat so you don't freeze to death."

He must have heard my whispers. Anyway, I do have my coat buttoned up. While trailing behind him, I start hearing the roaring of river rapids. We are now nearing the river bottom. There is just one higher place in the road and then it's downhill all the way.

He says nothing about the river noise but does notice measly little varmint tracks. "Look, James. Rabbit tracks. Let's follow them and see where they go." Dad crouches down, sinking his knobby knees into the snow, carefully looking at the tracks. "I don't see how he gets around on top of the snow like that, James. He will need bigger feet to walk in this stuff. It's starting to come down again."

Taking a slow, deep breath, Dad stands up then looks around. He says the cold air clears his sinus. For a moment, vapor hides his cold face, causing ice to form on his not-so-shaven face. "James, don't drift back too far."

Everywhere I go, he watches my every move. Knowing he knows best, I stay close to him, attach myself like a statue, and listen to his every word.

Most of the time I trudge quietly, waiting for him to say something to me. Down the snow-covered dirt road, he walks on. Distracted by the sounds of river water, I take my eyes off him and then look toward the river bottom. The bottoms are mostly fields of tall, yellow grass and blackberry briars surrounded by hardwood forest. There, the river flows alongside great fields. A lone young rabbit nibbles on a blackberry vine. Wondering if we should pursue the measly rodent, I turn toward Dad.

"Dad, the snow is getting deeper as we get closer to the river." Pointing my twenty-gage at my prey, I grin. "Mr. Rabbit should have stayed in his warm bed."

Dad stands beside me, blocking the wind from biting my cold body. Not saying anything, he looks down at me all wide-eyed.

"Spoken like a true rabbit hunter, James. On a snowy day like this, we can track him to his bed. What do you say, James? Do you want to blow him to pieces with your twenty-gauge? Or, while he is snug in his bed, be merciful and hit him in the head with a stick."

Snug in bed; that is where I should be, not caught up in traditions. His ancestors must have started this hunting thing on Christmas Day.

"Dad, you make it sound so terrible. You do it. If he runs, maybe I'll blast him."

Dad walks farther. "Stay behind me," he repeats.

Following orders, I drift back, watching the snowflakes cover little tracks. Suddenly, a chilling blast of icy wind blows snow through the trees into my face. To lessen the chill, I turn my head away from the wind and then pull my stocking hat over my cold, numb face. Just in time, a branch heavy with snow breaks loose, throwing me to the ground.

Dad lowers the big gun from his shoulder, turns, and faces me. "Are you all right, little man?"

He spreads a little sympathy my way. Trying not to let me see his face, I know there is a smirk behind his icy whiskers. Still, he fixes his face toward the roaring river.

"Yes, sir, I'm fine. Thank you." Looking down at my shoes, I feel humiliated.

After rising to my feet, I brush the snow off and walk toward him. Suddenly he stops dead still in his tracks. I am still a little perturbed from my treatment. A moment ago, I was the focus of a humorous pitfall. Now, for some reason, his demeanor shifts toward survival. I think he has been out in the cold too long. I still try to watch him. Now, with his fist tight and finger pointing, he violently stabs at a place down toward the river. He seriously captures my attention. Then, hurriedly, he points toward a stand of trees. They are not too far off our beaten path.

"James, take cover!"

No time for questions, I make a mad dash for trees, looking for a place I can hide.

"Dad, why do all this for a measly rabbit?"

Because wind is swishing about through snow-covered pine trees, he doesn't hear me. With all of his concentration, he focuses on something close to the river. After running from the snow-filled dirt road, I hide behind a large, curly barked hickory tree. I pray I am hiding from view and then press tightly against the tree's thick, rough bark. There I remain perfectly still, not even a flinch from me.

Slowly, I look up into the enormous tree. Beside its great trunk, it towers over me, quickly pressing myself into snowdrift at its base. I then blend in like one of the old tree's protruding knots. With eyes still fixed on Dad, as if leading a platoon, he motions for me to come to him. Before leaving my cold bed of snow, I hear a loud, dreadful scream echo through the forest. This noise is so loud it shakes snow powder loose from low-hanging branches.

A nippy, gusting wind blows falling powder throughout the forest. Before we move again, Dad wants to see what it is. His worried eyes still scan the river bottom where he stands motionless, not even a twitch. Then, at a snail's pace, Dad slowly lowers his hand, which means, do not move.

"James!"

I try to be motionless. However, my frigid hands go deep into my pockets. I mutter to myself. "Whatever it is, I hope it's friendly!"

I stand terrified and perfectly still.

"What was that, Dad?" My mind is still fearful from the scream that forbids us to come any closer.

"Keep it down, Son!" His voice is quick, strong, and exact. He then turns to look at me. His eyes are wide open. His face is pale from what must be fear and not like my Dad at all.

"What is wrong?" From my hiding place, I look up at him, waiting for him to speak.

Not saying anything for a moment, Dad takes a deep breath. He then slowly plunges his hand into what must be a warm pocket.

However, he does not leave it in there long enough to thaw his shaky hand. Quickly, he removes two large, black, ten-gauge shotgun shells. Like a handful of wishes, he grips the shells tightly. He then looks back at me. "I am not sure if this is enough ammo." His hand shakes and his face contorts. He acts as if there are dire consequences to having only two gun shells.

"Enough for what, did you see it?"

Without answering, he crouches into the snow. Now a blank expression covers his pale face. He solemnly mumbles words too low for me to hear. Finally, Dad rises to his feet. He then stands beside a large pine tree and calmly whispers to me, "I saw something at the bottom of the hill!" Now calm and matter of fact, he continues. "It looks like something I saw some time ago in New Guinea when I was in the army. It is a real jungle place there! The natives call it *Didi*."

"*Didi*," I speak the word to myself. "What is that?"

Sighing heavily, he replies, "I don't know. I only saw it briefly this time. It resembles what attacked us in New Guinea!" He then rests the back of his head against the tree's rough, brown bark. "The *Didi* killed four of my men! It happened so fast. A loud scream, and then it disappeared into the jungle. James, did you hear it scream a few moments ago?"

"Hear it? Of course I heard it! Its scream was so loud, snow fell from the trees!" Brushing snow off my stiff coat, I ask, "Is it animal or human?"

I try to cheer him up or make a joke.

In spite of my attempts, he looks at me with scared, squinting eyes. He then softly speaks. "Son, it's both. It's both."

I stare back at him, saying the first words that enter my mind. "Are you serious?"

Suddenly, I feel a cold chill creeping in on me. I begin to shake, no longer able to keep it from spreading through my body. I want to be at home in my bed, with the covers pulled over my head, where it is warm and safe. At home, the only scary sound has been a hoot owl outside my bedroom window.

Then I remember that sometimes during the winter nights, I have heard loud screams, as if a man is being tortured. When I run to Mom and Dad in terror, they both laugh and say bobcats are screaming for a mate. After hearing the frightening screams, I never stayed outside after dark. I have also heard strange stories about the vast Saluda River area. For many years, local lore tells about monkeys swinging from the old bridge's iron framework. Now we know the nighttime screams were never bobcats. All the while, Dad was hearing the murderous creatures at night, but he forgot what the *Didi* sounded like.

"Dad, what did you see?" I ask him, hoping for reassurance that our lives are not in danger.

"I'm not sure, James, something big and hairy. We need to get closer. Stay close to me."

Dad does not return to the snow-covered dirt road. As we slowly make our way to the river, we stay in the forest. The shadowy trees keep us hidden. While he creeps through the snow, little by little, I stay close behind him.

"Dad," I whisper quietly, "can it be Daisy?"

He speaks calmly, does not want to make any loud sounds over the quietly falling snow. While staring seriously behind me, his squinting eyes look right through me toward the river. Overpowered by his haunted stare, I am not able to help myself. I have an overpowering drive to jerk my head around and look behind me. A shadowy figure stands poised in the forest across the river. I reason to myself it must be what he is watching.

Dad says nothing about the figure, but he responds to my question. "There is a bell on Daisy! We would hear it!"

"Dad, Daisy is down here somewhere!"

He knows she is, but he offers no comforting reply. I follow behind him; his grip around the old ten-gage clamps down like a vice.

I follow behind him and the grandfather of all shotguns. Stepping slowly and suspicious of every sound around him, Dad becomes more uneasy with each step taking us closer to the river. He then holds his right hand up, makes a fist, and points toward the river.

"Look over there, James. There was a struggle in the snow."

"I see it."

Before leaving the cover of so many tree trunks, we look deep into the forest, beyond what meager eyes can see. We watch for any movement, even a rabbit scratching his behind in the grassy field, but there is no sign of anything anywhere.

Still on guard, we are now at the river's bank. With the barrel of his gun, Dad spreads apart the shedding cattails. Like little white parachutes, windblown seed-spikes drift downriver. After looking inside, Dad stands still for a moment. He then speaks with a broken voice.

"What! What happened to you, Daisy?" Swallowing loudly, he wipes moisture from his mouth. His face turns red against his snow-covered coat.

"Stay there, James. It's Daisy!"

"Why should I not look? Is she all right?"

"No. She's dead! The creature I saw must have killed her!"

I want to see her. Peering into the cattails, she lies there, mutilated, her throat and stomach are torn out, still bleeding into the snow. The muscles in her partly eaten hindquarter are still twitching, not long dead. Dad glances around. His thumb is still pressing down on the big gun's hammers, ready to pull the triggers at any time.

"Nothing around here kills like this."

"Look, Dad." My mouth gapes open like a fly-catching bullfrog on a sunny spring day. "She hasn't been dead long. Steam is still rising."

Looking back at me, he brushes the snow off his coat. The big gun is in his left hand. He then points with his right hand. "Look, James. The kill was made over there. It takes a very large, strong animal to drag a heavy carcass to the riverbank." He closes the cattails and then steps back. "Remember where she is, James. As fast as the snow is falling, before long, snow will completely cover her."

"I will."

While standing over her, a chilling moment of sadness overwhelms me. No more watching her go past my window to the barn at night. I will miss her. I watch Dad as vapor rises from his breath, remembering his every word. He talks as his eyes glance up and down the wide Saluda River.

I can see what he is looking at. Spread out across the water, snow covers all the steppingstones. They make a trail that leads from one side of the river to the far bank.

"James, you have better vision. That big, flat rock in the middle of the river, does it have blood on it? Is that Daisy's bell I see?"

"Yes to both questions, Dad." He looks out across the river then down at me. "The rocks have snow on them. Stay here. You might slip. I will be right back. Hold the Belgium until I get back. I don't want it falling into the murky river." I panic when I realize he means to leave me alone on the bank. "Wait!" I shout at him in a small, meek voice. He plods across the stones toward the river crossing.

While he crosses the river, I look at the heavy gun clutched uselessly in my hands. I see that the heavy firearm is too much for me to fire and aim. Why did he give it to me? I shout, "What if the creature returns when you are gone?"

Out there, almost in the middle of the river, Dad stands on a large, flat rock that is about two feet out of the water. There, snow covers most of its surface. As he steadies himself on the rock, he then points to the far side of the river. "Look, Son. It crossed over to the other side of the river. If it screams again, it will come from over there. God only knows where it went!"

He makes me feel no safer. He is still standing on the same rock, looking down at Daisy's bell. Like a soldier, Dad looks for signs of the enemy. He looks very hard up the river and then down the river.

I shout at him again. "What are you looking for?"

Although he doesn't answer me, I said it loud enough for him to hear. I stand there afraid, biding my time, looking up into the falling snow. I then shout again.

"Dad, the snow is really starting to come down now! Can you hear me?"

Big flakes fall heavy on resting snow. Falling to the ground, they make a creepy sound. You know, it is something hard to describe. It must be a warning to get out of here. Nevertheless, Dad is still standing out there. Now I can barely see him. Standing in one place, fidgeting about in the loose snow, I feel abandoned, separated from him. One more time, I take a deep breath and then shout.

"Dad, did you hear what I said?"

Finally, I catch sight of him. He is carefully making his way back across the river, stepping from one snow-covered rock to the other. I wait where he left me. I then look down at Daisy. Snow is covering her lifeless body.

"What were you doing out there?"

"I was looking at Daisy's bell and some tracks in the snow."

Now that he is back, I return his ten-gage. I feel safer knowing it is in his hands.

"What kind of tracks?" I ask him.

"Can't make them out; there is too much snow covering them. But something did cross here."

While Dad investigates the river, snowfall completely covers my grief lying in the snow. I know he too feels safer back with the ten-gage. Feeling more at ease now, I reach for my little twenty-gage and then look up at him. While he grips the heavy gun, his large hand swings down beside me. I feel dwarfed, standing beside him. After placing his hand on my head, he looks down at me.

"Son, someday you will be the master of this big gun. Not long from now, you will fire it and remain standing."

Speaking softly, he smiles at me. He must sense how small I feel. Grateful, I then look in the direction of home.

"Let's go home, Dad! I'm getting hungry."

More than hungry, I am scared and want to be at home, where it is safe and warm.

"Dad, maybe we'll see a rabbit when we go home. I do not want to be down here any longer! Can't we take some of Daisy back home for supper?"

"That's good thinking, James. Luck is on our side. I keep my knife with me."

He reaches for the blade on his hip. Smiling as he reaches for it, he pulls a long, sharp hunting knife from a worn-out sheath emblazed with *US Army*. Reaching out with his arm, he leans his gun against a dead tree.

After crouching down on his knees, he grips the knife tightly. Like a chef slicing a rump roast, the razor-sharp edge glides through Daisy's still-warm carcass. Soon, she will turn to ice. Now standing up, Dad wipes the bloody blade on his trousers and then slides it back into its sheath.

"Let's get out of here, James."

The snow is still falling. It makes the road hard to see. To make a step, I lift my legs high over the snow. The way I walk reminds me of what Dad calls goose-stepping. He always says something bad about the German soldiers.

"Look, Dad! Goose-stepping! Is this how the German soldiers did it?"

I should not ask that question. Immediately, with an expression as cold as a winter's night, he hesitantly speaks. "I don't think you would make a good German soldier, Son."

I try to keep up with him, but walking uphill away from the river bottom is hard on me. Perhaps I should take his mind off what I asked him.

"My legs are getting tired."

"James, I know the snow is getting deeper. Hang in there a little while longer. Soon we will be home."

Sometimes I wonder who I am—a soldier or a son.

Not so far away, I see dark, black smoke drifting our way. It can only be coming from our chimney. Watching it fall to the ground, the smoke settles fast on a cold day like this. I hate to have it around me. We will have to hurry. Thank God the cabin is not far away. Then I remember that there will be no more listening to Daisy's bell when she passes by our cabin.

"Dad, you forgot Daisy's bell!"

For the moment, Dad wants to forget the awful things that happened to Daisy. Her bell will be another reminder hanging on the front porch. He acts disappointed, kicking snow into the air, mumbling words I dare not ask.

"We can get it another day." I hope to cheer him up.

Finally, we are nearing home and none too soon. I tire from lifting my feet over the deep snow. Dad's gun is still in hand and Daisy's remains in the other.

I run for the door and swing it open. Worn, squeaky hinges announce our arrival. Dad goes in first. Mom looks like springtime, standing near the heater, wearing a long, flowery dress. It's bright, yellow sunflowers. She reaches for a broom.

While looking down at me, Mom stops what she is doing and places the palms of her hand on top of the broom handle. With a voice like an angel, she speaks. "James, all of the warm air is rushing out the front door. Be sure you close it back. What does Dad have there? It doesn't look like you've been rabbit hunting to me."

"Mom, our cow is dead! No more Daisy!"

Dropping the broom, her hands fall to her side. Mom gasps, "What happened?"

CHAPTER 2

Mom stands close to dad as he carves the rump roast into meal-sized portions. "Jack, what are you doing with the rest of Daisy? We need the beef."

"Yes. I know, Ina. She will not waste."

Mom always looks out for the family. She has a good reason to. This is the worst winter yet, a bad time for making money.

"Dad, are you going back to the river tomorrow to get the rest of Daisy?"

"Yes, Son, if I can get there with Mr. Valentine's old tractor."

Before dark, Dad will leave and go to Mr. Valentine's house.

"Jack, when are you coming back?" Mom does not want him to leave.

"I'll be back as soon as I can, Ina. I need to be there before it gets too late!"

He keeps going away, never breaking his stride. Standing on the front porch, I watch him walk steadily toward the old man's house. He wants to hurry back. No telling what might happen with those creatures still out there.

"Come in and shut the door, James." While shaking her head, Mom mutters, "Your dad behaves as if he's living in a barn, always waiting for someone else to close the door."

Mom expresses her disappointment, feelings of hopelessness toward a situation she has little control over, waiting for Dad to change the way we live. My eyes glance back at Mom. I see the desperation on her face and then watch Dad's distant form disappear toward the old man's house.

While on my way to Mr. Valentine's house, I look back to see James disappear into our dimly lit cabin, knowing with every step that I get closer to Mr. Valentine's house. I do hope he is home.

Safe on a limb overhead, a familiar sound breaks a calm, lifeless night. An owl perches overhead in a high oak tree. It is James's feathered friend. It looks like the one that lives outside his window in the hollow tree. As deep as the snow is, what can he possibly catch on a snow-covered night like this? Keep a keen eye, Mr. Owl. It is a dark, silent night not good for hunting.

Another distant sound echoes in the night. What is that? It sounds like Daisy's cowbell. It cannot be! I must be hearing things. I step onto Mr. Valentine's porch with my footsteps hollow against the creaking wood. With his back to me, I can see him sitting in front of his pot-bellied stove. Everybody around here has one. His hearing is poor, so I raise my fist and hammer hard on his thick, wooden door. Mr. Valentine senses everything. He is mostly deaf, not blind.

Immediately, he notices me standing on his porch. Slowly, his tired, old bones rise from his warm chair. He once told me, "I have a good heart, Jack, but am worn out from the waist down. I can hardly walk." More so, he is quite right, worn out from working his fingers to the bone on this old farm. Like a tired, old turtle crossing a country road, he slowly shuffles his way to the door and then opens it. "Youngster, what are you doing out on a cold night like this?" Like the fire in his heater, his voice crackles with each breath. He must be coming down with a cold.

"Good evening, Mr. Valentine. Are you keeping warm?"

"What? You'll have to talk louder, son. Lost my hearing in the war!"

With few words as possible, I speak to him in a loud voice. "I need your tractor!"

Mr. Valentine leans his right ear toward me. "What'd you say?"

I shout, "I need your tractor!" I try to speak to him loud enough the first time. Sometimes I think it is more old habits than bad hearing.

"Sure. What are you doing with a tractor? You can't work the soil in this kind of weather."

"No, sir, my milk cow is dead! I need to fetch her from the river bottom!"

He reaches out his frail right hand then takes hold of my arm, pulling me inside. "Come in by the fire, son, and let's get warm."

He is a good old man. He treats my family like his own, but he will talk the horns off a billy goat.

"Here, son. Take this pad. Write it down. Tell me what happened to Daisy."

He gives me a pencil with no point. I then stand up from my chair, reach into my pocket, and pull out my little, green, Case pocketknife. My father gave it to me before he died. I want to make sure I do not leave it here. I sharpen his pencil as wood shavings fall around the stove much like squirrels dropping pine nuts from a lofty tree.

Facing me, he can read lips. "Is your family staying warm in that little cabin?"

"Yes. It stays nice and comfortable as long as we keep a fire going!"

I lean back in the chair then place the tip of my pencil on the paper, wondering how I should begin telling him my story. My tired body tells me it has been a long day. I do not feel like going deep into what happened on the river bottom this morning, even though, like a heavy rock, it still lies solid on my mind. There is probably more than one of those creatures. Them being so close to James and Ina, it burdens me to no end.

Having nothing better to write on, he gives me paper torn in places, old and worn from age. I used this same thick paper in the first grade. Reaching down, I brush snow from my coveralls before it turns to water. I struggle to write a few lines, describing what I think I saw moving among the cattails on the riverbank. It is so hard to see what I am writing. Not much light comes from his smoky-colored lantern. It flickers like dancing candlelight. Mr. Valentine keeps nodding his head until his chin rests against his chest. I should hurry so he can get some sleep.

Finally, I finish writing, tuck the pencil behind my ear, and push the paper into his outreached hand. Half asleep, he slowly reaches into his gray flannel shirt pocket. His stiff, swollen fingers fumble with wire-rimmed glasses, scratched with age. Smudged coal dust still covers their worn, hazy lenses.

"Here, Mr. Valentine. Let me help you."

Like him, his glasses are old, fragile, and needing care. I clean them the best I can and then give them back to him. He fits the earpieces around his ears and then pushes the rims toward his nose. At his age, there is no reason to hurry. His eyes squint. Seeming interested in what I wrote, he looks at the words curiously. I look at his aged face and wonder how his life had been growing up during Depression days. Did it make an old miser out of him? Is that why no electricity is in his house?

When we moved in, I asked him about wiring our little log cabin. He held his head down, stirring his foot around in circles, and then he hesitantly spoke.

"You kids don't need that stuff!"

I am taken back in time while he reads what I wrote. Firelight flickers on his aged, wrinkled face. He reminds me of my father. My father died some years ago. It still feels like yesterday. My eyes fix on

Mr. Valentine. Sitting across from me quiet as a mouse, he sits there, reading my words, mumbling just like my father.

Then, like a creeping chill from a cold winter's night, his face slowly changes from serene to fright. His expression becomes increasingly serious. He lifts his dowdily covered eyes up to me as he speaks.

"Put some more coal in the fire for me, son."

I get up from my squeaky rocking chair; go to a nearly empty wooden box, and then gather a handful of the black, filthy stuff. I wonder what is on his mind. I slide aside the hot, round eye from the top of the heater and then drop in coal. Wanting to be free, the orange flaming embers try to leap out of the heater.

"Turn the damper down for me, son. Sit back down." As he leans forward in his chair, he places the palm of his hand under his chin. "Tell me what you did, Jack."

Yes. Just like Dad, leave it to me to do something wrong. I write on the old, tan, decrepit paper, *What do you mean, Mr. Valentine?* I give him back the writing paper.

"Jack! Did you take anything from the site?"

Not knowing exactly what he means, I write the first thing that comes to my mind.

I took some meat from her.

"How much did you take? Did you take all of it?"

"Not yet. I took just enough for supper, why?"

I watch his face and mouth form the right words to say.

"They kill because they are hungry."

They kill? I wait on him to make a long story short. If I do not hurry, Ina will be on her way here.

"I had an encounter with them many winters ago. In nineteen oh two, when I first came here. That's when I built the cabin you live in."

Still sitting in his rocker, he holds onto his chair and then slides it around to face me.

"When I first built your house, my wife and I lived there for twenty years. She was a beautiful girl. I love her so much. God bless her heart. I miss her so much."

He still has tears in his eyes for her. I feel so sorry for him, spending his life alone with only memories. Makes me think of Ina, how fortunate I am to have her.

"Mr. White said this is the worst winter in fifty years." I interrupt him.

"It is a bad one all right, but it's been longer than that. He is in his seventies. Been in that general store for a long time, but I'm much older than him."

Out of kindness, I sit in a hard chair and yawn. Trying to stay awake from a tiring day, I let him talk. He hardly ever talks to anyone.

"Of course, Mr. Valentine, you have seen a lot take place around here."

He looks straight into my eyes. "Jack, I know you are struggling. During the winter, everything is in short supply around here. No one gets enough work to buy food. Like you, I also turned to hunting and fishing for food. You might not believe me, Jack, but you're competing with a creature whose survival instinct is just like humans."

I sit there with dead concentration on every word coming out of his mouth, knowing not to interrupt him again.

"Jack, they don't want humans around them. You took what they consider theirs. When are you going back to the river?"

Oh, bother! Some Christmas day this is turning out to be. That northerner is responsible for this. Last night, standing on the front porch, looking north, I did have dreadful thoughts but did not see this coming. This gives a new meaning to going to the river.

"Tomorrow, Mr. Valentine. James wants to go with me. Because it's so cold, Ina said something to James about waiting till the temperature rises a few degrees."

Mr. Valentine continues. "Now everything is a risk."

Taking James to the river does not have the same meaning. Still, he wants to go with me. Most of the time I am working, do not have much opportunity to spend time with him. I know what it is like not to have a father to spend time with growing up.

"Good. If you take him, make sure he stays in your sight at all times. I know they snatch children. Parents seldom see their youngsters again."

Hearing him tell me to watch out for James, he reminds me of Ina. She is forever telling me to keep an eye on him. I always keep him within sight.

"Because of our confining situation, I can't let Daisy die in vain, Mr. Valentine. We need the food."

"Yes. I know. If you go back for your cow, be on guard. They will most likely want to keep it for themselves."

"True enough, but they are no match for the Belgium gun. Where do they come from anyway? What are they doing here?"

"They stay somewhere in the mountain area where the Saluda River begins. In the Great Smokies when food gets hard to find, the creatures follow the river here, looking for food."

Our little family has lived here for quite a while. I admit, sometimes in the evening, loud screams reach my ears from the river. That is not strange. Some creatures are hard to identify. Driven by the lure of plenty on the bottoms and the river, they never come close enough to harm anyone, whatever they might be. That is, until now.

"Mr. Valentine, when did you come in contact with them?"

It seems like people see them in the winter mostly. I swear I also hear their screams during the summer months. However, they never leave the river; not yet anyway.

Mr. Valentine continues with his story. "A day I will never forget. February nineteen twenty. In those days, sometimes I would sneak off down to the river bottom to check on my sheep. Too much hard work on the farm, it makes me want to get away. Grady, my Great Pyrenees, watched over the sheep. This old body is a wreck now. I was a youngster then. When I was a youngster, the cold made me tough. I could take anything. I felt that way then. I also liked to fish."

The old man rambles on about his past. I listen to him, knowing he will feel better telling me about his encounter with them. In addition, I need to know as much as I can about them.

"What were you and James doing down there?"

The fact is, I would not have been on the river if not for Daisy and Christmas. Before he rambles on, I reply to his question. "James likes to go hunting on my days off work. Here recently, many of my days are spent hunting. It being Christmas, James wanted a chance to fire his twenty-gage shotgun. Santa brought it to him. There is not much to do when stuck inside the cabin. To keep from being bored to death, James and I took a little hunting trip." Mr. Valentine continues on with his story.

"During the summer months, it is easy to spend a lot of time down there. You know how it is, Jack. If a lot of rain falls in the mountains, the river floods. When it is dry, you can see the rocky shoals, even walk across them. When you first get down there, if you look to the right, there is a deep hole in the bend of the river."

Tired, my mouth opens wide with a great yawn. I can hardly hold my eyes open. I then think of Ina. If I do not hurry, she will be on her way here. I try my best to hurry Mr. Valentine. "After arriving at the fishing hole, I cut a forked branch from a dogwood tree. Those dogwoods are beautiful trees that bloom white everywhere around here in springtime. That riverbank is mostly sand. I found a soft spot in the earth and then pushed the fishing pole in. You know how it is down there, Jack. The wind blows a lot around those sandy curves. With all that wind, my pole plunged to the ground several times that cold morning and made me feel like giving up. Finally, my luck started changing. Grady, he just laid there. He let me do all the talking. He and I were two old dogs. I said to him, Grady, that old, black skillet at home sure is going to make catfish taste good."

Mr. Valentine points to the floor as if talking to Grady. Grady is long gone now. He now owns another mutt. It barks at everything that moves. I let him keep talking so he can get it all out. Poor man. I know he gets awful lonely up here. If I stay here much longer, I will start talking to myself.

"Go on, Mr. Valentine, I am all ears."

"Grady, he didn't rise to the occasion. I told him to just lie there and say nothing. There was no movement out of him at all. However, nothing stays the same very long. The float bobbed around, but nothing took the bait. Then down it went. The thing went completely out of sight. That fish wanted hook, line, and sinker. I caught a big one then another. Then, like a pointer, Grady rose to his feet. He spotted something up the river. Up the river a distance, I noticed movement in the forest."

Finally, the old man gets to what I want to hear.

"After a while, I saw what looked like a person with a heavy coat on walking out on the sandbar. I said to Grady, 'That is what I need, a heavy coat to keep warm.' You know the sandbar, the one where all those mussels wash up during a storm."

Those nasty things are everywhere after a rainstorm. "Yes. I know the place. In summer, we sometimes go swimming there. Go on, Mr. Valentine. What happened next?"

"Slow down, son! Let me tell it! At first, I believed them to be people fishing."

That place is close to where I saw the creature.

"Then I heard a loud scream. Grady's ears suddenly pointed straight up. The noise really startled me. To me, it sounded like a man in great pain. Everything was easy to see. It walked upright like a human onto the sandbar. A trail crosses the river there. With his nose pointing upward, he sniffed the air. 'I think he smells my presence,' I told Grady. The creature didn't take many steps. Instead, he was cautious when he came into the open area. After that, two more came walking out of the forest, one behind the other, to the water's edge."

While he tells his story, I sit in my hard, wooden chair, astounded. He makes it sound so real. No one can make up such a tall tale.

I finally get a chance to ask him, "What do they look like?"

If the creatures are the same as my encounter, I want to confirm it. Mr. Valentine keeps talking.

"They are large and hairy, a kind of reddish brown, about seven feet tall. They look like an ape. I thought to myself, 'No apes around here.' They are a distance away yet so close. While he looked around, smelling the air, I could hear him making grunting sounds. What must have been his females; they were the last to come from that shadowy cane forest."

I know exactly the place he is talking about, all those canes in one area of the river.

"All around them, mussels wash onto the sandbar. They cracked them open, washed the sand away, and then ate them. Curiosity got the better of me. So to get a better look, I moved closer. The male then saw me. That was a mistake. He stood there for a moment, staring at me. He was just as curious about me as I was about him. He then slowly walked toward me, swinging his arms. For no reason at all, he went crazy, slinging his arms about, running to the other creatures and then back toward me. I looked behind me and started backing up. When I did, he ran toward me. 'Grady, he is not very friendly.'"

He stops for a moment, catching his breath.

"Grady was growling as if he could do something. I did not stay around to find out. He scared me so bad. I wet my pants. After scuffling around on the slippery bank, my feet found firm ground. Then, toward home, my feet scurried like a frightened chicken. Wishing won't make it any closer. Home is a long way off. Finally, I made my way to the top of the hill and then stop to look back at him, but he was nowhere in sight."

"Did he go back to the others?"

"I suppose he did. Jack, you saw them too!"

"I believe so, Mr. Valentine. Just as you say.

"The one I saw must have killed Daisy. When you saw him, Mr. Valentine, do you think he only wanted you to leave?"

"If I had stayed around, I believe he would have killed me!"

"You were no threat to him."

"Jack! If I had stayed around, no telling what he might have done. One killed your cow."

"Yes, but I made it easy for him to find her. Daisy had a bell on her."

"Whatever it was, Jack, it will be back for more."

Taking heed of his warning, I quickly rise to my feet and ready myself for the walk home. Turning back to Mr. Valentine, I said, "If you don't mind, I will be here in the morning for your tractor."

CHAPTER 3

"I will let you know what happens. Wait. I almost forgot. You need coal for your fire."

I spy a threadbare burlap bag on the front porch. Underneath a mound of snow, I find a dwindling pile of coal. I know the ice will make my hands hurt. After opening the dirty, brown bag, I place it close to the pile of frosty coal. Like icicles on a frozen day, the bag stands upright, frozen in place. It rather reminds me of a dirty snowman. All it needs is coal for eyes. Freezing my fanny off, piece by piece, I loosen the coal from its icy mound. I then toss it into the stiff, frozen bag. A swishing sound from wind blowing through pines is the only sound I hear. At last, the bag is full. Too heavy and too stiff to carry, it is easier to drag. Standing beside the old man, I know I need to hurry back home. If I do not hurry, Ina will be on the front porch, shouting for me.

"Thanks, Mr. Valentine. I will let you know what happens."

"Be careful, Jack. Always expect the unexpected."

I close the door behind me, walk off his porch, and then hurry home. I was at his house for about an hour. Once again, heavy snow starts falling. Even though snow is coming down heavy, my tracks coming from home are still visible. I stop, curiously looking around. This night is strangely silent. The only sounds I hear are the big flakes falling on frozen snow. When I look east over the cabin, every now and then a rising full moon peaks through the thick, heavy clouds.

Suddenly, silence is cut short when a great cry comes from the river. I wonder if the creatures ever leave their watery sanctuary. How many other people have seen them? Has anybody ever been killed by one? Now getting closer to the house, I see a dimly lit light coming from the cabin.

Ina frequently asks, "When are you going to put lights in this house, Jack?" She always gets the same answer: "Working in Odell's body shop, I only make fifty dollars a week. We cannot spare the money."

While on the way back to the cabin, slow going and stepping high over the deep snow, I have disturbing thoughts. I hear Daisy's bell clanging in the distance. Am I really hearing it? Telling the difference between what is real and unreal is getting hard to decide. What does such an animal want with a cowbell?

While trying to run in the deep snow, I begin to panic. The snow is too deep. I am already clumsy just trying to walk on dry ground. I cannot lift my legs up high enough. I then fall flat on my face. Feeling brainless, I lie there, covered in snow like an arctic fox hiding underneath its thick layer. *Slow down, Jack,* I say to myself. *There is nothing out there to be afraid of, only your thoughts. Collect yourself.* After getting to my feet, I finally step onto the porch, reaching for the frozen handle of the front door.

I try to get inside, but frozen ice is holding the screen door shut. Hesitating for a moment, I stand still and then look back over my shoulder. Peering out through the open field of yellow grass and snow, I think I see a hairy head slowly rise up. My imagination is getting the best of me. I have a childish feeling that something is after me.

"Let me inside!" I shout with a loud voice, pounding with all my might on the door.

I did everything but break it down. *What can she be doing?* Even though locked, my hand wraps tightly around the door's handle.

Pulling hard, still trying to pull the door free, I kick and pull with all my might, but nothing happens. Ina then appears before me.

"What is wrong with you, Jack? You almost tore the screen door off. Are those creatures out there? You keep looking back toward the field."

I pass by her and then go to the kitchen. She still stands at the door, looking outside toward the grassy field of snow. With woman's intuition, I am sure Ina knows something is going on out there. I have the same feelings myself.

"I will be glad when things go back to being normal, Jack. First, we are snowed in. And then strange creatures kill our milk cow. I hope tomorrow brings a better day. I grow tired of being in this little cabin."

Ina sighs deeply and wipes her brow. I know how she feels. There will be better days.

"Come on, darling. Sit down. It's the best part of the day, all of us around the table. Our little family, we can make it through anything that comes our way, Ina."

"Bow your head, Son. Lord, we thank you for the food on our table, and help us to accept the things we do not understand. Keep us safe through the night. Amen."

Ina looks suspiciously at me. She knows I am hiding something. My quirks always give me away. It is a good thing I am a one-woman man. I would not be able to hide anything.

"Do you like the steak I cooked?"

It is not cooking she wants to talk about.

"Yes, I do, sweetheart."

"A sad way you came by it. Do you think the rest of her will be fit to eat?"

"Mom, Dad saw what killed Daisy."

"Not now, James! It is getting late! Son, you need to finish eating and then go to bed. Ina, I'll make sure the heater fires all night."

I try not to broach the subject again until James goes to bed. Trying to keep him quiet long enough to get him in bed is impossible. Eventually, he will let everything out.

"Jack, it's going to clear off tonight. The temperature might go down to zero. You need to make sure everything outside is safe and everything is closed tight in here, or we will get cold tonight. I don't want James getting sick."

"James, you hurry up now and go to bed. So you don't get cold tonight, Mom will be in later to make sure you have plenty of covers on you."

Patting my full, round stomach I look at Ina. "Supper was wonderful, Ina. I ate too much. I'm going outside and gathering some coal for tonight."

After helping me into my coat, Ina opens the door for me. She is standing in the open doorway, watching me struggle with the heavy, frozen bag of coal.

"Jack, do you need any help with that?"

"Ina, I don't need any help. Close the door. You are letting all the heat out." She slams the door tight with no reply.

Perhaps it is not only me. She is right. Getting out of the house is what she also needs to do. First, I will drag the coal box onto the porch. Unlike Mr. Valentine's pile, I can only afford a hundred-pound bag. After removing the frozen snow from the bag, I fill the wooden box and then drag it back inside to the heater.

"Jack, I'm through with the kitchen. Is James in bed?"

I nod my head affirmatively. Ina smiles and brushes her dress, smoothing out the wrinkles.

"Now we can have a quiet evening listening to the radio."

I turn the radio on only to find the volume is fading. The batteries are getting weak. Ina looks at me with a crestfallen expression.

Now back inside with the coal, I try to explain to Ina why times are so hard right now. "Mr. White said this is the worst winter we've had in forty years."

I then go back outside and leave Ina inside the cabin. After making my way to the edge of the woods, I pull my stocking hat over my face. Its heavy wool keeps the cold wind from biting. Through a window, I can see Ina talking to herself. Confined in this closed space too long, she acts a little troubled. I close the door to the henhouse and then lock it. Now the fox won't be in the hen house and hungry bobcats won't have a reason to hang around. Off in the distant night, I hear that bell again. Old lady Wilson's house is across the field. I think she also has a cow with a bell. I am talking to myself again.

"Jack, are you all right out there?"

I yell back at her, "Darling, before long, I will come inside!"

I wonder what is up with the bell. Surely, the creatures have no use for them. If so, where are they now? I have a bad feeling about this, but sounds do carry a long way at night. Better get back inside. Ina will be calling again. In the evening, she enjoys our time together. I had better make the most of it. Not much she can do confined in this little cabin, but become overwhelmed with boredom. I step back into the warmth of our cabin.

"What time is it, Ina?"

She answers quietly, "It's almost eleven o'clock."

"Ina, if you will, wind the clock before it stops? I nearly froze out there. I want to warm my bones by the fire."

Even though I dread telling her, I know Ina needs to understand the danger surrounding our family. She deserves to know everything. I nervously rub my eyes, trying to remove the memory of Daisy's carcass and the hairy beast screaming in the woods. I take one more sip from the bottom of my cup. Nothing remains of my hot chocolate but the froth on my lip. After taking a deep breath, I begin my story.

"The old man had a lot to say about the creature that killed Daisy. They have ventured into this area at least once before."

Ina's eyes widen with surprise. "What do you mean by creature? I though Daisy was killed by a pack of wild dogs?"

"No, Ina. What I saw near the kill sight was eight feet tall, hairy, with powerful shoulders and hands. You know the place we go swimming during the summer, the sandbar. Old man Valentine saw three of them on that very same sandbar. The old man said during a bad winter, they come down from the mountains, looking for food."

Ina looks directly into my eyes.

"Do you think we are safe?"

"I think so, even though the old man said after watching them for a while, the male started running toward him and then back toward the females. He said the male made him run for his life. You know how it is in all life. The male protects his family. The creatures were not interested in us. At the time James and I were looking for Daisy, they were hungry and looking for food."

My legs ache, and I try to rub the deep soreness away. Walking around in snow is very hard work and wears me out. My limbs are weak and heavy from the effort of trudging through deep snow.

"We should go to bed a little early tonight. I will pack the heater with as much coal as possible. Then it should burn for hours. Maybe I can get some sleep before the fire burns out."

Ina rubs my shoulder with sympathy.

"I do not mind getting up and stoking the fire, Jack. You need to rest."

For a moment, I stand there, looking at her, and then briefly sigh. I hope she does not think me helpless. James long ago retreated to his room and sleeps under heavy comforters in his pajamas. Ina and I finally go to bed. Before she falls asleep, lying beside her, I get my words out.

"That's my job, sweetheart. Taking care of you and James is my job."

I lie there in bed beside her, face-to-face. She puts her arm around me. I turn over on my back and lie there, remembering what happened at the river. I remember what Mr. Valentine said to me, hoping the creatures will not come during the night. Not likely. Daisy's body is still lying beside the river. I move closer to Ina. She snuggles up to me. Her body feels soft and warm. A thought enters my mind. Daisy is frozen solid. How can they eat her? I get up and look out the window toward the river.

For peace of mind, I check on James and then spread another quilt over him. While watching him sleep, I am convinced we are blessed with him. After leaving his room, I sit down in a chair beside the heater and then turn its damper down. Before returning to bed, I check each window and the front door lock. Purposefully stepping over loose, squeaking floorboards, I make my way back to the bedroom. Now I can rest and settle in next to my sleeping Ina. Pulling the covers over my head, I snuggle up to her warm body. Soon, I fall into a deep sleep.

The night slips by without incident. Before morning, I wake only once to load the cooling heater. After lying back down, I dream there for a moment, half asleep, and then drift back into a deep slumber. Again, a dream of being at the river fills my head. It is a hot summer evening, and we are at the river cooling off, a refreshing dip on a hot summer's day. Then, in the morning, I wake when warm sunlight strikes my face. I lie there for a moment, hating to leave my warm bed. *No time to lie here. I need to get up.* Ina, warm and toasty, after pulling covers back over her head, drifts back asleep. Now wide-awake, this morning is like any other. When I open the heater, it is still hot with bright, orange embers. They warm my hands.

Nothing comes easy. This morning, I have to grapple with the coal box. Struggling, I slide it close to the fire. I also find my lost asbestos gloves under the coal box, using them to protect my hands while I fill the heater's belly. It takes a few minutes to start blazing. Ina is now banging pots and pans around in the kitchen.

"Here, Ina. Let me put these pine knots in the stove. It will get hot faster." Ina stands at the kitchen entrance as if guarding her territory.

"I can do it, Jack. You have enough to do. Who do you think does it when you are at work?"

"The milk man?"

"That's a good idea, Jack. Why don't we start getting milk delivered to our door?"

I suppose we will have to now that Daisy is gone. It should not cost much. I should say yes.

"I should have kept my mouth shut. But if you are serious, go ahead."

She says nothing else about the matter.

"What do you want for breakfast?

"Surprise me. Everything you cook is very good anyway."

I lower the oven door and look inside. Just like country living should be. The smell of Ina's hot bread hits me in the face.

"Are they brown enough on top, Jack?"

She knows my face is in the biscuits.

"Yes, dear.

They look good and smell wonderful but are not quite finished cooking. Bread tastes so good when baked in a wood stove."

"What other kind of stove is there, Jack? I would not know anything about that. We still live in the backwoods, far from civilization. Do you know what I mean?"

Shaking my head at Ina's sarcasm, I do not believe she understands where the money comes from. In order to give her everything she wants, I will have to become a rich man.

"Yes, dear.

I get the message. Things will change. If you are patient, good things will come."

I leave the kitchen behind me, go to his room, and then stand just inside his doorway. The little man is still fast asleep.

In a soft voice, I say, "James, wake up, Son."

He scuffles around in bed, stretches a couple of times, then sits up in bed.

"Dad, it's so warm in bed."

"I know, Just the same, you need to get out of bed."

James rubs the sleep from his tired eyes.

"Do you want something to eat?"

James nods his head eagerly.

"Then go wash your face and hands before coming to the table."

James yawns widely. "Do I have to?"

He asks the same question every day. "Yes, you do. I am not asking for much. Think of Mom. Early every morning, she cooks a great breakfast for us."

James smiles brightly, still sitting upright in bed with heavy covers pulled up to his chin. "Dad, are you going back to the river today?"

"Yes!"

"Can I go with you?"

"We will see. First let's make sure Mom doesn't need you around here."

A cloud of danger falls upon our happy morning with the mention of the task that waits for me at the river.

I know James wants to go to the river so he can be with me, but Ina might need his help around here. He needs to spend more time with his mother. Not withstanding, the trip to the bottoms might be dangerous.

James argues hopefully. "I can carry the Belgium for you."

Growing impatient with his persistence, I command him in my drill sergeant's voice, "Wait. Let's talk to Mom first. Go on. Wash up."

I stand at his door and then watch him walk past me to the washbasin. Yesterday, I closed all the shutters on the windows so the back porch will be warmer. He hates to get out of his warm bed and then go to the cold porch. He hates cold water on his face—or any other water as for as that goes.

"James, the water is warm for you this morning, thanks to Mom."

He cups his hands, lowers them into the basin, and then splashes water into his face. I then walk back to the table and sit down beside Ina.

"Everything looks so good, Ina."

"Where is James?"

I reach for hot bread and start to spread butter on a steaming biscuit. "He's coming."

"Leave that alone!" Ina reaches over and takes the butter knife from me. "You need to give thanks first."

That's always the response, but I still try every morning just the same!

"Sit down in your chair, Son. Bow your head. God, thank you for the food we eat. And forgive our sins. And please watch over my family. I ask in the name of Jesus Christ. Amen. What do you think, Ina? May I eat my buttered biscuit now?"

Ina does not answer and turns her head away from me.

"Darling, should I go back to the river and fetch the rest of Daisy?"

"Will she be fit to eat?"

I am thinking to myself that surely those creatures believe she is. Instead, I answer, "I believe so. It's still freezing outside. The thermostat on the back porch shows five degrees. What about James? Do you have something for him to do around here?"

I look at James to see his response. He sits, still looking at his mom, hoping she says, "Go with your dad."

"Even though the snow is deep and cold, I know he wants to be with you. He wants to go with you and that gun! Someday, I'm going to have myself a daughter." Ina then looks at James. "She will stay at home with me."

"I don't think so, Mom. She will want to go with me."

"No! She will want to do girl things! I am only teasing you, James. Go with your dad. You will have to wait until the temperature climbs a few degrees before riding Mr. Valentine's tractor to the river."

Before going to the river, James and I wander around the house, finding things to do until nearly noon. The temperature finally reaches twenty-five.

"Dad, is it warm enough? Can we go now?"

"I don't see why not. Get your thermal underwear on and heavy coat. Be sure you wrap a thick wool scarf around your neck. Get some wool socks also. I do not want you getting sick."

James stays in his room for a while, putting his winter clothes on. Finally, he comes out of his room, walking toward the front door. He looks well prepared for the occasion. I kiss Ina quickly.

"Before James starts turning red from overheating, we should leave right away."

CHAPTER 4

The sun is getting high in the sky. I need to get the tractor and leave before animals start on Daisy. The old man should be up by now.

"James, you and Mom will be safe. Stay here with Mom until I come back with the tractor and its trailer."

"Can I ride in the trailer, Dad?"

"Yes. Ina, I will be back as soon as I can. Keep a good heart."

After stepping off the front porch, I look out over the snow-covered countryside. It is a beautiful day. Snow fell late into the night, deep on the ground. Animal tracks are everywhere. This winter wonderland is unlike anything I have ever seen. Snow covers the cedars. They look like Christmas trees, shimmering like diamonds on a snowy blanket.

I take a few steps in the deep snow and then shout at Ina, "The snow is about two feet deep!"

The cabin door is now closed, and she cannot hear me. I have to lift my feet high to make footprints in the snow. Lucky for me, the old man's house is not far away. Looking around the yard, birds, rabbits, and some fox tracks are scattered everywhere in the deep snow. Where are the rabbits when we hunt them? My tracks from yesterday are no longer on the path leading to Mr. Valentine's house. Snow completely covered them. When snow is this deep, a hunter only needs a wooden club. Because a rabbit does not run well in deep snow, today is not a good time for him to leave his bed.

I look up into the sky, seeing brilliant blue. No clouds mar the perfect horizon for now. A red-tailed hawk soars overhead. It catches my attention. He is calling to his mate as if to say, "Where are you, Red? I am hungry. Let's have rabbit for breakfast." He soars so high in the sky, almost out of sight. A full moon is out as well. We should come out on the porch tonight and see how bright the night is. James and Ina will enjoy any chance for them to leave the cabin. The deep snow is hard to walk in. My feet crush through layer of snow. With some distance behind me, the old man's barn is getting closer. A couple hundred feet, and I will be there. Thank God for Mr. Valentine and his tractor. I cannot get to the river without it.

After reaching the barn, I try to open the old, wooden doors. Snowdrift has obscured part of the barn doors. Freezing out here, even though I have thick gloves, my hands are numb from trying to move snow from the barn door. I will need to remove a lot of snow before the doors will open. It is an old barn built in the thirties, a little rundown but still in good shape. Once I move enough snow, a heavy iron latch also bars the door. I hammer on the iced-over latch. Finally, the ice breaks free. After that, the door opens enough to squeeze through. I feel a little drowsy from the cold and exerting myself.

It has been a long time since anyone has been in this seat. I turn my head to the right, looking over the fender toward the ground. Snow comes up to the axle. Slowly, it makes its way forward. Tire tracks break the snow's splendor. Now a much larger animal is making tracks in the snow. Pushing its way forward like an ancient beast, the tractor makes its way downhill through the snow and then finally to our little cabin. I pull into the yard, easing the tractor to a stop. Climbing down from the tractor, I leave the engine running. My fingers are still numb from digging snow.

I trudge through the snow, go inside, and warm my hands by the heater.

"James and I are now ready to leave for the river. We will be back in three to four hours. I hate to leave you alone."

"Jack, be careful down there. Don't let James get out of your sight."

Just like a wife, while we are gone, she will worry about us. It does not matter what I say to her. She will be frantic until we get back. I feel horrible leaving her alone. She is standing by the table, holding her hands behind her. I slowly slip outside and then stand beside the tractor.

"Dad, these tires are awfully bald. I hope we make it back."

"I know, James. I cannot do anything about that. Climb onto the trailer, and get a firm grip on something. Hold on tight."

I sit down on a cold, metal seat, but at the same time I am looking at Ina. She is now on the porch. I hate it when she makes me feel this way. I cannot help the way things are. I must get underway. With every puff of smoke coming out of its tall, black stack, the tractor runs stronger. I look over at James and make sure he is gripping the trailer firmly.

"Are you ready to go?"

He stands there boldly with both hands firmly planted on the trailer's cold rail. He is ready to get underway, gripping it with his thick, furry gloves.

"Dad, this is going to be fun."

With my foot, I hold the stiff clutch in firmly and then push the shifter into first gear, easing the clutch out slowly. It jerks a couple of times and then moves forward.

"Hold on tight, James! Don't fall off!"

After getting underway, I shift to second gear; but the pace is still slow enough to manage the deep snow. In places, the snow is deeper. Instead of running over it, the tractor performs like a dozer, pushing snow out of the way. Finally, we make our way to the river bottom.

I hop down from my perch. Surveying the edges of the forest for tell-tale prints, I find there are no signs of the creatures. Daisy looks untouched. James clambers down from the trailer, stepping into the deep snow. Facing the woods toward our cabin, James looks intently into the brambles.

"What are you looking at, James? If the creature comes from over there, we will have plenty of time to leave. Look, over there on the left side of us is a dense, wooded area. If they come, they will most likely come from there. Keep a good lookout, Son. Don't let them sneak up on us."

"Dad, you need to turn the tractor around and head it back up the hill."

"Good thinking, James. I do need to head out. That way I can back the trailer down to the river's edge."

I take James's advice. He positions himself away from the tractor, giving me plenty of room to maneuver. Because the snow is deep, I have to struggle when turning the steering wheel, even with both hands. I turn to the left and make a circle. It is not so bad pointing the tractor back toward the house. Daisy will be easy to load. James is still in sight, standing on a rock in the river.

"James, be careful. Those rocks look slick. You can fall and hurt yourself or drown."

"Daddy, I don't see the bell!"

So as not to slip off, James carefully positions himself on a snow-covered rock, confident he is making a great discovery.

"What? Are you sure, James?"

"It's not there, Dad!"

I stop what I am doing. Trying to make sense of it all, I stand perfectly still. Was that Daisy's bell I heard last night? It must have been. My body is tight with concentration as I try to decide my next move.

"That's crazy, Son. What do they need with her bell?"

A chill runs through my body like dread. I like to think of the creatures as mostly animals without intellect. Why would the beasts keep Daisy's bell? Is it a trophy of a successful kill? Do they like the sound it makes? The bell rang out several times last night in the not-far-away distance. Now I know I was not just hearing things. I peer into the dense woods across the river, looking for the clever hunter responsible for Daisy.

"We must hurry and get out of here! They have not been here yet. They could be back at any time. Come on, Son. Help me load Daisy so we can get out of here."

When I take hold of her, her dead body will not break free of the ice. I step back from the trailer and look around. I spot a rope lying on the trailer. James stands by with his hands deep in his pockets, trying to keep them warm. My fingers hurt from wrapping them tightly around the frozen rope. Just the same, I manage to tie one end of the rope to her leg. The other end I tie to the winch at the front of the trailer. With both hands, I grip the handle and begin to turn the winch as fast as I can. As it tightens, ice breaks free from the frozen rope. Ice then scatters onto the trailer like broken glass. It seems like an unlikely task, but she finally breaks free from her frozen grave. Finally, the winch turns with greater ease. Slowly, Daisy's stiff carcass begins to inch toward the end of the trailer.

Encouraged by success, I put more effort into cranking the handle. Soon, the carcass is ready to load. The work causes me to breathe heavily, so I stop for a rest.

"James, get those two boards off the trailer and bring them to me. We will use them like a ramp to slide her onto the trailer. See if you can turn the handle on the wench. Use both hands, Son. Almost there! Let me help you."

James strains with all his might until the handle slowly begins to move.

"I can do it, Dad!"

I watch as he manages to rotate the handle four or five more times. Finally, James's face turns beet red and beads of sweat dot his forehead. Daisy now rests in the middle of the trailer.

"You did a very good job, James. Climb on board, and let's get out of here."

The tractor chugs and strains as I steer it out of the river bottom. At last, we are on our way home. A few minutes later, we are back on higher ground. When the river bottom is far behind us, we will be safe. James unexpectedly lets out a distressed shout.

"Dad, they are at the river!"

His sudden cry startles me. I jerk my head around and look back toward the river bottom. Three ape-looking creatures stand at the river's edge, watching our steady departure. We left just in time. I hate to think what might happen if we were to face-off with them.

"Dad, do you think they will run after us?"

"I hope not, Son. I hate to kill such a magnificent creature. Do not worry, Son. They are no match for the Belgium. You watch them so I can keep driving. Warn me if they charge after us. A rifle slug would reach them long before they get to us."

James sits with his legs dangling off the back of the trailer, watching the three figures. One of them is taller than any man I have ever met. I am six feet four. Even bent over, he is still much taller. The other two are shorter, about six feet. Suddenly, the big male swings his arms around in the air in defiance. He then bends his massive upper body over, picks up a large jagged rock, and hurls it through the distance between us. His loud scream fills my ears.

"James, what do you make of that?"

"He is angry at us for taking his food."

"I believe you are right, Son. We need to get out of here fast."

Now that the tractor is packing down the snow, maneuvering is easier. I grip the shifter tight and shift the transmission into third gear.

"Tell me, James, if they come over the hill so I can be ready with my gun. Hang on tightly; we need to get out of here fast!"

The cabin is now in sight. I am glad to see it. Dimly lit amber light comes from its windows as black smoke from the chimney drifts across daisy's pasture. I am relieved as I pull the trailer into the yard. Before bringing the tractor to a stop, I look toward the river. The creatures are nowhere in sight. After a sigh of relief, I turn the ignition and listen to the tractor's engine chug to a stop. Stuffing my hands deep into my pockets, I am satisfied they stayed at the river. Before smoke settles from the now-lifeless engine, James quickly leaps from the trailer, relinquishing my heavy gun that will someday be handed down to him.

"Mom, we are home!"

Sore and aching from being shaken about on the tractor, I slide off its hard, metal seat and then walk away from the old, noisy, cooling beast, thanking it for not failing me. Taking a last look back at the trailer, I consider Daisy's mangled body, moreover, reminded that after tomorrow, she will become a fading memory. After kicking a porch post to remove snow from my shoes, I then spot Ina through a window combing her long, silky, black hair.

"We are back."

She turns her head my way. "Did you have any trouble down there?"

"When the tractor made it to the top of the hill, we saw the creatures by the river. We left just in time. There are three of them. The strangest thing is they look almost human but much taller. The big one was about seven feet tall, a male."

James joins in, adding his opinion to the story. "They were not happy, Mom."

I look toward James, hoping he doesn't get his mom more upset. Seeing that it's hopeless, I offer a small comfort.

"They stayed at the river, Ina."

Ina's face becomes griped with fear. "Jack, James was with you! I thought it was safe! I don't believe we have seen the last of them."

"Don't worry, Ina. I can see that for myself. We've been here for ten years and never any kind of trouble."

Ina twirls a loose hair around her ear.

"Jack, what are those things? We are not living in prehistoric times."

I plead with her to calm down. "I don't know what they are."

While I stand in the kitchen doorway, Ina is sitting at the table with her forehead in her hand. She has a great imagination that sometimes gets the best of her. I try to get her to talk about other things, so I can distract her. She should not fixate on the creatures, and I change the subject.

"Before you make bread tonight, you should go to Mr. White's and get some cooking oil. That will give you a chance to get out of the cabin."

"Yes, dear, must have your biscuits." She lifts her head suddenly.

"Take it easy, Ina. Don't be so afraid."

While she is still frozen, I should take Daisy to the general store, as soon as possible. If other animals are as hungry as the creatures, they will be climbing on board the trailer where her carcass lies.

"I don't have the tools to cut her up or a place to refrigerate her. I need to get Mr. White to store her in his walk-in freezer."

She answers, "He won't do it for nothing, Jack."

"I know. He can take a small part of her for payment. There is a lot of her left."

The yard is still full of snow. Everything is still frozen solid. If I don't go out and free the Ford from its icy tracks, Ina might start walking up the road. She is in very bad need of a break from this place.

"Wait, James. There is a lot of snow in the yard. I need to take the tractor and pull the car into the road. James, you can steer the car for me."

James glances at his mom.

"Jack, are you sure that is safe?"

"Sure. He can do that. Right, James?"

He stood there, looking at his mother, waiting on her approval.

"Go on, James. Do what your father tells you to do."

CHAPTER 5

"James, first, I need to unhitch the trailer."

I climb on board the tractor and then back close to the car. Daisy's bloody rope is still lying on the trailer. Red snow covers it from end to end. It's better than having to find another. It's a bit hard to manage, stiff as it is. If I'm not careful, my fingers will mash. James is in the Ford, looking back at me, waiting for instructions.

I shout over the tractor's noisy engine, "Are you ready, Son?"

I said it loud enough for him to hear. I hate having to repeat myself.

"Yes, Dad! I am ready!"

"I will go slow, so keep your eyes on me and stop when I do!"

I climb onto the tractor and began to pull until the rope tightens. Finally, it creeps slowly backward into the road, free from its icy tracks. I leave the tired tractor parked on the side of the road, belching black smoke. Through a window, Ina watches every move we make.

"James, you did that like a professional! I am so proud of you! Are you ready to get your driver's license now?"

He glares at me. "Dad, I cannot get my license. I'm not old enough."

Hearing him, recalling when I got mine, I'm reminded how short life is. My father was dead, but I had an uncle who took his place. He would let me drive his car on dirt roads. I think it was because he was too drunk to drive.

"Jack, you do the driving, and I'll do the drinking." That was his favorite saying.

"When summer gets here and we go fishing, you can drive to the river bottom. How about that?"

"I would love that!"

I see Ina still looking out the window, eager to get on the road. Now that the car is out of the yard, she can get underway. James did very well. I can see him under the wheel more often as soon as the weather allows.

"Let's tell Mom so she can leave for the store."

Eager to tell his mom what he did, James runs to the door.

"Mom, Dad said when we go swimming this summer I can drive to the river bottom!"

"He did? You won't drive into the river, will you?"

"Mom, a professional doesn't do that!"

Ina looks at me with a look of curiosity. "What have you been telling him, Jack?"

Ice covers my blue nineteen fifty Ford. After opening the door, I sit down and turn the engine over. Just like always, my V-8 did not disappoint me. *Do not move her yet, Jack,* I said to myself. *Let it warm up first. Do not damage the engine.*

"James, do not touch anything. I will be back in a moment."

While trying to reach the porch, I slip and slide across a frozen ground, nearly falling flat on my face.

"Ina, the car should be warm and ready to drive. Be careful on the road. There is a lot of ice still out there."

Eager to get out, she sits on the couch, putting her warm shoes on. These are hard times for us, closed up in a little cabin hardly big enough to turn around in, trying not to bump into one another.

"I will be back in an hour or less. James will not get out of my sight. Be careful not to let those creatures get you. You do not know what those things are going to do. I will see you later."

She is not teasing me.

"I know, darling, I love you."

"I love you too, Jack!"

I prop myself up in the doorway and watch her drive up the road. She believes there is more going on than what I am telling. Perhaps there is, but I am only trying to protect her from a vivid imagination.

"Why are you so quiet back there, James?"

"I am thinking about school, Mom. When do you think I will go back to school?"

He misses going to school. It is very hard on James living here. There are very few friends for him around here. Like his Dad, he is a nature boy. Still, he hardly ever complains about anything. I know he misses his friends at school. I wish things were not the way they are, him growing up alone, no brother or sister.

"Do you miss your classmates?"

"I like learning new things, nature and math, you know, things I like."

"You are a good student, James. Your teacher has many good things to say about you."

"Watch out for the black ice under the mulberry tree, Mom. Dad said to pump the brakes in snow and ice."

"Yes, Son, your dad is a smart man."

James is very close to his father. The two are alike. Sometimes I wish he was more like me.

"Mom, I like to go hunting with him. He is going to let me shoot the Belgium when he gets a lower-grade, ten-gauge shell."

I watch him in the rearview mirror, a brave and adventurous young man in a hurry to grow up. Thinking of him and that big gun makes me shiver. I mumble a few words of discontent to myself and hope that day is a long way off. When that day comes, he will want to take it out by himself. I will die a million times over. Farther up the road, tree limbs hide the stop sign at the end of the road. That mulberry tree will get someone killed someday.

Slowly coming to a stop, I stop under the mulberry tree. James is right. Ice hangs from the sign, and black ice covers the road.

Not wanting to play demolition derby with a passerby, I wait for other traffic to slip and slide by before driving across to White's General Store.

"Come on, James. Let's go inside and get what we need so Dad can do what he needs to do with Daisy."

"Can I have some candy?"

"Yes, you can, but do not get a fistful. You watch your manners around Mr. White."

The store keeper stands at the counter watching Ana Marie sweeping up the floor for the next days work. Mr. White tiredly wipes the counter clean of smudges. He looks up at us as we open the door.

"How are you today, Ina?"

"I am fine, Mr. White. How is the day treating you?"

"It has been a long cold afternoon."

"What can I do for you and James today?"

"I need a few things to cook. Jack wants to have his biscuits every day, and now I have to get milk too."

"Did Daisy go dry?"

"No. Something killed her at the river bottom."

"Did Jack see what did it?"

I begin to walk down the aisle, looking for what I need.

"He said he saw it, Mr. White. But whatever it is, it did not stay around long."

"Did he say what it was?"

"I don't believe he even knows what he saw. When he came in sight of the river, he saw something in the ducktails. He said it was ape looking, whatever that means. It was gone when they got there."

"Well, if he wants to process her, tell him to bring her to me."

"He's bringing her up after I get back."

I steal around the aisles, searching for what we need. There is not much of a selection. If the weather doesn't let up, there won't be anything to eat. I do not want much. Finally, I find everything I came for and lay them on the countertop.

"James, take what you have and put it where Mr. White can see it. Hurry up. Dad is waiting on us."

I look around for Anna. She is usually here this time of day.

"Where is Anna Marie?" I ask Mr. White. He couldn't run this store without her.

"She is in the back, doing some inventory. I am very low on supplies."

"Tell her we miss seeing her. Come, James. Let us go home while there is still daylight. Dad wants to take care of Daisy before dark."

"Mom, I don't see Robert anywhere. Will Dad need him to help unload Daisy?"

Robert has been here all his adult life. Just like Anna, he will be here forever, until the doors close.

"He is around somewhere. When Dad gets here, Robert will help him. He's probably in the back, helping Anna."

When we get home, I can see Jack pushing snow off the porch with a shovel.

Now that Christmas is gone, I hope he goes back to work soon. Hunting for food is not what I want him and James doing. When he is home, he stays gone with James too much.

"How is everyone at Mr. White's? James, I see you have candy. Do you want to rot your teeth out? When he starts complaining about a toothache, Ina, you can get his teeth fixed."

Why not? I think I do everything else around here.

"I know, Jack, one of the responsibilities of being a mother."

"I can't argue with that. How was Anna Marie?"

"She was in the back, doing something. And yes, Mr. White was in good spirits. I told him you would be at the store soon. You need to go before it gets any later, Jack."

Ina is right. Perhaps this is not a good time to be around home. Ina needs time alone, and I need to get this taken care of.

"I don't think there is much of a chance of it getting any warmer. Just the same, I had better get it done before Daisy spoils. I need to hook the trailer to the car first. Did you leave anything in the car?"

"No. I got everything out except James. See if you can get a refund on him."

"No! He's my boy! James, are you leaving with me or staying home with Mom?"

I wish he would spend more time with Ina. I feel horrible, her spending so much time alone.

"I want to go with you, Dad!"

He wants to hit me up for more sweets, but that isn't going to happen.

"No more candy, Son. I mean that. Come with me while I hitch the trailer to the car."

After hitching the trailer to the car, I stand quietly, staring at Daisy, remembering the way it used to be. When she saw me coming with the milking pail, she knew what I was about to do. She was always happy when milked. After hitching the trailer, I pull away from the house and head for the store.

The road is nearly clear of snow. I hope I can go back to work. The general store is only a couple of minutes from home. Maddox Bridge Road, the road we live on, runs into Highway 25, better known as the Dixie Highway. Across the road is the general store.

I pull in and park next to Anna Marie's house. She lives in a small, two-room house to the left of the store. In the store are tables where people come to order food. Some have coffee. Some people have whole meals. Most of them come to talk about what is going on around the countryside.

The store is like others: longer than it is wide, with a large porch across the front. Across the front are sacks of feed. Right of the door, as you go in, is a large, wooden box with salted fatback. Like a farmer's market, in summertime, carefully arranged on the porch are boxes of fruits and vegetables. Also, in the unpaved yard are two gas pumps. Where in rainy weather, people drive through the mud, slipping and sliding while waiting in line to have gas pumped, ten cents a gallon. If the price gets any higher, we will have to stay at home. Mr. White tries to keep the store stocked with supplies.

"Come on, Son. We need to get Daisy taken care of and get back home to Mom."

James is following behind me. Mr. White is at the counter, helping people. Now four o'clock in the evening, hungry people visit the store for a hot, home-cooked meal. I push the squeaky door open and walk inside. Always busy, Anna Marie busily collects plates and wipes off tables.

She is a beautiful, black girl about twenty-four years old and has worked here all her life.

"Evening, Mr. White.

Looks like I caught you during the wrong time of day."

He places his hands on the cool countertop and leans toward me with a smile.

"Nonsense, Jack. What can I do for you? Do you need your cow processed? Ina said something killed her."

I try not to strike up a conversation about the killing of Daisy. This is not the right time.

"If you have time, I will appreciate it."

"I will get Robert right on it. Pull around to the side door so Robert can unload her. Robert, Jack's cow needs processing!"

While talking to Mr. White, John Jakes walks by and interrupts us. A big mountain of a man, he came out of the army the same time I did. They say he never hid in a foxhole. How can a man big as he is dodge a bullet?

While speaking to Mr. White, John steps between the counter and me. He pushes in with a firm hand on my shoulder and places his bill on the counter without apology.

Looking at the bill then the store keeper, he impatiently jabs at the paper. His voice rises loudly, "See right here? Steak and eggs!

Mr. White obediently takes the receipt and files it away beneath the counter as John pushes his way through the front door. As the door clangs shut, Mr. White flushes red saying, "Sorry about that, Jack. John is short tempered and not much for small talk."

Thinking of John's large hand on my shoulder, his tall stature towers over me, I am glad Mr. White took care of him first. With a smile, I indulge in some gossip. "Mr. White, I hear people say that while in the war, that man killed most men in hand-to-hand combat. I have to respect him as the kind of man I want on my side with a history like that."

Mr. White smiles and reaches across the counter holding out his hand. "Jack, I guess we are going to do some business together with Daisy. It's too bad John could not stay to help unload the trailer, seeing that he's on our side."

I shake hands with the store keeper over our bargain with Daisy. "That's okay, Leon. She is frozen solid and will slide right off the trailer with a little elbow grease."

"I better move the trailer around the side of the store before Robert comes looking for me."

"Sure, Jack. Pull it around to the platform. Robert will hook her up to the hoist and lift her off your trailer."

I say, "James, I will be back in a moment. I'm going to help Robert unload the trailer."

I leave by way of the front door, get into the car, and pull the trailer around to the side platform. Robert is already there, pushing the old chain hoist in place where the trailer will park. The hoist is easy to slide on the big beam.

"Hi, Robert.

There sure is a lot of snow. Biggest ever, isn't it?"

"I have been here forty years and never seen so much snow, Mr. Jack."

Robert is now doing something else. Daisy is now inside the building, lying across a large, wooden table. Robert will do a good job.

"I will see you later, Robert."

I walk around to the front of the store and back inside. Mr. White is already checking out my cart.

"He will cut and wrap her in no time at all, Jack."

My son sits on a bench by the soda machine sucking on a lollipop.

"James, I hope you did not find that on the floor."

"No, Dad. Anna gave it to me."

With his two feet side by side, as if waiting for a command, James stands in front of me. Mr. White smiles and shrugs his shoulders.

"I cannot say no to Anna. She is what the world needs more of—a loving person who thinks more of others than herself. However, some of those others do not love her back. Although she does work for me, I cannot stop her. When she is working, she gives children candy."

"Yes. I know, Mr. White. Everyone loves her. Well, nearly everyone."

Anna Marie was an abandoned newborn. Someone found her in a box wrapped in a pink-and-blue cloth flour bag. She was the talk of the countryside for a long time. Robert is also a long-time employee, for thirty years now.

"Mr. White is a good man. He has been my friend for more than ten years. Never says a bad word to anyone, no matter the color of his skin."

Anna Marie did that to him.

"When do you think I can get some of the meat back, Mr. White? Can I charge a few things until you get her cut up?"

"Sure you can, son. Get what you need when you need it."

Hearing the word *need* is good to know. With a bit of luck, soon, life will start having with it normalcy. So much is hanging over my head.

"Come on, Son. Let's go home. Mom will wonder what happened to us. Thank you, Mr. White. I will see you tomorrow evening after work."

"All right, Jack. Take good care of your family."

I pull into the driveway, turn the engine off, and get out of the car.

"James, watch your step. You might fall. The porch is very slippery. Grab that bag for me," I shout back at him as I walk across the frozen ground.

We then go inside and place our groceries on the table. Ina is standing next to the stove, wearing an apron painted with bright red strawberries, a little dusty with biscuit flour. The kitchen is warm and toasty. I look forward to her commanding voice.

"It is on the table!"

"I have a few more items, my sweet! Robert is processing the cow. Mr. White said Robert would finish processing her tomorrow. He also said it will be tendered if frozen for two weeks or more."

"That will make the meat tender?" She brushes flour dust off her apron.

"Yes, Poor Daisy. All that is left of her is a memory."

"Jack, before you come home from work tomorrow, stop somewhere and get some coal. We are almost out."

Checking on the heater, I leave the kitchen and see how much there is in the coal box. Before I spend what little money I have, I need to hold onto it as long as I can.

"Ina, I can get some coal off Mr. Valentine's pile. He will not care."

She stops what she is doing long enough to ask, "What else did you get?"

One of life's little pleasures, the only thing I can afford right now.

"Look what I got us: three Cokes. Want one now or after supper?"

This is a good time to ask her if there is anything I can do to help. She will say no. "Stay out of the kitchen," she likes to say.

"Is there anything I can do, Ina?"

"You can put the milk in the icebox."

CHAPTER 6

As cold as it is, there is no need for ice.

"Jack, I want you to install electricity in this house this spring. There is no reason why we cannot have some comforts of life just like other people."

"Yes, dear, as soon as I get a few things to work with, I will do that. Now, let's talk about supper."

Ina's apron rustles softly as she whisks the gravy thickening on the hot stove. As usual, I end up talking to myself. This snow has slowed down my work. If I don't start working, we will have to survive on beans and rice. I need to repair some of the damaged vehicles in the shop. Then David can collect some money.

"How much does he owe you, Dad?"

"One hundred dollars." Not much for what I do.

"What are you going to do with it?"

"What I always do with it: hold it out and then give it to your mom. Then she will do what she always does with it: spend it on you, James."

Ina pours the smooth, white gravy into a blue, clay bowl and looks up at me.

"We also need food to go in this house, Jack."

Ina wants much more than food—things like running water in the house, indoor plumbing. Those things are wonderful to have.

However, they are completely out of reach. There are far more things needed now, like food. I look at Ina as she finishes our meal and agree with her.

"Yes, darling. I know food is a priority. I need to buy some more ten-gage shotgun shells for the Belgium too. I still don't know if those creatures are friendly. When James and I were at the river, they came back for a second helping. They were angry that we took away their kill."

I think about their blazing eyes burning into us as we drove away and picture them lurking in the woods with revenge in their minds against us. The last thing they saw as we drove away was James.

It was a tiring day, and the night passed by fast. So Ina can sleep a while longer, I get up at five and put more coal in the heater. Trying to hurry, I go into the kitchen, build a fire, and open the damper. The old cook stove takes about an hour to reach three hundred and fifty degrees. Frozen from being on the back porch, I bring the last of Daisy's milk inside where it is warm to give it time enough to thaw out before breakfast. Before long, it melts enough to drink. After an hour, the stove, once a mass of cold porcelain and black iron, is nice and warm. Now it's time to get my sleeping beauty up.

"Darling, need to get up and get those pots and pans rattling."

Lying on her back, her eyes slowly open to her asking a question.

"I was talking to our daughter, Jack. A large animal had her in its arms."

A puzzling moment.

"We don't have a daughter, Ina."

Still not quite awake, she asks, "What are you talking about, Jack? I know we don't have a daughter."

"Ina, if the drive-in theater is clear of snow this weekend, do you want to see a movie? If you want to, we can leave James with my mom. He always falls asleep anyway."

I hug Ina's waist, hoping to convince her, but she only turns away from my grasp.

"Instead of doing that, Jack, perhaps you should buy some supplies and start wiring this old cabin."

After James washes his face and hands, we sit down at the table and eat breakfast like civilized people. So we can have life a lot easier, we talk about wiring the house. "Breakfast was good, Ina. I have to go now. Give me a kiss. See you this evening. James, I love you. Help your mom by doing what she asks you to do."

I put my coat on then go out the door, get in the car, and think to myself, *I need to put the tractor and its trailer back in the barn.* Nevertheless, I will do that this evening. I pull into the road and then leave with the house in my rearview mirror. Parked by the stop sign under the mulberry tree, I slowly pull out into the Dixie Highway and turn right. The place I work is not far down the road, about five miles. A small town, Ware Shoals is about four miles farther down the road—a cotton mill town.

Here, the Saluda River falls over a dam about thirty feet high and four hundred feet long. Its spillway opens to beautiful but angry rapids that run for a mile or more. Every now and then, we go there and have cookouts, fish fries, catfish stews, and turtle stews. In the springtime we get together with others and just have fun on the river. After a snow thaw, water runs over the dam and creates a great, roaring mist. Then the rapids become wild and furious, dangerous to the best of kayakers. Before long, the shop comes into view. I then come to a slow stop, pull into the shop yard, and get out of my car. Mike O'Donnell comes out of the office and speaks to me.

While standing before me with a heavy coat on, his hands in his pockets, Mike seems a little upset.

"I thought about sending a search party to your house."

Mike's eyes squint against the glare of the sun as it reflects off the cold snow.

"Did you forget where you work? Did your family fare well during the storm?"

He is spiteful and concerned. Way to go, Mike. I pass it on, as in keeping with the way things are.

"We did all right. There is still a lot of the stuff still around."

Mike nods his head as if to say my absence is forgiven.

"Are you ready to make some money?"

"Oh yes. I am ready to do that, more than you will ever know! Do you still want the fifty-five Chevy out today?"

"Yes, I do. I got paint for it yesterday. I knew you would show up eventually. The owner wants the whole car painted now. Remember, no runs in the paint."

Insulted, I turn back toward Mike, asking, "Have I ever put runs on any of your cars?"

"No. But there is a first time for everything."

Mike has owned the body shop for ten years now. He is a perfectionist and sometimes hard to work for. He said that is why he hired me, a perfectionist. I start taping off the chrome and windows, making it ready to paint. I take some paint thinner and wipe all the dust from the body.

"Jack, given it's Friday, a perfect shine and then I'll give you an extra hundred dollars."

His generosity takes me by surprise. It's not like him. I now finish papering the chrome and windows. The Chevy is ready to paint.

"What did I do with that paint gun?" I glance around the garage, looking carefully before I spot it hanging on a nail over the air compressor.

Mike snaps with irritation, "Take it down from there. Jack, was it cleaned?"

I always do. I remember what I had to listen to when someone did not clean it.

"I used it last, Mike! It should be clean."

"Take the top off it and make sure before you pour new paint into it. One of my boys might have used it and not cleaned it. That can ruin some expensive paint."

I peer inside to find lumpy, old sludge. "It is not clean."

Mike stops what he is doing and walks up the hill to his house, mumbling to himself.

I shout to him in a loud voice, "Do not be too hard on him, Mike!"

I take it apart and thoroughly clean it. I hear a commotion up the hill and turn to see what is going on.

Doug, his son, thunders across the yard, gets into his car, slams the door, and leaves in a rage. Doug does not look happy judging by the cloud of dust he leaves behind. Mike must have come down on him hard. The boss is on his way back to the shop to see if I am able to get all of the dry paint out of the gun.

"Did it clean up?"

"Yes, Mike. It did!"

"Looks like I will have to start locking the thing up from now on. These kids, they think money grows on trees! I have told him repeatedly, 'Leave things the way you find them.' Get that Chevy painted, you can take the rest of the day off."

Is he being funny? It will take all day and then some. Every coat will have to dry under the heat lamps. Mike walks by and looks my way.

I finish up at seven o'clock. So that no dust will collect on the Chevy, I put it in the ready room. Mike is already home. While thinking of Ina, I close the shop up and go outside.

Standing by the car, I look at the Milky Way spreading north to south as it lights up the night sky. I wonder how long the skies will remain clear. My eyes are drawn to the heavens. I have to force myself to get into the car. After being on the road for a few minutes, I reach the general store and then turn onto Maddox Bridge Road. Turning in, I notice the tree that hid the stop sign is gone. Suddenly, I just remember I am supposed to go by the store. Annoyed, I quickly turn around and go back. After parking next to the store, I open my door and step into the frozen mud. It makes a crackling sound. Mr. White is at the counter, going over the day's receipts.

"Good evening, Mr. White. How did your day go?"

"Today was a fine day, Jack. At my age, every day is a fine day. God let me live another day."

"How did I make out on the beef?" I hold my breath with anticipation.

"All cut up and ready to go, but do you want all of it now?"

"No. I don't have a place to store it just now. Can you keep it here?"

Not having what I need reminds me of Ina and her complaints. She would say, "When are we going to become civilized and buy a freezer?"

Mr. White interrupts my thoughts. "Before it is eaten, your beef needs to stay frozen for two weeks so it will cure."

Lessening the pain of asking, I keep quiet and hope.

"Jack, if you want to, I will swap pound per pound, for what you owe me in trade, if you want to do that. Is that what you want to do? Is there anything you want now?"

"I would like some ground beef."

"How much?"

Ina usually does this. How many pounds will she need?

"I think two pounds will do. I also need a sack of coal. I almost forgot about the coal."

"Do not want to do that. From the looks of the sky, it is going to be cold and frigid tonight. Ina will send you right back here. When are you going to wire that old cabin for her?"

There is a time and place for everything. Soon, I hope. The way things are happening, there's no way to keep things from spoiling. I need a fridge, electricity, indoor plumbing...it just keeps adding up.

"Ina wants me to start right away. She wants to be like everyone else. I should not say that. I love her so much, and she deservers everything I can give her."

Mr. White consoles me. "You will, Jack. You have determination in you. You have a wonderful son too. He is growing up to be a fine young man."

I know Anna speaks highly of James. She loves all the children around here, but James is special.

"Yes, Mr. White. I know. Where is Anna?"

Mr. White looks toward her house. "She went home to get some rest."

Speaking of home, my mind wanders toward my warm cabin.

"Ina is at home waiting on me. I had better get back home."

It is getting late, and the moon rises brightly in the sky. She might be afraid, the two of them there by themselves. I like coming home. Seeing my family there on the porch, waiting for me to arrive, makes a man feel loved. Mr. White hands over my order.

"Here, don't forget your beef. You know where the coal is."

I go out the back door and step into the frozen mud. It has been frozen for weeks. To the right of the porch lays the coal pile. Robert is already there, filling hundred-pound bags.

"Getting late, Robert and colder. Time for you to go home, isn't it?"

"Yes, Mr. Jack. It's been a long day; them cornbread and beans going to be good tonight."

My car is on the other side of the store, just a short walk away. My toes begin to get numb, and there is a need to hurry. So not to tote the dirty, heavy stuff a long way, I need to back my car up to the pile. Robert is a strong man, but I do not want to take advantage of him. Too many people do. Robert thumps his hand on the roof of the car after I back into the yard.

"Open the boot, Mr. Jack. Let me lift it for you."

"Thank you, Robert. I do appreciate you."

Robert's hands—old, black, and worn from age—lift the damp, cold, dirty, black bag and place it in the back of the car on top of newspaper. I dare not offer to do so myself. He takes pride in doing his own work. By now, Ina is standing at the porch window, looking for me with every tick of the clock. Most of the time, I am not this late, but the cabin is only a moment away. Soon, I will pull into the driveway.

James sits in his wagon like a captain on the front porch, waiting on me.

"Hi there, wagonear, are. are you waiting on me?"

"Yes, Dad, why are you so late getting home?"

"I had to stay late so I could make some money for you and Mom. Come on inside before you end up in the road with that red flyer."

"Dad," he shouts, "They came back and cleared more of the road today! They also cleared the driveway and the yard."

"I see they did. Come on inside. It is too late to be outside. Want those creatures to get you?"

He scuffles out of the wagon and stands beside it. With eyes fixed on the surrounding area, he cautiously looks around the woods and snow-covered, grassy field.

With a bag of groceries in one hand, I patiently stand in the doorway, holding the door open for James. Now late in the evening, tall shadows fall all around the naked trees of winter. "Get in the house, James."

Ina, with broom in hand, takes the bag from my hand. "Did you remember where you live?"

I knew that was coming. "That sounds like what Mike asked me, Ina."

"Why are you so late?" she asks again.

In her hurried life at home, she must have forgotten what I said.

"Do you remember me saying I might be late?"

James is enough to keep her mind busy all day. I do not blame her for not remembering.

"Yes, but I didn't expect two hours."

"I know, I would much rather be at home with you." I pull her to me. "Did you miss me?"

If she was not at home waiting on me, how would life be?

"Yes, I did. But when I don't hear from you, I worry."

"Are you saying we need a phone?"

"No, but now that you mention it, for such occasions, we do need a phone."

Well, from my hand to yours. I know where my money is going now.

"Mike wanted me to finish the Chevy, so he gave me an extra hundred dollars."

"What were you paid?" Ina asks in an eager voice.

"Would you believe two hundred dollars? We can put this money to good use."

I reach down and untie my shoes and slip them off my tired feet. I am sure it will not go toward anything I want but shells for the gun. Can never let the Belgium be without gun shells. I might have to depend on it, a matter of life and death.

"Yes, Jack, put it to good use, like wiring this house and a phone and whatever else we need to make this place a home."

I also bought some ground beef for supper. However, I see supper is ready. Even better. I do not have to wait. I am starving.

"Supper is already cooked."

"Do you need any help setting the table?"

"No. You and James go out on the back porch and wash up."

"Okay, James. Mom said it's face and hands time."

Ina orders us to hurry. "I will take it out of the warmer and set the table."

"Come on, boy, and let's do what Mom told us to do."

I walk onto the porch with a kettle of warm water and then pour it into the washbasin. James stands by, waiting on me to get out of his way. So as not to scald him, I put my hands into the water.

"Just right.

Go ahead, Son. Take a handful and splash it into your face. Get those hands lathered up. Use the washcloth on your face. You won't melt!"

I am going to set down over here and rest my feet. My feet hurt from standing on a hard concrete floor all day.

"I believe Mom is waiting on you at the table."

By the time I get comfortable, James is sitting at the table, waiting on me. While standing at the washbasin, I ponder the idea of having a nice house with a bathtub and shower, no more bearing cold winters on the back porch or scorching heat. Someday, everything will change for the best. A dry towel hangs on a large, rusty nail.

Reaching for it, I ask Ina, "What is for supper, dear?"

"Salmon stew, cornbread, and tea."

"Good! I love your salmon stew. What happened to the Cokes we bought?"

"They are still here, kept nice and cold by Mother Nature. I was tempted to drink one while you were at work but did not."

I look at Ina with a smile. "I think after supper, I will rest by the heater, put my feet up, and have myself a cold Coke."

Ina ladles the steaming soup into our bowls. "Jack, I am so glad it doesn't take much to please you."

"Not so fast. I didn't park the tractor back in the barn yesterday. Oh bother. I will have to put it away tonight."

"No. You don't have to put it away, Jack. When they were clearing the driveway, Owl came by looking for you. He wanted to know why the tractor and trailer were down here."

I sigh with relief. My brother always wants to be up to date on everything.

"He put them back into the barn. I told him about Daisy and the creatures. Your brother has another side to him. He was shocked! I have never seen him that way. He claims to have heard of them before. Owl said they have killed people in northern Canada."

"Did he stay long?"

"James was in the floor, wiping fingerprints off his twenty gage. Owl kept leaning over him, teasing him about rubbing the gun bluing off the barrel."

Listening to Ina, a little nostalgia takes me back. Teasing me about the ten-gage is one of few memories I have of my father. Owl is a lot like Dad. He even talks like him.

Ina reiterates, "Before he left, Owl kept teasing him, saying the same thing over and over: 'Jack junior, that thing is going to be so shiny every rabbit in the county will know you are coming.'"

Dishes make a clattering sound as Ina hastily places them on the table, saying, "Albert's long, red hair kept getting in James's face. James kept pushing him away. Looking at Owl from behind, he looks like a girl. He needs to get it cut."

Owl means no harm. There must be something he wants done, something he doesn't know how to do himself. That is the only reason he comes around.

"Why was he here?" I ask Ina. "He wants help with his carburetor."

Ina knows him as well as I do. She stays on him all the time about his lifestyle.

"If he does not stop drinking, his carburetor is going to stop working forever." Ina makes a joke.

"Ina, Albert, needs to leave the liquor alone, find him a woman, and settle down."

"Maybe someday he will, Jack. You know how your brother is."

Yes, I know. Living life in the fast lane is putting him in the ground much sooner.

"Ina, things are not always what they seem to be. He is afraid to be serious with any woman. When Cheyenne died, he never got over her. That is why he wears his hair long. That Indian woman has a hold on him."

"He drinks her memory away! I feel sorry for him. I want you to help him."

Ina does not realize how many times people have offered him help. I can lead him away from the watering hole, but I cannot make him stop drinking.

"I can't help him unless he wants it, Ina."

Ina keeps her back to me, does not want me to see her expression, how serious she is. "By the way, Jack, Joni, the old woman on the hill, made her way down here this morning. When I was in the yard, talking to Owl, she was all crazy beating on the hood of his car with her walking stick, angrily saying the same thing over and over: 'Your boy has been shooting out my windows with his bb gun!'"

"She kept saying it over and over. Owl got out of his car and sweet-talked her out of the cane. Jack, the old woman is crazy!"

Ina doesn't know how fortunate she has it. We have friends. The only time that old woman shows her face is when she goes to the mailbox. With my feet propped up in a chair, I listen to Ina making friends.

"One morning, when James was in school, I met her at the mailbox. She invited me to her house for coffee. I was curious, so I went up there. She lives like a hermit on that hill. Boxes line the floor in every room. You barely can get around. Her house is like a maze. The place is dark and dusty like a dungeon. Old, heavy drapes hang all the way to the floor, a creepy, gothic look.

James interrupts with youthful exuberance. "Can I have one?"

"I wish you would not speak before your mother is through, Son. One what?

James leans forward and pretends to have his sights on a target. " A bb gun! Pow, pow!"

"Son, you just got a twenty-gage."

That boy, will there ever be an end to his wants?

"Jack, I am talking to you. The house is so dark inside it is hard to get around in. When we got to the other side of the room, she pulled the drapes back and let the light come in. A small, round table was there with four chairs, her little spot."

"Ina, maybe she likes her own little space in that house. What does she need with that place anyway? She is too old to live by herself."

Maybe she and Ina can be friends. It was bad on Ina losing her mom at such a young age.

She was only two years old when her mother disappeared from her life. The loss still haunts her. Sometimes she can be very insecure about herself, getting all upset about unimportant things.

"Jack, the house is full of antique furniture. You know the way the house looks, ancient like her."

I know what Ina is thinking: Old, but it has electricity, Jack!

"Too bad, Ina.

Most likely, she will die there and no one will know or care. She is probably a good person, crazy from being alone."

She is like so many forgotten people. It reminds me to go see my mother. Ina's voice changes from excitement to concern.

"She told me she has no living relatives. I told her James has no bb gun."

"Ina, what do you want to do tomorrow? It's Saturday. You said Owl is coming over today. I was thinking about him and me walking down to the river and looking for signs of those creatures."

"Darling, before the day is spent, I need to go see Mr. Valentine, give him some money for rent."

"Why? He never takes it."

"I need to offer it to him anyway. I'll be back in a little while."

I close the door behind me and then walk away. As always, going to the old man's house is a short trip. I have made it a thousand times. After walking up to his porch, no one has been here. The only footprints on his porch are mine. In addition, there is no sign of him being out of his house. I step onto his porch and hear the same old, squeaky boards. Knowing how bad his hearing is, I pound my fist hard on his door.

As I stand there, a cold, hard wind blows against my back. I wait. There is no answer, only a whishing of wind blowing through snow-covered tree limbs. I step away then look through a porch window. There is no fire in his heater. Built strong and sturdy, his oak door is heavy. I stand there, leaning against it, and then push hard with all my might. It opens. I slowly step inside, taking a quick look around.

"Mr. Valentine, are you home?"

I scream it aloud. He is nowhere in sight. After walking through the room past his heater, I opened the door that leads into his kitchen. The room has a musky odor. I stand there for a moment, looking around. I do not see him. Remembering that getting around for him is not easy, he cannot be for away. Maybe he is outside. I do not see him anywhere. I then open the door to the back porch startled by what I see. The frail old man lies facedown on the floor.

CHAPTER 7

I gently place both hands under him and slowly roll him over on his back. I don't know what happened to him. I hope he is still alive. Now I see him. His face tells a story of a frightful death. His eyes are lifeless, hollowed out, a look that reflects a terrifying night. Leaning back, with a deep breath, I gasp. My heart pounds in my chest. Like a choked man, his tongue hangs out his mouth. Still kneeling beside him, my knees begin to tire and then throb. I ask myself, *What is happening here?*

Mirrored explanations reflect the day's events. I look around the room beyond the broken dishes. Splintered chairs, a room now destroyed where there once was a back door; it looks like a tornado ripped through here. The back door is off its hinges. What could have done this? Then, in a flashback, the answer brings me to a sober awakening. Those creatures.

Once I get to my feet, I walk to the back door and look outside. His black lab lies dead in the backyard. Part of his body is missing. I then remembered what Ina said.

"We have not seen the last of them, Jack!"

Immediately, I think of Ina and James.

My heart starts pounding with fear that the worst is happening. Without thinking, I slam through where there was once a back door. After losing my footing on slippery ground, I fall facedown. I have no time for this. After rising to my feet, I make a mad dash toward the cabin. A rush of panic runs through me. My head pounds, my heart beats in my ears. Running hard toward the cabin, I reach the porch. My hard-soled shoes make a pounding noise on flimsy, loose boards. In a frantic state, my body crashes into the door. I burst inside and look around.

In horror, I shout at the top of my voice, "Are those things gone? Ina! Where are you?" Ina stumbles into the room.

"What has come over you, Jack?"

"Where is he?"

James is still not in sight. "He is on the back porch."

"Who is?" I ask her.

"James. Who else?"

Ina stands there, waiting for me to say something.

"Why so many questions?"

I take a deep breath.

"The old man is dead, killed by those creatures! His dog is torn apart like Daisy."

I watch Ina's face go from shock to a twisting shape of fear.

"My God, Jack!

Those things have left the river? Where are they now?"

She asks questions I have no answers to.

"They might even come here, and all we have is that old ten-gage shotgun of yours, Jack."

"Ina, let's not panic!"

"Looks like you are already doing that, Jack!"

She is right. I need to calm down, need to keep my thoughts straight. I do not want Ina and James thinking they are not safe.

"What do you expect me to do? I saw something terrible."

Fidgeting about, trying to gather my thoughts. I need to think! Owl will be here in the morning.

"You need to go get the sheriff, Jack."

"Ina, calm down. I cannot do that, not just now! If I do, all three of us will have to go. If we do that, just as they did at the old man's house, those things will come. Then they will destroy everything we have."

I try my best to stay calm. *Think! What do I need to do first?* Under this pressure, it is hard to think.

"See why we need a phone, Jack? We need to change the way we live!"

I hear this enough while I am around her. This is a bad time to bring that up.

"At the moment, darling, I'm doing the best I can!"

"You're right, Jack. I'm sorry. I am so afraid."

It's a bad time for anything to happen. There is snow on the ground. We are confined to this cabin.

"Ina, in the morning, when Owl gets here, I will send him for Sheriff Pickens. Tell the sheriff what happened. That's what I'll do. The old man saw them at the river. I saw them too. Whether the sheriff believes me is another question."

"Jack, the sheriff can go to the store and see what happened to Daisy."

Ina is right to be concerned. It is my responsibility to tell him much sooner. I have been treating this like just another happening around here.

"Daisy is already cut up. That's not important right now. Before daylight is gone, Ina, we need to think of our safety."

Ina is relying on me to keep our family safe. Her face is still gripped with fear.

"Jack, did you get more gun shells?"

"Yes. I have a box, twenty-five shells. They had better be smart enough not to go up against a ten-gage. It will bring an elephant down. At least the thunder from it should scare them away."

Thinking of Ina and James, I know we are going to have a cold and fearful night. I should bring in enough coal to last all night.

"Ina, before dark, I need to bring all the coal in. We also need to close all the shutters and lock them. When I go outside for the coal, I will unlock the shutters and then close them. All you have to do is lock them from the inside."

Ina is right. The way we live is so fragile. These old, wooden shutters will not even keep a raccoon out.

If the creatures come, they will be much more damaging here than at the old man's house. Ina is afraid. A drab look covers her face.

"Jack, you should have left some for them."

After the fact, I see no reason to state the obvious.

"Yes, Ina. After taking Daisy away, they are leaving the river looking for food." Mumbling to myself, I say, "Yes. That was selfish of me. I should have left something for them. What have I caused?" I turn to Ina. "Ina, don't be afraid. If they come back, we will be ready for them." I don't know what to expect. At least in war, I know where the enemy is coming from.

"Jack, since they are wild animals, they might be hungry enough to do anything."

Holding my hammer in hand, I grip its smooth handle tightly as I walk around to the back of the cabin. There in the snow, three creatures left enormous wide-toed footprints in the deep snow. My eyes follow winding tracks through Mr. Valentine's barren peach orchard.

No time to whisper crazy thoughts, I focus my eyes beyond the pasture to where the dirt road to the river starts. Without a doubt, they did come by way of the dirt road. Looking at the tracks, burdensome thoughts fill my mind. They did follow us from the river. I keep repeating it to myself. I now feel responsible for Mr. Valentine's death. I took their kill from them because we needed food, and now a long night will follow.

I am no Moses, but waiting to see if the Grim Reaper is coming is like Passover; it is going to be a long, stressful night. Trying to get blood flowing through my cold, numb fingers, my hands close tightly into a fist. Releasing my grip, my hands then plunge deep into my wool pockets as if directed by some unknown force. My fingers throb. So I can get warm, I need to finish what I am doing and go back inside. I make my way around the cabin, unlocking every shutter.

"Ina, I have unlocked all the shutters. All you have to do is lock them from inside."

"All right, I will do that now."

Stepping in the cold snow, it covers my shoes and sticks to my coveralls.

After returning to the front porch, I lift my feet high and stomp hard to remove snow from my paint-splattered work shoes. I lift one dirty bag of coal, drag it inside, and empty it into the small, wooden box behind the heater. Now with my entire task finished, I am ready for them. If they come again, I will be ready. The sun is on its way down. In the east, a nearly full moon is breaking through barren, wintry trees. Soon, because of snowy reflections, the night sky will be lit up.

"Ina, are we ready?"

She stands before me, holding a broom with her hands, resting on top of its handle.

"Yes, Jack."

Looking around for my son, I call out, "James, where are you? Ina, where is James?"

"I saw him a moment ago. He was here in the house with me."

A sudden look of terror moves across her face. She drops the broom on the floor and runs room to room, shouting. Then she goes out the front door, screaming for him.

"James, where are you? It's getting dark outside, Jack! Where is my son?"

I pause for a moment, trying to think of something to say. She is terrified and crying.

"Ina, he must be in the john. Earlier you mentioned something about Joni. Do you think he went up to her house?"

"He never goes up there. Go see if he is using the toilet! Hurry!"

I run fast as I can down a trail behind the cabin to where most of the newspapers end up. He is not there. The john—another reason to change the way we live.

"James, where are you, Son?" Terror grips my mind as I run toward Joni's house. Reaching her porch in seconds, with my fist balled tight, I beat on her door.

Hurry, Joni! Where are you? I pound my fist on the door again. *Where is she?* Before I could kick the door, she opens it.

"Have you seen James?"

"No! Why should I?" She spoke in a frail, soft voice.

I can barely hear her. Looking away from her, trying to think of places he can be; I cannot think straight. I speak aloud.

"Where can he be?"

"Jack, is something wrong with your son?"

My thoughts run together. I can hardly understand what she is saying.

"James is missing! Mr. Valentine is dead!"

Fragile as she is, I hate blurting it out.

"*Dead?* What happened to him?"

"Last night, some creatures from the river killed him."

Her aged face slowly changes to a look of fear.

"Jack, this time they're back to kill all of us."

Perplexed, I say, "Joni, you need to come back to my house with me."

After telling her about the old man, I feel responsible for her safety.

"I can't walk that far."

"Wait here. Go back inside and lock your door. Listen for my car. I'll hurry back."

Like a runner running for the finish line, I storm through the front door, screaming at Ina, "I can't find him! He is not at Joni's house! Joni is waiting on me to fetch her. We cannot leave her alone in that old house. They might kill her too." I should never have said *kill*.

She held her hair back with her hands and screamed at me, "Jack, you better find my son!"

I hold my hands up in surrender. "Darling, I am only one person. I am doing my best!" I hold back my tears. "Joni is waiting on me. As soon as I get back, I will find him."

Ina interrupts me. "I will go get her! You find James!"

"I need to think this out, Ina! You stay here with Joni while I go to the store and get help. I will hurry back."

I leave the house, run for the car, slide under the steering wheel, and drive frantically away.

I arrive at the store in no time at all. Several people are there as I push my way to the counter where Mr. White is standing. He knows something is wrong.

"What is wrong, Jack?"

"I need help finding James! I found Mr. Valentine in his house dead, killed by those creatures from the river. I cannot find James anywhere. My son is missing."

People are starting to push in around me. Seeing the severity of the situation, Mr. White reaches behind the counter for his rifle. He then reaches out and gives it to me.

"Here, take this. I have more on a wall in the back room."

Concerned about every passing minute, I need to be on the river. I then speak loudly so everyone can hear me.

"I need strong, able men to help find my son! Who will help?"

All but two older men step forward. A boy about eighteen raises his hand high above the others as he speaks.

"We are only five. We need more people."

I know he must be thinking. What can five accomplish?

"All of you arm yourselves. I need to go back to my wife and let her know what I am doing. Half of you go east down the river. The other half goes up the river. Meanwhile, meet at Maddox Bridge

Road. Don't forget, be sure to organize yourselves. Be careful. Watch over your shoulder. I am going back home and then to the river. Remember to tell Sheriff Pickens what happened to Mr. Valentine! I might be ahead of you on the river, west of the bridge. If you hear me fire off a round, I might have found my son or I am defending myself against those creatures."

One of the men asks, "What do they look like?"

I pause for a moment then say what comes to mind.

"They walk upright like a human." Unsure of my words, I continue, "But they look something like an ape."

The onlookers mumble among themselves.

"If you hear me fire this ten-gage more than twice, I need help."

Don't forget the weather, Jack, I say to myself. There is still a lot of snow on the ground. Still, I hurry back home as fast as I can. In a way, the snow is good. In a way, it is bad; good for tracking, bad for slowing me down. The 30/30 Mr. White gave me is loaded. I take no chances with it. Better to unlatch the door and then push it open with my foot. Too many bad things have been happening. Rather than to take a chance by being empty handed, from here on out, my weapon stays in my hands. After driving to an abrupt stop, I run and push the front door open.

Ina is still standing in the same place I left her. Her eyes cast a desperate stare across the front porch into a lonely field of snowy, yellow grass.

"Ina, I'm taking the Belgium with me. Keep this thirty-thirty with you. Most likely, the creatures are on the river and won't be back. You know how to use this weapon. It will stop anything. Don't worry about them coming into the cabin. It will keep them out."

"Is anyone going with you?"

"People are meeting at the bridge to organize a search. I cannot waste time. Close and lock the door behind me." I hate to leave her, but I have no choice. "There is no idea how long I will be gone."

"Be careful."

Ina's words ring in my mind. I reflect back to that time in the jungle. My sight is no longer superficial. This time, I keep a keen eye.

"Don't take any chances. With the full moon's light, they can see you at a great distance," she says, staring me in the face.

Ina holds me tight as if it's the last time she will see me. Letting go, her left hand grips the 30/30 tightly as she swings it down beside her slim body.

"I can see tracks at a great distance also, darling."

Walking out the front door, I sling the heavy ten-gage across my shoulder, once again in pursuit of the enemy. It gives me a feeling of nostalgia and hatred all rolled into one. This is something I know. Focusing my eyes down toward the river, deep snow still covers the old, winding, snow-covered, dirt road. After reaching the decline to the bottomland, I soon pick up their trail. There are still three of them. They are in a hurry.

Why do the creatures want James? These tiring hours will not go by fast. They have at least a two-hour head start on me. Trodden deep in the snow, I follow them as fast as I can. Breathing silently, listening, I can see that having the eyes of a point man, I can search for signs of them passing. Finally, I come to a stop.

I think aloud to myself, "Which way did they go, up the river or down the river?"

In this location, humans and animals wear the river trails until deep and wide. By following a trail, I will have it easy for a while. They go for miles up and down the river. Finally, I come upon James's tracks in the snow. One of the creatures must be carrying him. "Look," I said to myself, "a skirmish in the snow. James must be trying to get away from them."

Caught up in the moment, I stand still and listen to a great wash of sound passing through my ears. Over my head, black bats dart about here and there, a hallowed witching hour. It seems appropriate. A nervous, insane laugh engulfs me.

"It all seems so crazy!"

I feel as if I am playing a part in a picture show. There is no time for fantasy. This is no act. The prize is too great. I know in my mind that if things turn bad, Ina might lose her mind. *Hurry, Jack!* From looking at their tracks, they crossed to the other side, using the river stones.

What kind of animal am I dealing with? Are they communicating with James? They went to the same place they left Daisy then crossed the river. Where are they taking him? Jumping from rock to rock, they went to the other side of the river. After they crossed, their large footprints go west, up the river, back to the mountains where they came from. I know they crossed a while ago. Except for some wet footprints on the rocks, there are very few anywhere. I can do this, but it has been a long time since I tracked an animal. I am not used to tracking in the forest anymore. I need to slow down and pace myself. I try to move at a faster pace, but I am a bit out of shape. After a while, I reach the old, steel-frame bridge. It stretches across the Saluda.

As I get closer, standing among the bridge's silhouette of iron is a familiar face: Jim Darkman. *One man,* I say to myself. *Did he come out of the woods because someone said something about the disappearance of James?*

"Where is everyone?" I ask, hoping to get an intelligent answer.

"I told them not to come! Too many men are just as bad as not enough!"

After saying that, I see his point.

"True. Tracks will disappear, making catching up difficult."

He said nothing back. When I came down the frozen dirt road, the thought of too many men entered my mind as well.

"Come, Jack. We must go before the tracks get cold."

The tracks are already cold. After all, there is snow on the ground.

After climbing down from the bridge, we make our way up the trail alongside the fast-flowing river.

"What do you think, Jim? What will happen if they cross back to the other side of the river? Will they use the rocky shoals to try and throw us off?"

"Your boy is still alive. I know them. They need him for some reason unknown to me. For them to snatch him out from under you, they want him bad."

I listen to him with patient curiosity.

"You talk about them like they are people! They're not people," I say to Jim to get him to talk.

"Not people like you and me, but more people than animal."

He keeps talking in riddles as if he knows something I don't. He doesn't want me to know he spends most of his life in the forest. Maybe he is a blood brother with all of them.

"Jim, have you any idea where they are taking my son?"

"Back to their lair, no doubt somewhere in the mountains, a place where they have lived a very long time."

Right, I have lived here a very long time too.

"Darkman, what do you want me to call you?"

"Call me Jim."

"Okay, Jim. What do you know about these creatures?"

I figure if anyone understands them, he should know everything. How can a man live like a wild animal and not think like one? The black man then speaks.

"First of all, they are not creatures but early man. They still live in the forest like animals. Sometimes they take humans and make slaves of them, mostly children."

While listening to him, a hateful chill runs through my body.

"James a slave! I don't think so, unless they want a war with me!"

I see no sign of him covering up for them.

"Most of them came from northern Canada."

Before this is over, they may wish they never left.

"Why come down here?"

Jim gives me a confident look.

"They have always been here. Now people see more of them because there are more of them. They try to stay away from humans and guns."

Thoughts ramble through my mind. They must not want to stay away bad enough. They take big chances coming this close to humans and their guns.

"They didn't mind coming to my home and taking James. They know what there are doing if, indeed, they are smarter than animals." I then ask him, "Do you ever come in contact with them?"

While waiting on him to answer, white ashes rest heavy on his cigar as he thumps its burnt remains to the ground. "Jack, I am both trapper and tracker. In my line of work, I encounter them. The first time was in the Great Smokies. When trapping mink, there is a good place to set up camp. Plenty of hairy, big-footed creatures roam those hills."

He then lets out a quiet chuckle. Jim sounds a bit wild himself. It has been a long time since I lived in the woods and survived off the land and ate what I could find. That will be a last resort. I have heard it said before, "Eat what the monkey eats. If you can't do that, eat the monkey." However, that was then, the jungle's motto.

I patiently wait for him to answer as he braces himself against a pine tree, kicking it hard, trying to remove ice from his shoes.

"I have come face-to-face with them in a cave behind a waterfall. It was only because I had to take refuge from a thunderstorm," he says as ice falls from his shoe. "I don't mind the rain, but when lighting starts striking around me, my mother always comes to mind." He looks my way out the side of his eyes. "I can hear her say, 'Do not tempt the Lord, son!' So I take cover."

He must be like Mr. Valentine. He needs someone to help him pass the day.

"When I ran into the cave, there stood two youngsters, hairy feet and all, against the opposite wall. It was the first time ever seeing one. They didn't know what to think of me either. You know what I mean, me being black." He pauses long enough to unlace his shoes and pull his socks up.

"Eye to eye, they just stood there, curiously looking at me. I did not want to enrage them. They were huge. It was the longest few minutes of my life. When the lighting stopped, they snorted a few times then walked out and disappeared into the forest."

"That is quite a story, Jim. The creature and you both have something in common. You know when to get out of the rain." Distracted by my painfully cold feet, I sling the ten-gage across my shoulder. As Jim searches the ground for signs, he mumbles a few words just under his breath then speaks what's on his mind.

"I know they have a good head start. They might even be moving much faster than us. In any case, it doesn't matter. If they don't want to be found, they will stay far enough ahead to stay out of sight."

Still, I have to ask, "Do you know how far they have gotten?" I know it cannot be very far, as distance goes, not in miles.

"Jack, I don't see your son's tracks anymore."

Just as I thought, James is giving them a hard time. Make friends, gain their confidence, and then slow them down—an old military tactic he learned from me. That means they are carrying him. Jim takes it out of his mouth and then lights the smelly thing, puffing on it as he speaks.

"Now, that might mean he is slowing them down or he might not. As I said, for some reason they want him bad. If we stop following them, they will take it easy."

Why won't he come out with it? "Are you saying they know we are behind them?"

"That's right, Jack, so no slowing down. They will do anything to get him there, even kill us."

That shines a different light on the situation. He makes it sound like a bloody fight.

If that happens, James might get in the line of fire. How do I handle a monster like that in close combat? This is not like any other battle.

"Jim, I suppose you heard about my neighbor getting killed by these creatures?"

"A man called Fatso told me what happened. When I came into the store, they were all talking about what they were going to do. I stopped them in mid conversation and told them only two men need go after the boy, his father and me. After some convincing, they agreed."

"Concerning your neighbor, the creatures, as you call them, they don't needlessly kill. Someone said the creatures ate his dog. They do eat dog, but I'm not sure they killed your friend."

You say that, but everything points to them. "What else could have done it in that fashion?"

"Another person could have done it. Did you look to see if anything was missing?"

Yes, I wanted to say. Most of the dog was missing.

"Jim, at the time, everything pointed to them."

"If what you told me is true, a killer could still be out there. That makes me uneasy. I do not like leaving my wife at home. She can be emotional."

"Is someone with her?"

Yes, I say to myself. *A little, old woman, she is lethal with a cane.* "My neighbor, Joni, is with her. But she is very old and sometimes out of her mind."

CHAPTER 8

Pacing across the cabin floor, I worry about James. Nervously chewing my nails, my thoughts turn to busy work.

"Joni, can I get you a cup of hot tea?"

"Yes, Ina. Will you please? Get us some tea then sit down at the table. Let's talk."

I make some red tea and place a small, white cup on the table. I will have some too.

"Ina, I know you are having a sad time, but they will find James. In two or three days, he and Jack will be back at home."

I watch Joni's face carefully. Depending on the situation, Joni's voice makes certain sounds. Anxiously, I wait for her to speak. Lifting her hand to me, she places it on the top of my knee.

"What happened to Roy will not happen to James. Is anyone else with Jack?"

I pause for a moment, gathering my thoughts. "While in the store, Fatso pushed his way past me. He told me the hunter, Jim Darkman, is with him."

"See there? You have nothing to worry about. Darkman is a great tracker. He lives in the Smoky Mountains. He has a reputation for doing what other people cannot."

After talking to me, Joni falls silent.

Still drowsy, I am taking in everything Joni said about Jim Dark-man. I guess everyone around here knows the tracker. I hope this hunter is as good as his reputation, and James will be found in good health. Joni's face has a distant look as her finger traces the edge of the tea cup.

"What is wrong, Joni?"

"We all have our troubles, young lady. Let me give you something to take your mind off of yours."

"I was thinking of Roy. He was a good man. I wish he could have died peacefully in his sleep. Instead, he died brutally at the hands of a beast." Joni rubs her careworn eyes with knobby fingers as tears choke her voice. "I knew him most of my life." A look of sad regret covers her face.

Both of them are the same age. She must know his history.

"What happened to him, Joni?"

"He gave up on life when Ruby died."

Joni is not the only person who will miss him.

I consider the ten years our little family has lived in Roy's small cabin. James was just two years old when we moved in—a lifetime ago. Roy never acted like a typical landlord. When lean times fell on our family, he refused rent payment. Judging Joni's grief, Roy must have meant a lot more than she is willing to tell.

"Were Ruby and Roy close?"

Joni smiles broadly. "He loved her so much. They were always together."

I suspect a deeper reason Joni feels the way she does.

"Were you close to Ruby?"

"She and I were like sisters, but sisters do not tell each other everything. I kept a secret from her. Secretly, I loved Roy too. But he was loyal to her. So I kept it to myself until she died."

Sudden understanding clears my puzzlement over my reclusive neighbor's odd behavior.

"I see why you spent the rest of your life alone. Did you ever tell him the way you feel?"

Joni's face once again falls with grief. "He knew my feelings. Even so, he would not let his memory of her fade away."

Right away, a chill of dread runs through my mind, thinking of Jack while I listen to her talk.

"He showed no affection for me. I became an old woman and Roy a lonely recluse. He hardly ever came out of his house, even for food."

Jack did a lot for him. I know Leon White delivered everything he ate.

"Joni, what happened to his wife? All I know is that she drowned in the Saluda River. He must have taken her death horribly."

Joni looks at me with a pained expression. "I will try to tell you about that night, Ina, if I can remember everything. It all seems so distant now. It was April sixteenth, nineteen thirty-five. Ruby began a long labor with her first child. I was with her most of the time. Roy was afraid to leave her alone. Roy sent me for the doctor, but he was about two hours away. When I finally found him, he was drunk. I was gone so long Roy thought something happened to me. You know how the bridge is now, old and worn out with only one lane? Then, it was much worse. It had rained for days. The river was out of its banks. No one took care of the bridge at all. Boards were missing in places, a lot of them rotten. Roy was so afraid he was going to lose Ruby that he ventured into the night with her.

"He left with her to find the doctor. Like most men, he knew nothing about delivering a baby and panicked. On the way there, Ruby birthed the child, and it seemed like the worst was over. When they turned back toward home and crossed the bridge, the deck fell through. He was holding the baby when they fell. When he came out of the water, he still had the little girl in his arms. But Ruby washed down the river. For a week, he and fifty other men looked for her.

"After the river went down, they found her lying on a large, flat rock a mile away. She crawled out of the water onto a large rock where she then died. Roy could not bear the thought of her dying alone. He put flowers on that rock until he died."

I think of Jack and me, how it would be without him. What a horrible thing to live with. No wonder everything around him wasted away. He gave up on life. "What happened to his daughter?"

"When she was a week old, he gave her away."

CHAPTER 9

After Jim and I reach the great sandbar, we camp and rest for a while. Before taking it easy, I first walk to the end of our long, sandy spot. It is an isolated, appropriate place to set up camp for the night. Standing by the now slowly flowing river, I skip rocks across the glassy water as many others have done for millions of years. Leaves, twigs, and other debris wash onto the sandbar. During the hot summer months, people come to the sandbars to party and enjoy the cool river water. However, in winter this place is bare of vegetation and dead from the lack of activity. None of the river-goers have any idea what goes on in this thick, endless forest. Thoughts ramble through my mind. I wonder how many people will come if they know the truth.

Even so, no one comes when the trail is heavy with snow. It is still freezing cold weather. Now evening, the river is alive with pale, wavy moonlight. Remembering what the old man said, I see his fishing spot. In my mind's eye, I see him running for his life. Then, suddenly, a rustling behind me brings me back to the present. I cannot stay here any longer. I am not far from camp. A few minutes later, I scramble back into the dusk-lit campsite.

"Jim, did you know when Valentine was in his thirties he saw the creatures on this very sandbar?"

"I heard something about him seeing them on the river. But I didn't know it was this close to his house."

Watching him prop his rifle against a tree, I bet when the creatures see Jim around they do not shy away. Stooping down to tie his shoe, he speaks.

"For reasons I am not sure of, they don't shy away from me like they do a white man."

I move my head up and down in an agreeable fashion. *Strange. I was thinking about that.* "Jim, maybe they like black better than white."

"Sure, Jack. They are discriminating creatures. Jack, while the moon is still out, we need to take care of our needs. The creatures are not far from us, in their standards. However, if they get a whiff, they will put more distance between us."

I do not know much about these creatures, whatever they are. I have been in dense places where some furious animals roam.

Nevertheless, when they got a whiff of us, they did not run away. "What is their range, Jim?"

"Downwind, they can pick up a scent about five or six miles away."

Disbelieving, I stop. "How can that be? No animal on earth can do that. Jim, you've been in the woods to long." That sounds like a wild boast.

"Jack, you never hear of someone trapping one. Why are there no photos of them?"

That is easy to answer! I come back with a smug reply. "No one wants to eat one, and they won't pose for a photo. If what you say is true, Jim, we will never get close to them."

His self-confidence is high. "But we can follow them to their lair. Once getting there, I hope there is no need to kill a lot of them."

Jim has his reason for early camp. But unlike him, I believe the creatures are not a great distance from us. So as not to get to close to them, I know we need to pace ourselves. We walk around camp, trying to find dry wood to build a fire. We have to venture farther out from our campsite. However, the darkness of night is not here yet.

I have no idea of what to expect. For all I know, they might be out there, watching. With every snap of a twig, I pause. Then, suddenly still, my eyes scan dark shadows in the forest, wondering if they will come charging through the thickets.

It is good we are away from the forest and camped on an open sandbar. I do not like our back to the river. There is no retreat. A large log lies on the sandbar, close to the fire. Jim is standing across from me.

"Jim why don't you spread your sleeping bag over here, where the log is. We can put it between the forest and us."

He stands there with bag in hand, thinking. Unrolling the bag, he then speaks. "That sounds like a good idea. However, I have my own. It is better if I sleep away from the fire, out of sight. I sleep light as a feather and motionless as that log. I will hear them if they come."

Soon, daylight fades away, giving way to a moonlit night, making the night spooky even though the moon is full and the night is bright. Moonlight casts dark shadows all around. I hope I am able to sleep. Jim is already asleep early, with the birds. At home, bedtime comes early. Not tonight. Maybe it is the moonlight. I lie here awake until midnight, all cuddled up to a cold log rather than Ina's warm body. Oh what a night! Soon, orange and yellow flickering fire dies down to a pile of orange embers and then needs more wood.

After leaving my warm spot, I take white ashes and then cover part of the red cinders. A pile of wood dwindles as I stack more onto the dying flames. Now finished, I take a quick look around the forest. Jim is out there somewhere, not a thud out of him or the beast that might lurk out of sight watching us. Slipping back into my warm sleeping bag, I relax and then drift into a dream of home. We are living in a new house on the same property where we now live. It's nighttime, yet everything is lit up with bright light! James is stretched out on the plush, carpeted floor of his room, reading a book. A startling sound interrupts my dream, causing the warm vision of James to fade. I quickly jump to my feet and then grab my gun before I am even awake. Jim sits at the campfire, stirring the coals, smirking at my alarm.

"Didn't you hear that, Jim?"

"Hear it? I did it to wake you up! It is time to get the pots and pans rattling." That sounds like something I would say.

I shake my head and wipe the sleep from my eyes. I do not remember winking out last night.

"I am not very hungry this morning, Jim. A cup of coffee will hold me over until noon. How about you?"

"I suppose so. Not much kept me awake last night, and I slept plenty. Sure! I can go for that!"

Good. The pot is already on the coals and hot. "Here you go, Jim. Hold this cup while I pour it."

We sit on the log while we drink our coffee. Afterward, we put the fire out, immersing the coals with water. Then we gather our packs and begin our hike farther up the river.

The farther we go, the more our path turns into an animal trail. Not like a human trail, wide and trodden down, this one is narrow with animal tracks. Creatures of the forest; this is their world.

"Something's different."

"What do you see?"

Jim looks all around for tracks. "One of them has put James on the ground. That is a mistake. It will cost them." While slinging his rifle across his shoulder, he looks dead at me. "Your son is having an effect on them. The female is carrying your son, probably on her shoulders."

I know he is waiting on me to ask the obvious, but I do anyway. "How do you know that?" Jim slows down and turns toward me. "The female is falling behind. James must be slowing her down, making things worse for them. Late evening, the moon will come up, throwing their bedtime off. When it is bright, the male will watch the moon."

That will be a sight to see.

The big male will be moonstruck, staring upward into the night sky with his face glowing brightly. I have seen James do the same thing. Jim talks on.

"Their sleep will come a little late, about two hours. Even though the moon is still full, tonight is not a good time to overpower them."

How does Jim know all this? I never hear him say anything about living with them. I know a lot of what he says must be plain logic. Sometimes he is hard to hear over the noisy river. "Jim, can you speak louder? I can't hear you over the river!"

He turns toward me. "Jack, just like us, they will stop and find a place to sleep. As I said, it will be late. If we try to take James from them while they are sleeping, he might be hurt. They are still very much a primate. Just like monkeys, they sleep in trees. Nonetheless, just like us, the male will sleep on the ground."

"Sounds like a war to me, Jim."

"To see our strength, Jack, he might pay us a visit tonight. If he does, do not get trigger-happy. We must not kill him. If we do, they might kill the boy."

Jim keeps looking up at the sky. It is getting late in the evening. I hear him mumble something about the night sky. We try to put more distance behind us. It causes a late start on our next campsite. We need to hurry. A large, bright moon shines through tall trees, but soon it will be dark. We quicken our pace until we come upon an open area close to the forest.

"I will gather wood for the fire."

"Be careful where you put your hands, Jack. Cottonmouths kill. You might roll over a log and find him sleeping."

Reaching down to pick up a piece of wood, I look back at him. I do not believe they are out this time of year. He must have a thing about snakes.

"You don't have to tell me, Jim."

He leaves, walking a distance up the river. It looks like he is getting in the water. Only a crazy man would get in water with this kind of weather. I hear him shout, "I'll get food for us!"

I go back to the woods to gather wood for night. While on my last trip to the fire, Jim has returned with enough fish for the two of us. Jim cleans the fish, finally pushing a stick through them. He rests them on two wooden forks, one on each side of the fire.

Afterward, we sit by the crackling fire and listen to night sounds. We turn our dinner slowly over the searing flames. Soon, all the fish are cooked. By the warm campfire, we rest and consume our dinner hungrily. Jim does not have much to say. To break the silence, I ask how he caught the fish.

"I pinned them under the rocks with my hands."

"What about snakes?"

"I don't eat snakes. Only fish."

I did not carry the conversation any further. I can see he is at home in his surroundings. We unroll our sleeping bags and then spread them on a nearby *sandbar. This sandbar is clear of mussels. Those smelly, dead things attra*ct every creature in the forest. Tonight, we will rest on clean sand and pebbles with clean water flowing nearby.

The flow of water makes a rushing sound. I lay beside the flickering fire, listening to a great, horned owl fishing for his food. Without making a sound, he glides across the surface of the water. Thinking about the creatures, I remember what my father told me: "Don't worry, Son. Wild animals won't come around a fire at night." As I stare into the woods, I know that these are not the usual wild animals. Nervously, I scan the night for the large outline of the hairy creatures that killed Daisy and took my boy.

"Get some sleep, Jack."

Jim rolls over and drifts off to sleep without a care in the world. I lie there, watching the owl perched on a dead limb. Its branches stretched out over the river. My eyes slowly close. The sun comes up four hours later.

CHAPTER 10

As usual, as soon as the morning sun comes beaming through my bedroom window, I am up early. Joni, in bed with covers pulled up to her neck, is still resting comfortably in James's bed. As peaceful as she looks, she will be fine. There is no need to stay around here, waiting on her to wake. I need to go to the store. I will leave her a note telling her where I am and soon will be back. To keep my mind off James while going out the door, I sing a little song. While driving up the road, my song keeps running through my mind.

Soon, the stop sign is in sight. Fence posts go by slowly as old blue's brakes screech to a halt. It is early morning, and people are scurrying about, trying to accomplish their daily tasks. Waiting, I look up and down the Dixie Highway. *Someone please slow down and let me cross. Can't they see I need to cross?* Black ice still makes driving slippery. *Where is everyone going in such a hurry? Surely they know how bad the road is.* While waiting at the stop sign, I see Anna sweeping tracked-in snow off the walk area. She pays me no mind.

Trying to get to the gas pumps before anyone else, I lose traction crossing the road. As soon as I open my door, Anna props her icy broom against a porch post on her way to meet me.

"Did they find James yet?"

Her face is all a glow with hope.

"I haven't heard from them, Anna." I want to say they are at home.

"I am so sorry, Miss Ina!"

As long as I have known her, she still calls me *Miss*.

"We have known each other for a long time, Anna. Please call me Ina."

She can see I don't want to talk about them. I need to keep them off my mind.

"Do you want some gas, Miss Ina?" Robert asks as I open my door to speak to him. I hate this entire ma'am and miss stuff. I know he says it to show respect for me.

"Yes, Robert. Thank you. Will you fill it up for me, please?"

Pushing his smudged eyeglasses up his noise, he shoves the gas nozzle into old blue. The gas makes a burbling sound as it flows into my empty tank. Finally, I hear him tighten my gas cap. I need a place to park. Cars are parked zigzagged all around the store. Hopefully I can settle into a safe place. In their busy life, too busy to cook for themselves, they scamper about, trying to be first to find an empty table.

As they waddle along in trails made from footsteps in snow, some of them have a hot cup of coffee on their mind. But then again, before having to work all day at the cotton mill, most of them want their breakfast cooked for them, knowing they will have no time for a lunch break.

I almost forgot about Joni. She could wake at any time. I hurry away from my car. Before going inside, I stand at the door and then look within. There is a man around known as Fatso. He is as big around as he is tall—not short but tall. Rude, with a nasty, hate-filled mouth, he graces the restaurant every morning with his presence.

Full of the devil, he calls Anna a nigger. Nevertheless, wonderful as she is, she always shines it on. After I come into the store, everyone stops what they are doing and watches me. Anna is taking Fatso's breakfast to him. As always, he likes it piled on. In the back corner of the eating area, his table always waits for him. No one dares sit in his favorite spot. She doesn't show it, but I know she dreads serving him. Anna, trying not to show what she really feels, keeps her composure, walks over, and then gives him his food.

Holding his head down over his plate, without looking up he says, "Nigger, where is my coffee?"

Eating like a pig, he drops food on himself and on the floor. He effortlessly raises his head from his food as he speaks to me.

"I hear you lost your boy!"

His voice strong and pointed. If anyone else had said it that way, I would think nothing of it. Anna looks at me and then at him.

"Pay no attention to him, Ina!"

"You shut up, nigger. I did not speak to you!"

Still being polite, Anna Marie stands there.

"Fatso, you have no right to talk to Anna like that!" My face feels flushed, my anger rises, and I take his plate away from him and then hold it in my hand. Without as much as a smirk on my face, I reach out and slam it down on his head.

"Here Wear this. You look and eat like a pig. You might as well be one!"

He springs to his feet, knocking the table over with his protruding stomach.

"You taking up for that nigger? She's nothing." As he gets his words out, his fat face shakes ferociously.

"She is much better a person than you, Fatso!"

Without saying anything else, he stares around at everyone. No one says anything. After walking to the front door, he reaches for it and then slams it open against the wall. He leaves without paying.

"Mr. White, I'll pay for his breakfast."

"You don't have to do that, Ina. You do well. He does that every time he comes in, but Anna puts up with him."

I hear words coming out of Mr. White's mouth. I want to tell him what I thought about him, but I have too much respect for the man. Even so, he should not be reluctant to let people know how he loves Anna. Anna loves him very much. He's the only father she has ever known. After the encounter with Fatso, I gather my thoughts and then pay for my gas and eggs.

"I'll see you later, Anna."

Before long, I arrive home.

I remove a carton of eggs from the car seat and then go inside. Joni is comfortable in her chair. She speaks as I walk by.

"Good morning, Ina. How are you this morning?"

My mind is tired with worry over my missing son and absent husband. Even so, I manage a weak smile and a half hearted reply. "Fine...is the heater warm enough for you? Did you sleep well last night?"

"No, I didn't. It's hard for me to sleep in someone else's bed."

I can understand that. Jack is the same way.

"I'm sorry. Perhaps breakfast will make you feel better."

While I work in the kitchen, Joni sits there, rocking and talking.

"I need to stop drinking coffee. It is bad for my heart!"

She said it seriously. She smells the coffee. *Of course, Joni. I have a lot to learn about taking care of you.* I have never had a mother, not one I can remember. Perhaps she will like something else to drink while waiting for breakfast.

"Can you drink milk?"

"Yes, Ina. I like milk."

"Good. We will have breakfast soon."

CHAPTER 11

Now that morning light brightens the river, the hunt for James can continue. Jim is already up, preparing breakfast.

"Good morning, Jim. I see you are familiar with surviving in the wild. You are much better at this than I am. What is for breakfast?"

He walks around the fire and picks up a plate. "Eggs, coffee, fish, and some fried bread."

"Sounds good. I'm starving." Following Jim's example, I help myself to breakfast.

He stands by the fire, pouring himself a cup of coffee. He then pours some for me.

I reach out and take the steaming hot cup. "Where did you get the food?"

As if to say, "That was a dumb question." Jim shrugs his shoulders. "I packed it in."

"You must have it packed away tight and out of sight."

"That's the way I do it. All packed and ready to go on short notice."

Back home, everything happens so fast. Now I don't know what to expect.

"This is all new to me. I thought we would have caught up with them by now." I try not to show how disappointed I am.

"Not these creatures, Jack. They are smart and have heightened super senses. I tracked one for a week last spring and never came in contact with him."

That is inspiring insight. You make it sound like we will never catch up with them.

"Some crazy fool told me a wild animal took his wife. Looked like an ape, he said. Someone told him about me. When I got to his house, he was like you, full of questions. His name is Sam Burns."

"He said, 'They took my Jane!' After questioning him, I asked him to take me to where he last saw her. She and the creature's tracks were not far apart. After spending some time in the woods, the evidence left me a little suspicious. Not sure the creatures even took her, I began investigating in another direction.

Intrigued, I try to press Jim for the end of the story. "Did you think someone else took her?"

"No, but I eventually did suspect the husband." My tracker guide looks at me with a direct and piercing gaze.

I hope he does not suspect me. Okay, let us not step off the deep end and fall into a pit of paranoia. This is crazy, talking to myself! Jim may have doubts about the ape like creatures killing old man Valentine, but I have nothing to hide. I can see where innocent people can let misplaced guilt and suspicion drive them crazy. I need to get my mind off this!

"You say you had suspicions. Why do you say that?"

"He appeared nervous when I asked questions about Jane, as if blaming him. Doesn't matter what happened to her. Once involved, I'm obligated."

"If Sam Burns is anything like me, he was worried sick."

As Jim somberly thinks back, he removes a cigar from his mouth and then throws it into the river. "Keep all the gear packed away and ready to go at a moment's notice. Before the tracks disappear, we need to be on the trail."

His hot trails, lucky for me he never wastes any time. Biding for more time to finish my coffee, I press for more about the missing woman case. "Was the terrain like anything here?"

"Similar. He lives in the Great Smokies not far from Bald Mountain, Georgia. Have you ever been up there?" asks Jim.

"A long time ago, before James was born, we used to take a telescope up there and set it up. Up there, the stars are very bright."

Those days are gone now. So many years have passed. Now I find myself on the Saluda, hoping James is still alive.

"Then you know the lay of the place. I've lived there nearly all my life so I know the place like the back of my hand."

"Jack, you know how it is for us. We can track them forever yet still never catch up with them. I spent all day trying to catch up with his wife and the creatures. Something was not right about Sam, but I could not put my finger on it. Even so, I had to know if she was with them." Jim gathers up the campsite and our meager belongings.

As I listen to Jim spin his story, my thoughts return to Ina and home. I am going to make sure I give all those little things she wants: indoor plumbing, running water, even milk delivery.

"I figure at least, I could find out if his wife is with the creatures. Like a wolf on the chase, I stayed on their trail."

"When did you catch up with them?" I sling my pack onto my back and begin to trail behind him. "Five days later, I saw them cross a ridge not far away."

"Did they know you were tracking them?"

"They always do. They stopped and looked back at me."

Sounds to me like the creatures are playing a game of catch me if you can—a game Owl played with me.

"The woman wasn't with them?" I ask Jim, waiting to see if he heard me over river noise.

"No she wasn't, but that doesn't mean anything. Sometimes they release a captive when a tracker is close to them."

I flash back to my past war days, my captain's voice, saying, "Take no chances. Do not let the enemy slow you down." If, indeed, she is with them, she is lucky they did not kill her. Jim walks out to the water's edge, then peers up the river for any sign of them crossing.

"She could have been somewhere on the trail."

Jim quickly responds, "Could have been, but I would have known it."

"So when the creatures crossed the ridge some distance away, I threw my hand up and waved good-bye to them. And surprisingly, one of them did the same thing."

"He was mimicking you, can't be that intelligent."

We now follow a narrow animal trail.

"Look, Jack. They slept in this tree last night. Looking up, Jim points at a crude bamboo platform placed across large pine limbs.

Jim cracks a thin grin. "I wonder what James thought of sleeping in a tree."

"James did want me to build him a tree house."

I stand there, gathering a mental image of the tree where leaves press down flat on the ground. James and the other two creatures slept in the tree. The greater male must have stayed on the ground to make sure James did not sneak off. Jim walks to the water's edge and stands by a large weeping willow. Its roots stick out into the water bouncing up and down in the rushing current. The creatures must have stood in this same place. Tracks are all around where Jim is standing.

"We won't catch them today. They will zigzag across the river rocks several times. Perhaps they want us to believe they have left the river."

"What happened to the woman, you spent all that time looking for?"

Jim walks away from the river's edge toward me.

Taking his rifle off his shoulder, he says, "You want to know all you can about them, don't you, Jack?"

"Your stories help keep my mind off James and Ina. After he waved bye to you, what happened then?"

Jim walks away, trailing words behind him. "When I discovered they didn't have her, I went back to their house to see Sam."

Following the river while listening to Jim's adventure, we make our way farther upland. I try to stay alert, but the rush of river water is hypnotic. It tries to take me away, makes me drowsy. Still, it is not enough to take me away from this horrible experience. The truth is, you never know how much you miss someone until something takes him or her away.

"Was Sam Burns surprised to see you back at his house?"

"He wasn't there. Only Jane's sister, Elaine. A woman about thirty, blonde hair, blue eyes, and about five feet two came to the door."

He is so keen in his description of her. I wonder if he knows as much about the creatures.

"She sounds like a fine lady, Jim. You don't miss anything, do you?"

Smugly, Jim agrees, "Not in my line of work!"

"Did you keep searching for Jane?"

If Ina came up missing, I would never give up on her.

"No. I did not search any longer, not at that moment. 'Where is Sam?' I asked her. 'I haven't seen him since you left.' 'I thought he was with you,' she said to me. While standing in the doorway, she was very fidgety. Strange behavior, as if she was hiding something. After talking to her, I went to my truck, sat there for a moment, and then left. Elaine's behavior was very suspicious."

"I came back later and questioned her further. 'Sam did not go with me,' I told her. Where is Jane?' I asked her blatantly.

"'I don't know where she is!' She sounded very sincere," said Jim.

Just the same, she should have kept watch on her sister. I believe Ina would say the same thing.

"When did you tell her you suspected Sam?"

"I waited until the next day to weigh everything in my mind."

"When something so obvious is taking place, why did you put it off until the next day? The girl's sister had to know something."

"Were you trying to save her some grief?"

"You could say that. Why make her suffer?"

Jim is too trusting. I would have called the sheriff.

"The next day I came back, had coffee with her, and asked more questions about her sister."

I wanted to find out how Jane got along with Sam.

As we walk a narrow trail through a thicket of pussy willow, he continues telling his story.

"'Elaine, tell me, would Sam harm your sister?' She stumbled around my question before answering, 'How can I answer a question like that? I am so confused right now!' Sister Elaine knows more than she is telling.

While tracking the creatures, I had time to think about things.

I have a feeling Jim's story does not have a successful conclusion.

"What were you thinking about?" I ask Jim.

"I felt something was wrong back home, with the location of her tracks to the creatures. In the mountains, I never saw her tracks, only theirs."

"Didn't Elaine have suspicions about Sam? Seems to me she would have, him disappearing like that."

"Unfortunately, you never know, Jack. Elaine did not suspect anything bad of him. However, I think she knew more than she wanted to tell. So I asked her, 'Elaine do you suspect Sam?'"

"How did she react?"

"I believe she wanted to protect him. I thought this would be a good time to ask her why Sam left so suddenly."

She was silent for a moment then shook her head, silently crying. Ripping her heart out was not what I wanted to do."

"What did you tell her?"

"The only thing I could say to Elaine was 'things don't look good for Jane.' Then, in so many words, she wanted to know why he made up the story about the creatures."

"What do you think?" Jim turns and faces me as I answer his challenge.

"He planned it at last moment." Sam knew enough about the creatures to use them as an alibi."

It is obvious he had to come up with something, even if it was crazy and out of this world.

"He must have wanted to get rid of Jane for a long time."

"What do you think happened to her?" Jim asks me.

I feel like Watson measuring up to Sherlock Homes.

"Maybe he wanted the sister and believed with Jane out of the way he could have the blonde-haired beauty. In his mind, he could do no wrong."

That is the way it is for these crazies—let the devil come in and take control.

"How long did it take for you to find her? You did find her, didn't you?"

"I found her, but I'll save that 'til the end so I don't kill the suspense for you."

"Oh, thanks a lot. I can hardly wait!"

I let him tell his story, but I already know the ending.

"Before asking her a lot of questions, I wanted Elaine to believe I was not there to blame her for Sam's deceitfulness."

How can a person live with someone and not discover who that person is?

"Jim, she might have done something to cause him to turn wicked."

Sounds to me you want to protect her. Maybe Jim spent too much time with her.

"I told her I would never stop until I found Jane. Jack, it's the same way with you. I will never stop until I find James."

That is great to know, Jim, but these are different circumstances. No crazies here...only big, ugly beasts.

"I only hope James is still alive." Not knowing how James is brings tears to my eyes.

"Jack, these creatures are not like that. They kill in self-defense, and not old men."

"The old man is dead. How do you think he died?"

Perhaps I need to paint a better picture.

"I don't know, but I would be disappointed to find out one of the creatures did it. I will look into it when we get back. Now I have a mission, and you know what it is."

Don't need to tell me. I know why we are going without sleep. "Wait, Jim. Take a look at these tracks."

As I kneel down over them, Big Jim stands beside me.

"What kind of cat tracks are they?" I look up at him.

"Appears to be a big male cougar...I hope that's what it is."

What else is going to happen? While I entertain the possibilities, my ears quicken to sounds around us. "What else can it be?" I ask, rising to my feet.

"It could be a panther."

Where does he think we are? First, creatures, and now it's big cats. "Jim, there are no panthers in this country." No ape-looking creatures either, I say to myself.

He then says, "Most people believe that. They do migrate here from Central America."

"How will we know what it is?"

I feel like the new grunt in my old platoon. I have a feeling if I ask anything it will be the wrong question.

"Hard to tell, big enough tracks to be a panther, but I hope not," he says as he kneels down, brushing leaves away from the tracks.

"Are we in danger?" There it is—a stupid question. Of course, we are, and the rest of this rescue will be spent looking over my shoulder.

"Only if he discovers we are behind him," says Jim as he takes the cigar out of his mouth, holding it between his yellowed fingers.

"What do you mean by that?"

Jim takes his rifle by the barrel and places it on his shoulder. "Because of their large, powerful size, even a killer cat won't attack one of those creatures. But James is with them."

If the creatures want James bad enough, I don't see them giving him up. However, I suppose he is safe. Any cat would be out of its mind to go up against those hairy beasts.

"Is he after them or after us?"

I suppose the question is moot. Jim's knowledge of the apelike creatures is impeccable. Nervously bring up the rear, I keeping vigilance. What does he know of this feline that might be trailing us or has its sights on James?

"I don't know what he is after yet, Jack. It's too soon to tell. This is an animal trail. It could be after anything."

That is not reassuring.

"Jim, if he follows them across the river, we will know."

"Yes, good thinking, Jack. Let's hope he is hunting for deer. Just the same, we will keep a lookout behind us.

All of a sudden, I have a nostalgic feeling of being back in the jungle. Once again, I bring up the rear, looking behind me. Following behind Jim, listening to the sounds of the forest, I cannot help but think of James and wonder how he is holding up.

CHAPTER 12

Where is Dad? I hope he is looking for me in the right place.

With James sitting on her shoulder, she stops briefly to listen for any approach from unwelcome guests. Her large, black eyes shift about, looking at every possible hiding place, her big, hairy feet are planted firmly on a large table rock. I don't see anything, but she is in tune with every sound on the river. I keep looking back, but Dad is nowhere in sight. I now see why Mom is always saying, "Don't let James out of your sight." At the time, it made me feel like a little child, but never again. Staring down at the water, watching it run by, I worry about Mom, how she is surviving all this. I hope Dad did not leave her alone, surely not.

At first, I was terrified of them. Although they are very primitive, these creatures have a gentle way about them. They act lie monkeys but much smarter. They gave me raw fish to eat last night. I will watch the large male. If I see him reaching his hands under the river rocks, I will have to do something to build a fire and then do some cooking. Where are they taking me? The female behaves as if she likes me. Sometimes, she amazes me. To be so large, she jumps from one rock to the next. I don't see how she does it with me on her shoulders. Large Black eyes searching the area, she raises her large, rough hand up to me, lowering me to the ground.

They do not stay in one area very long. Somehow, they know someone is behind them. Every now and then, all of them stop at the same time and then turn their big, hairy heads down river. They hear, or maybe sense someone off at a distance. So much has happened since I saw them in the forest near our cabin.

Mom and Dad tried to keep me near. When he said they might be in the woods, I thought he was teasing. I should have paid attention to him. He was not teasing, and now, here I am, with them. Hopeful, I look down the river for Dad. If he is back there, he is ever so silent. The female is smart with keen senses. I watch her hold her head upward into the air, nose pointing upward, sniffing the air. Lowering her primitive skull, she stands there, looking at me with dark, black eyes as cold as night. She knows what I am thinking. I can see it in her face.

I ask her in a harsh voice, "Why did you take me?"

She confidently grunts and then steps to another rock, jerks her head around toward the others, and then eerily howls in the direction of the males. They stop. Eyes on me, she is waiting on me to catch up.

"I'm coming, beast!"

A distance up the river, I can see large rocks in the water. Brown in color, some still have snow on them. I still try to slow them down.

My diligence is to no avail. For some reason, she wants me to hurry. This female is the dominant one. She waves her hands around in the air as the big male did after noticing us at the top of the hill with his kill. Staring back at me, it wants me to climb atop her shoulders.

"What do you want?

Fine! I hate riding you. I am coming. Please don't put me on your back again! You smell like a wet dog!"

I shout loud at her. If Dad is back there, he should be able to smell you! I try to slow the creatures down, but the beast is so demanding. When I saw them on the river, I never thought this would happen. Mom and Dad said there is no such thing as monsters, but they are wrong. Are they nomads, or are they going to their home? So many unanswered questions; it's a frustrating situation. Now all my unanswered questions are useless gibberish. All I can do is talking to myself. Bewildered, I looked up into the sky. Clouds are starting to move in. Is Dad back there, watching them? Last time Dad watched the sky, three feet of snow covered the ground.

It is so cold. Snow can start falling again at any time. It makes me shiver even more. At first, it was an oddity. Now I wish it were summer. Looking down at my worn shoes, my coat is warm, but my shoe's stitching is coming loose. They think I can go where they go. If I could be as hairy as they are—hair even covers their feet—then I could go naked like them. That would be a sight. Mom should see me then. Mom, I miss her so much. My new mom wants me to know that, if I don't stay up with her, she will toss me onto her shoulders again.

If I try to get away from them, they will surely come after me. I should gain their confidence. Last night, I slept in a tree. I am still sore from that. When I go back to school, I will be the envy of everyone. Dad, please discover my whereabouts. They are not going to harm me. If they were, they would have already done it.

The same question keeps coming to my mind. Where are they taking me? Yesterday, they heard a gunshot a distance away. I was somewhat excited at it being Dad. When is he going to catch up with me? Now back on her shoulders, I wish she would put me back on the ground. She smells like a dog. These things killed Mr. Valentine. I know they can do the same to me. If they were going to kill me, they would have already done it. Dad told me if someone ever snatched me, it is my duty to escape. I told him I am not in the army, but escape does enter my mind. The only place I could go would be back where I came from. I don't believe I would get very far before they caught me, so I will wait for Dad to catch up.

CHAPTER 13

Joni and I are now at the table, eating breakfast.

"Joni, it is so nice having you here. I have always wanted to be friends with you. You seem so lonely up on that hill by yourself."

It's strange how conflict can bring two people together. I have lived around Joni for years and never knew her.

"Since Roy stopped seeing me, I am not used to being around people anymore."

I believe it is more, as if, she lost the will to socialize.

"You and Roy were more than friends?"

I have seen a painting of Joni hanging on a dusty wall in her den. In her youth, she was a beautiful woman.

"Yes, Joni. I remember. You told me you loved him?" *He must not have loved her back, or her life would have turned out much different.*

"Yes. For a long time, but most of the time, his wife occupied his mind. He could not find a place in his heart for me."

"What happened to him?" I ask.

"Whenever I saw him, he was always on his front porch, in his rocking chair, rocking his life away." Regretfully remembering the past, she throws her hands up in the air.

That never changed. During the summer, he still sits in a rocking chair, watching cars go by. "He must have taken Ruby's death very hard."

Joni becomes silent. A distant look covers her sad face. She then speaks.

"He could not do anything for himself."

I amuse myself with a little thought. *If he was like most men, he needed a housekeeper.*

"Did you do his housework?"

"Most of the time."

She loved him a lot to do his work for him and not live with him. "You loved him a lot?"

"I did for a long time. After a while, I gave up. I felt taken advantage of, but now I wish I had stayed with him." Joni tries to hold back her tears.

"You cannot blame yourself for what happened to him, Joni."

She then says, "A friend does not forsake you ever."

You went more than the distance, sweet Joni. "Joni, you had to put up with a lot?"

"I waited on him a long time, hoping he would get over her, but he never did. Now he is dead and everything is gone. Now I am old. And soon, I will be gone too."

If she will give me a chance, I will do my best to make her feel needed before that grim day comes.

"Now who can that be?"

Persistent knocking rattles the door. I rise from the table and then cautiously open the door. A man wearing a cowboy hat and a sheriff's badge stands in front of me.

"Hello. I am Sheriff Pickens. I need to ask you some questions about your neighbor, Mr. Valentine."

Well, here goes. He does not look like a man to believe fairy tales. "I will tell you what I can. I never went over there."

"How long have you known him?"

Why do they always start out with that question? What does that have to do with him being dead? "We have been living here for ten years." *I should know everything he wants to ask by now. I have been living here long enough.*

"Ten years, and you never went over there?"

He looks down at a small paper pad. If he would remove that ten-gallon cowboy hat from down around his ears, he might hear what I say.

"I did not say that. I was not there the night he died."

"Did he have many friends?"

If he could have gotten around, he might have. Nevertheless, he had us. "Hardly any." I felt violated and unwilling to answer questions

"Do you know what happened to him?"

I hate answering these questions. He is not going to believe anything I say. "Has anyone told you anything about what went on over there?"

"Something about a monkey killing him. What do you think killed him?"

How should I know? I am a homemaker. "I don't know. I only know what Jack told me."

"Where can I find Jack?" asks the sheriff.

"Jack is looking for James, our son. Those monkeys took him, as you call them. Before you ride off into the sunset, sheriff, can you go help him?"

"I was told by someone at White's General Store that Jim Darkman is with him. If your son can be found, he is the man to find him."

When the sheriff is talking to me, he does not like to look at me in my face. He glances around, looking at everything in the cabin. I guess he does not want to help find James.

"Well, that sounds very encouraging, but I have faith he will be found. Thank you so much."

He pauses for a moment and straightens his white hat, much larger than his head. He then speaks.

"The coroner has Mr. Valentine's body. If you happen to remember anything else or need any help, please call my office."

"Aren't you going to help find my son?"

"Mrs. Palmer, Darkman is with your husband. He doesn't want anyone else on his trail!"

Somehow, I expected that answer.

CHAPTER 14

"Joni, is there anything you need from your house?"

"No, I think I need to go back home. Maybe things will be better now." She moves her thin body around in her chair, trying to find a soft spot. "I have been in your way long enough. Your life needs to return to normal."

Ina crosses her arms. "I do not know why you say that. Things will never be normal until Jack and James are back. Miss Joni Hill, you are in a big hurry to get home. Don't you like my company?"

"That isn't it. I just need to get home."

Why does she want to go back to that cave? "I understand there is no place like home. Are you sure you won't stay for lunch?"

Gathering her thoughts, she answers, "I guess I can. The truth is, I haven't eaten so well in years."

I do not know how she has gotten by this long. She's lucky she hasn't burnt that old house down with her cooking. She need not stay there any longer. "I am so glad I got to know you, Joni."

She sits there, rocking in a chair given to us by Jack's mother. It is like Joni. It's old and in need of care. *Oh my, I need to finish breakfast.* Suddenly, Joni stops rocking, looks into my face, and then speaks tenderly. I listen carefully, leaning in close to hear her.

"You will get your son back, Ina. I saw him last night in a dream."

Her prophesy reminds me of Jack. He sometimes glimpses the future. Those little things, given the right set of circumstances, come true. Truth can be stranger than fiction. Therefore, I wanted to know her thoughts.

"Joni, what was he doing?"

"He was shooting at me with his bb gun."

She seems tired. Perhaps she needs more sleep. Hearing her voice waver, I worry about Joni's health. What little time I've known her, her strength comes and goes. I say nothing about James's gun. He just doesn't have a bb gun. She is probably thinking about one of her brothers when they were youngsters.

"Joni, in a little while we should go to the store. It will give us a chance to get out and see other faces."

"Oh, I don't know. I haven't been around people in a long time. I wouldn't know how to act."

"You will be all right. I will take care of you. It will do you good."

I leave the kitchen and face the hungry heater. Only orange embers remain. I drop a few pieces of coal through its partially open top. After turning down the damper, I hear a car idling in the driveway. Looking out the window, I call out to Joni, "We have company. Jack's brother, Owl, just drove up."

Joni's face lights with a cheerful smile. "I don't think I have ever met him. Is he older than Jack?"

He is older than Jack is, about five years. He comes around now and then when he wants something, hardly ever when we need him.

"Yes, he is a little older but not much. He should have already been here. Oh well. I didn't expect him anyway. He never shows up on time."

Owl walks onto the porch, and I open the door. He has a beer in his hand.

"Good to see you, Owl, but you know the rules."

"Oh yes! Let me get rid of this." He tips it up and finishes it. "No use wasting it, Ina. If not for you, I'd be a drunk." He walks in reeking of beer.

I shake my head and close the door. "You are a drunk, Owl."

"You did say that with a smile, didn't you?"

What other way would I say it? Owl is a needy person. Need to stop for a beer. Need to blow through like the wind. Never stay more than five minutes. I should not put him down, but sometimes he can really be a pain.

"Yes, of course, Owl. We love you, even with all your faults."

He looks around. "Where is the young master?"

For a moment, I didn't know what to say.

"Did I say something wrong, Ina?"

"Something horrible has happened, Owl."

He looks at me with an expression of waiting disaster. "Tell me, Ina!" Then he quickly shouts, "What is going on?"

I try to get it out without being emotional, but I cannot help but bury my face in his chest. "James has been kidnapped." I say it with tears in my eyes.

"Kidnapped? Who would kidnap James?" He asks with an expression of awe.

"By a creature or something that killed Daisy. Mr. Valentine was killed by it also."

I pull away and face him. Owl looks mortified. I am sure he feels he is never around when we need him.

"Where was James when this was happening?"

His green eyes are wide open. He has no problem at all staring me in the face. He loves James, said James reminds him of himself. Don't see how. James is nothing like him.

"James was in the woods, playing next to Joni's house. Earlier in the day, Jack discovered Roy in his house, dead."

Owl paces about the floor. "How did the old man die?"

I hate telling how he died, afraid the same thing will happen to James, but I blurt it out anyway. "The creatures strangled him to death!" Nervous, I try not to babble but stay focused.

"Is Jack sure they did it?"

Is Owl trying to confuse me? Of course, we know what happened to Daisy and the old man. If not, James would only be missing. "Jack knows a human didn't do it. No human will do what those things did—something that looks like a human did." This is a ridiculous situation. It all seems like a bad story.

Shaking my head in disgust, I think I should be able to change this situation.

"Owl, behind the cabin, their tracks lead to Mr. Valentine's house. Besides that, when he and James were going to the river, Jack saw one of them in the cattails close to the riverbank, where they mutilated Daisy."

Owl snaps a question at me. "Ina, where is Roy's Lab?"

"Owl, these things are not afraid of dogs. They eat them. Labs are not good for defending anyone! He must have been trying to defend Roy."

Joni looks up at me with a sad face. "Roscoe was an old dog. Lived his life and then died honorably, all for the sake of being man's best friend. I hope the Lord doesn't let me go like that, Ina."

I think to myself, *Joni, you will not die like that. Those things are better off back where they came from.* "If the creatures come back here, they will surely die. Joni, you are with me. If they come through that door, they will surely die from gunshot wounds."

CHAPTER 15

"Jack, they know we are behind them. Every now and then, I see where they stop and listen for our sounds. Or they might be sensing the big cat following somewhere behind them."

Whatever their reason is for looking back, it is much harder for us to keep up with them when they sense our every move. If the cat is following them, I hope James is on guard. Snow falls out of a tree and settles on my hat. Taking it off, I brush it against my trousers and then put it back on my head.

"Jim, about a hundred feet up from us I see a trail crossing the river. The creatures can cross the river there."

"I see it. There are no shoals there for them to walk across, but the river is shallow."

We walk to the crossing and look around.

"Look, Jack." Jim points to the opposite riverbank. "Over there, the trail is deep, where many animals have crossed."

I look across the river to where Jim is pointing and then notice tracks at my feet.

"Jim, what kind of track is this?"

After taking a step back, I stoop down and then brush snow and wet leaves away from one of several prints.

I ask him again, "Jim what kind of tracks are these? They look like dog tracks."

Leaning forward, he looks down over my shoulder.

"No. It's a timber wolf, judging from the tracks it's a big one."

Resting the butt of the ten-gage at my feet, I look at the tracks and then say to myself, *This place is like a wild buffet. Every animal is following the trail, looking to kill for food.* I crack a smile and then snicker aloud, catching Jim's attention.

I ask him, "Is everything big here?"

He walks away, taking the lead again.

"Not everything, only the predatory animals." He turns his head sideways so I can hear him. "Be sure you don't become fodder for them."

Now, after a while Jim drifts a small distance from me and then looks back.

"I have been much further up the river before!" he says, shouting back at me.

Jim wants me to feel reassured in his expertise in knowing this place.

"Any animal here is bigger. It gets plenty to eat. Even though this is a small distance, about twenty miles up the river, it's farther than most people want to go."

Jim is right. Most people around here never venture out of their county, must less ten miles upriver into no-man's-land. Amazed, I notice there are many different tracks still preserved in snow.

"At my little cabin, I never see wolves around."

The cattlemen would mistake them for wild dogs after their cows.

"If you did see a wolf around, it would not live very long." That's Jim's explanation for the diminishing wolves. "Let us cross over here. Jack, if you pull your clothing off, they will be dry when you reach the other side. You will appreciate that later."

That sounds freezing but wise to me. I proceed to take my shoes and pants off and then follow Jim into the icy water. It is not so deep. After I make my way to the other side, my feet are numb. I nearly freeze to death before climbing the opposite bank. I'm still shaking from the cold.

"Burrr! The water is so cold!"

Jim, still in water, is last to reach my side. After making eye contact, he makes a comment.

"Jack, it's not that cold. Don't think about it."

While putting his clothes back on, he leans against a dead poplar tree, shaking, freezing his fanny off. Said he did not want to be caught with his pants down. I don't believe he knows what that means. While lacing my shoes, I watch him walk up the trail. After tying my shoes, I catch up with him. He reminds me of a point man, always up ahead and out of sight, locating the enemy. From where I am standing, I can see farther up the river.

Something moves. I can barely make it out. Jim leans against a large water oak with large, low-hanging limbs that sweep out over the river. Jim blends in like a chameleon. As the limb brushes the water, it bobs up and down, but Jim remains motionless, frozen in time. While stirring around, trying to get my jacket on, all of my toes are throbbing. What is he looking at? I stop and wait for him to signal me. Is he looking at James and the creatures? Straining my eyes, stretching my neck, I try to see what he is looking at, but I do not see anything. He then turns his head toward me and motions with his hand.

Come, but stay low.

I leave the trail and move closer to the forest floor. At a snail's pace, I crawl next to him, whispering, "What do you see?"

"Look up the trail about three hundred feet, that low place, do you see it?"

A sleek black cat crouches against a low crop of dead blackberry bushes.

"It's your panther." Still trembling from the cold, I softly speak. "You are right. They are here in the deep woods."

Knowing how dangerous the cat can be, Jim cautions me, "He's shy but cunning. He lies low, waiting on his prey to come by. He is also upwind of us or he would not be so quiet." Jim turns around and looks in my face. "Do you know what he will do if he spots us?"

I am no fool, Jim. It makes me realize we are only visitors here. "Yes. There is no doubt the cat is not where I thought he was, waiting for us."

Jim sighs, reluctantly shaking his head. "I hate to kill him, but they have a sneaky reputation for attacking from behind."

"For our sake and James, better he should die than us. I want to go home in one piece."

"If I let him go, he might kill James and us."

If that happens, Ina will surely go crazy.

"Wait here, Jack."

What is Jim doing now? Is he giving that black devil an equal chance to get him? "What are you doing, why don't you just kill him?"

"Keep down, Jack, and have your sights on him. When he sees me, he won't run."

With rifle ready, Jim rises to his feet and then starts walking slowly toward him. Bracing myself against a pine tree, I have my rifle ready in case he misses. Taken by surprise, the big cat springs to his feet, head lowered and facing Jim. With every step toward him, black paws grasp the crunchy, icy snow. Now creeping slowly with head low to the ground, he fixes his piercing black eyes on Jim. Suddenly, the big cat quickens his pace. My heart pounds from terror. If Jim misses, will I be able to bring down such a stealthy target? Suddenly, the cat leaps from the ground. Jim raises his rifle. A blast from the 30/30 brings the animal down. As fast as a blink of the eye, it is over.

Now the natural flow of time returns. Once again, there is rushing water, wind blowing through the trees, sounds of the forest come rushing back to my ears. Now feeling safe, I take a deep breath. With gun in hand, I come out from behind the tree and then walk over to Jim. He stands over the lifeless blackness brought down with one shot.

CHAPTER 16

"Owl, I promised Joni we would get out amongst other humans. We are on our way to the general store for lunch. Do you want to join us?"

He needs to go with us. Perhaps we can take his mind off other things, such as spending all day in Hobo's Tavern.

"Sure, I can't turn two fine-looking women down for lunch."

"When you get the bill, you might wish you had."

He might as well spend his money on something worthwhile.

"White's, nobody can spend that much money here. Are you girls ready to go? Come on, young lady. Let me help you to the car."

Owl takes Joni's arm and then loops it through his. She smiles up at him.

"Come, pretty lady. Let me show you off."

Owl really knows how to pour it on thick.

"You are such a nice young man. Being old does have its rewards."

Finally, we make it to the car. As usual, Owl helps her into the car. We are in the car only a few minutes before we arrive at the store.

Right away, Owl goes to Joni's door and opens it for her.

"Come on, Miss Joni, let me help you out."

"This is all new to me. I don't know what to think about all this attention."

I don't know what to say. There is a side of Owl never seen before.

If Joni were much younger, they would be a perfect match.

"Are you hungry, pretty lady?"

Owl takes care to protect her from falling.

"I believe I could eat a sandwich."

She slowly climbs out of the car, and Owl helps her inside.

"Miss Hill, I haven't seen you in here in a long time." Mr. White is wearing an apron covered in cow's blood and walks from behind the counter to greet Joni.

"Leon White, you haven't changed any since I last saw you. You're still covered in blood."

"Yes, Miss Hill, I need to get this thing off. I forgot it was on me."

Mr. White leaves the room and disappears into the back storeroom. Fatso slouches in the corner of the room next to the heater, watching and listening.

"Why don't you ask her to have a chair before she falls down?"

"Is that you, Fatso?"

"Yes, Miss Hill, they ganna talk you to death before they ask you to have a seat." Fatso at his best is friendly to Joni, respectful to his elders.

"You sound as genteel as ever."

"Yes, Miss Joni. I am always the same man. About time you got out of that old house and caught some light on your pale face."

Anna walks over to Fatso and wipes the table off. "Fatso, why don't you get up from there and let Miss Joni sit next to the heater?"

"Don't tell me what to do, nigger. My people were here before you."

Joni, close enough to hear him, is angry at Fatso for saying what he did. Yielding her cane like Earl Flynn, she lifts her walking cane and begins to beat it on his table.

"Don't talk to her that way! You still got that awful tongue of yours. You should be ashamed of yourself," she says, still beating the table.

"Yes, Miss Joni. You're right." Fatso keeps his eyes on the cane, hoping she will not strike him. "Say you're sorry!"

Fatso scowls toward Anne Marie. "What? To her?"

"You heard what I said! Yes to her!"

Fatso looks at Anna hesitantly. Sheepishly, he says, "I'm sorry, Anna."

Mr. White places his hand on my shoulder, then leans over and whispers in my ear, "What do you make of that, Ina?"

"Leon, Fatso must have a weakness for older ladies," Owl buts in with his quick opinion, cutting me off.

I look over at Owl. He stands there, leaning back on the counter, thumbs tucked down in the waist of his blue jeans, fingers wrapped around his belt, acting guilty as sin from butting in.

"Sorry, Ina," he says to me. "I interrupted you."

Mr. White is still behind the counter. I turn to face him.

"Joni still has a spark in her."

I try my best to hold my joy in, but laughter did burst out of me.

"I hope she comes in more often." Leon chuckles.

Owl and I walk over to Joni, take her by the arm, and then sit down with her.

"Joni, you straightened him out. It does no good for anyone else to call him down, but he listens to you."

"My cane has that effect on people."

I say little. I just smile broadly. "Yes it does, Joni. Yes it does."

Anna walks over to our table. "What do you ladies want for lunch?"

"I'll have some hot tea and a ham sandwich," said Joni.

Looking into Owl's face, he and I speak at the same time.

"Little lady, she asks for so little."

Owl must have read my mind.

"And you, Owl. What do you need?" asks Anna.

"A good woman…that is what I need," he says, smiling at Anna. "I cannot have that, so I will have a Coke, a hamburger all the way. Hold the onions, please."

"How about you, Ina? What will you have?" Anna is waiting to write our orders down.

"Same as Owl, only I would like a sweet tea."

In a hurry, Anna scribbles our orders down.

"Not many people in for lunch, Anna."

"Ina, most of them will come in later. It is still early yet."

Her thin, black face smiles down at me. I remember when Anna was twelve, as old as James is now.

It took a long time for people to accept Anna. Even so, not much changes around here. People still work for the mill, and others work for the farmers. It's the same day in and day out. After sunset, they trudge in tired and hungry. After James was born, we started coming to the store as a family. I hope those days are not gone. Owl is no Jack, but he does make me think happy thoughts.

"Is your mother working today, Owl?"

"Yes. She starts at four o'clock on the second shift. I only wish she did not have to. Working in the bleacher around all that chlorine has damaged her lungs."

Owl lowers his face then shakes his head in desperation. His face is misshapen, distorted from worry. He sounds so passionate, a serious side he always hides. For the past twenty-five years, my mother-in-law, Edna Palmer, has spent one third of her life slaving in a dangerous environment. She does not make much money, but Ware Shoals would be dead without the Regal Textile Mill. Jack worked there once but prefers to come and go when he pleases.

"Is your food good, Joni?" I want to be sure she has enough to eat before we go home.

Not able to see well, her face is close to her plate. When I speak, she lifts her head. Her eyes make contact with mine. In a soft voice, she speaks slowly.

"It's wonderful, Ina."

Owl's glance surprises me. Again, we are thinking the same thing.

He leans forward and then whispers to me, "Joni is very thin. Does she ever eat?"

Anna was behind the counter, listening to us curiously.

"I will be right back, Miss Joni. Would you like something else to eat?"

"No, Anna. I feel so full now."

"You hardly ate anything. You can take it home with you if you like."

Anna then walks to the end of the table. There, she motions for me to come over. Her smiling face comes close to mine as she whispers, "Ina, Joni is nothing but bones! She spends too much time alone. I take groceries to her house when she orders them, but she is not eating them!"

Still face-to-face, Anna and I solve a problem that will change Joni's life. She is getting too old to live alone.

"Is she going to live with you, Ina?"

Slow to reply, her deep, black eyes take me away for a moment. Actually, I thought they were brown, strange.

"I feel responsible for her now, Anna. Don't you think I should take her in before she is found dead?"

"I do not want that, Ina. She is such a sweet woman. Joni needs someone to care for her."

CHAPTER 17

The black cat lies dead at my feet. Just a moment ago, it crouched low, waiting for its prey. I hate to see it dead, but it would not let us pass by. Eventually it would have been downwind of us or perhaps caught up with James. By killing it, Jim did save our lives. However, I know for sure they will not face off with the great hairy beast protecting James. Soon, we can move on upriver with our task. The sun now reaches midpoint in the sky.

Still standing next to the cat's lifeless body, I look up the river and ask, "Are we getting any closer?"

"Jack, I don't think we are close enough for them to abandon James. I have a feeling something is up."

He speaks a little loud, as if he wants them to hear him. He seems suspicious about something. For the life of me, I find it hard to notice that anything is different.

"What are you talking about, Jim?"

"Panthers do not lie around, waiting on their prey in the open. When the forest is this thick with trees and ravens, the big cat always stalks its prey through the uneven terrain. Then it strikes."

Creatures, man-eating cats—all this is so outlandish. When back at the cabin, life was somewhat normal. Then they came, and nothing has been normal since then.

For Jim to see something abnormal, what is so different now? It all seems a bit ironic.

"Jim, perhaps your senses are telling you the big fur ball knew the creatures are close."

Silent for a moment, scratching his head, he then speaks.

"That can be so. The big male might be doubling back to check us out, see how much of a threat we are. When the creatures are around, no animal wants caught off guard, not even a nasty cat. Never underestimate the creature that walks upright. They are very much like us, and yet they are wild animals."

What Jim means is, they are animals but not far from being humans.

"I see what you mean, Jim. Like humans, they have instinct and cunning."

Dealing with them reminds me of warfare. A big, hairy scout could be out there, watching us now. They will never ignore us. Remembering how it was in those days, we must never drop our guard. Jim stops pondering over the cat, what to do with it. I think he is having a hard time deciding. Standing beside him, I hear a branch break some distance away in the forest. Jim jerks his head around in its direction. Eyes squinting, he listens. He removes his gun from his shoulder and holds it in his hand.

The thought of another beast coming out of the forest, rushing us, brings back memories of the past. I will not let that happen again. I look around the forest cautiously, knowing it can happen.

"Jim, that breaking twig, is that him?"

"Hard to say. It could be anything."

I stand still for a while, but it makes no effort to come out of its hiding place. Normally, James makes a loud noise like that, but I know it is not him. I speak up. "Jim, do you think they will lead us to where James is?"

"I have tracked them for many years, but I have never seen a cave with them still living in it."

What's up with that...Were they kicked out for being bad tenants?

"Well, it sure is strange. They have James. They are going somewhere. There must be some kind of cave. They don't build houses."

I listen for a response. Not a snicker out of him. He is probably like me, scared to death.

"As I have already said, I found a cave in the Great Smokies north of Bald Mountain. Discovered it long ago, but there were only relics of the past in it."

The relics go back further than humans do. Makes no difference, if they harm my son, they will be lucky if I do not kill all of them.

"Every year I meet with other tracker friends at a place we designate to discuss what we encounter, compare scars. But we all come to the same conclusion."

"What is that?"

"The creatures are left over from a time when man still lived in the state of nature."

That does not sound so bad, no more money than I make, we could end up living in the woods too. Ina would love that. She would revert to nature. No more, "Jack, when are we going to get lights in this house?" It would be more like, "Jack, you kill that bear. I need a new loincloth, sounds good to me...living in the state of nature."

"If that is so, they still have all the senses God gave them long ago. How can we compete with that? We will never find them."

Standing there, thinking about what he just told me, he then says, "I do know this. They will not let you close to them unless they want you there. The creatures I saw on the ridge must have smelled me at least a mile away."

We spend too much time talking. We need to get the ball rolling.

"Jim, what should we do with the cat?"

He stood there, looking around.

"What are you looking for?" I ask him.

"A tree—- I need to string him up so he can be skinned. He has to account for something. Jack, do you want the pelt?"

"No, you take it. It is such a waste!"

CHAPTER 18

The day is nearly at an end. Again, I look up at the sky and see the first twinkle of starlight. The sun is sinking fast. I ask myself what I might do after darkness falls, after the creatures have made our bed in a tree. While walking along the river, I make certain that I notice every landmark that would keep me out of their line of sight if I manage to escape. If I manage to get away from them, will they think me worthy enough to recapture? The prehistoric-looking man from the past finally reaches up toward me. He wants to remove me from her shoulders. He frightens me.

I yell, "Get your hairy hands off me!"

In the struggle, I fall to the ground. Grimacing over me, the creature screams loud and menacing.

"Get away from me!"

I crawl away and hide behind the female for protection. Afterward, I poke my head out from behind her and shout at him. "Leave me alone!"

Without blinking an eye, he grunts at me. Then the female takes my hand. *A motherly female,* I think to myself. *Perhaps she lost a child to a wild animal or the male ate it.* I look up at her.

"How is it in your world?" She looks down at me while gesturing her head sideways.

"I see a sign of intelligence in you, Eve. I need to teach you English. Are you going to make me a member of your family? You only make animal sounds, but I will change that."

CHAPTER 19

Now that the three of us have left Mr. White's store, we are on our way back home. I try my best to occupy my mind with positive thoughts. If I start thinking about James, insanity will surely creep in, taking my mind. There has to be a brighter side. If it is true that good comes from tragedy, then getting to know Joni is proof. I am always fortunate. Although my parents are no longer on God's Earth, Jack's family is mine. Unlike Joni, she spent her life living alone in an old, rundown house, waiting on a man who would not bury the past. Now Joni has a friend, and she is the mother I never had. No more dark and dingy living conditions for her, those days are now gone. After leaving the store, everyone is silent. The road's vibration makes everyone feel warm and comfortable.

I try not to take my eyes off the highway. Everyone is so silent. They think about Jack, wondering where he is, if he is safe, if he is on the river by himself. I glance over at Joni. Her head leans against the door's hard window. Poor darling, she is unable to stay awake. For Owl, it is another all-nighter. He sits in the backseat, silently nodding his head.

"Are you okay back there, Owl?"

"Yes, Ina, trying to stay awake."

I know how he feels. Owl thinks he is his brother's keeper. Sometimes I wonder if he really comes over to check on his little brother rather than get Jack to work on something.

"Is there anything I can do for you, Ina?"

"No, Owl, I cannot think of anything."

His red hair lights up my rearview mirror. I prefer not to call him carrot-top, but many do. Like a young child, he keeps it long and in his eyes. It needs a trim. Every now and then, he squirms about like a worm in hot ashes and then glances at the floor of the car. He is preoccupied with something.

Not able to be silent any longer, he blurts out, "I need to check on Mom! I have not been home since last weekend. If you girls need anything, let me know. When Jack comes back, tell him to get that place wired for a phone so we can keep in touch."

Not only a phone—many things will replace the emptiness of the old cabin.

There will be changes when Jack and James come home. The most important thing is James can no longer wander around in the forest by himself. The days when Jack does not have to work, he will have to spend those hours with James. Not only that, our family will have a new addition. Once James and his new grandmother become acquainted, they should spend a lot of time together. James takes a shine to older people. He once told Edna, Jack's mother, that she is living history. Living in Ware Shoals has taught James a lot, but Joni offers something greater. In the short time we have been together, we have grown very close.

There are still icy spots in the road, but I manage to stay clear of them. Everyone is silent. Joni is tired out from a long day and nearly asleep, but we are nearing home. I lay my hand on Joni's shoulder and gently wake her.

"I keep telling Jack, people have telephones now. Joni, do you think we need one?"

She removes her head from the window and then takes a deep breath. "I was dreaming about picking cotton. Someone there asked me about a telephone. I said no phones out here."

I thought she was awake enough to hear me. Oh well. She is awake now. I wonder what she was dreaming.

"Joni, now that we are back at the house, I hope you stay the night."

Still drowsy, she slowly lifts her head to me. "Yes, but I need to go home and give my kitty something to eat."

"Okay. When we stop and let Owl out, why don't you stay in the car? Afterward, we will go to your house."

Owl, already out of the car, reaches in through my window and then taps me on the shoulder.

"Ina, if you have any need, call me. I am still at Mom's house."

He purposefully walks away, and then climbs in his car and is gone. It is good to have him around. Daylight is now fading and nearly gone. Joni and I feel drowsy. My hands tightly grasp the steering wheel as we roll up Joni's driveway. The icy snow crunches under the wheels as it presses tightly against the earth.

We park near the back porch, close to her kitchen. Being home and as weary as she is, Joni is now at her back door, fiddling around in the dark for her keys. It opens easily. Before stepping through the door, I cannot help but look around the dark woods, wondering if creatures are out there watching us. While still looking back over my shoulder, I step carefully through the kitchen door so as not to fall.

The lock clatters shut after I close the door. Some old house—it knows when to lock its doors. I wonder how it did that. I turn to Joni, but she offers nothing. Slowly looking around her kitchen, the semblance of reality comes back to her. She is in her own surroundings. From the expression on her face, there is no place like home. Joni motions me with her hands.

"Come on in." She smiles broadly, happy to be home. "The place is a wreck. Watch your step, Ina."

I walk slowly from her kitchen to her living room. Joni must like dim electric lights in her house. When the door opens from the kitchen, a pale light spreads over the dusty antique furniture, making it hard to see.

"Reach over there behind the door and turn the light on for me, Ina."

Watching her, I wonder what these walls would tell if they could talk. A dim light hangs at the end of a clothbound electric cord, swinging ever so slightly. Eerie, it casts dancing shadows everywhere. I look back at the kitchen door to see it still locked.

Still staring at the door, "Joni, there is so much history in your house. You should let me take care of it for you."

She is busy doing something else. I try to find my way to a piece of covered furniture in a corner of the room. I pull a heavy, dusty tarp draping across a large object, and the cover slides to the floor. Although grimy and dirty, it is a beautiful pump organ.

"Joni, does it still play?"

"Yes, it will, just needs cleaning, my mother bought it in eighteen fifty. I brought it here from Jacksonville."

"A dealer would kill for it."

Being in her house is like stepping back in time. I watch her move about the house as she has done so many times before. Unlike her, I have a hard time seeing where I am going. I can see why she hardly ever leaves her house. Like inseparable twins, she and the old, rundown house are one.

After shuffling her way through her cluttered house, she stops. I rub my tired, blurry eyes. Joni does not seem tired and clearly does not need as much sleep as I do. I hope we soon leave.

"Before returning to your house, Ina, let us sit down and talk a while. I will make some hot tea."

I make my way through the overstuffed house and sit down beside a small, round table. Like an act in a play, she places cups on the small table, laying spoons beside them on top of lacey napkins.

Proudly displaying a dainty teapot, she fills our cups with hot tea. She must have been a Southern bell, a very fine woman.

"Where are you from, Joni? Are you from around here?"

"No, child, my family came from Jacksonville, Florida. I spent my younger life there."

"How old were you then?"

"I was twenty years old." She hesitates before speaking. "That was so long ago. My sister was five years younger than I am. She is dead now. Merry lived in this house with me until she died, ten years ago. Tuberculosis killed her. She was seventy. My parents have been dead for a long time now. Those were the covered wagon days. Life was so hard then."

I am sure those days were unforgiving in their own right, but life is hard around here for us, especially now.

"Making the trip here was hard on your family?"

Joni takes a sip of tea. "It was hard then, but life was simpler. Does that make any sense to you? Not like now. When you need sugar, you get in your car and go wherever you want. Then, everything was seasonal. We left Jackson early spring hoping to cross the Savanna River before it got too high. Dad drove the oxen nearly day and night until we reached the river. It did not matter. The river was too deep to cross. Finally, after four days of following the river west, we came to Calhoun Falls, a little town just on the other side of the river, not far from here. There, we were able to cross. Still, the river was treacherous, and most of our supplies were lost."

Sitting at the table, I shiver, wishing for the warm fire in my cabin. Joni is getting sleepy and yawning. No wonder she is so fragile. It is no wonder she is not dead and cold as a corpse.

"Do you take cream and sugar, Ina?"

I hold the cup in both hands, breathing in the warm, fragrant vapor. "No. I like it black."

CHAPTER 20

Even though Eve is big and hairy smells like a wet dog, the odor does not bother me so much anymore. Her hairy hide insulates me from the bitter cold. If not for her keeping our pile of leaves warm, I would surely freeze to death. Before climbing the tree, I do what I need to do and then sit down beside her. Her eyesight must be like Dad's She sits next to me, head pointing up, squinting at the moon. Sad to think she cannot see it well. Even though she is a dumb animal, Eve looks at the moon as much as I do. On a cold night like this, it is big and bright. I believe they like it that way, high above the treetops. I see clearly. The creatures now move about at a slower pace than before. Clearly, again, their eyes have found a needy tree. Spotting the big male down the river, like an old man falling behind in a march, he slowly drifts back and then disappears into the forest.

I shout at Eve, "I wonder where he is going. You are not so dumb. You do not fool me, Eve. You know who is following us. He is going back to spy on Dad. It's sad to think what my father might do to you when he catches up with you. I am beginning to like you, Mother. I hate to see him kill you. If he has the granddad of all guns with him, the noise alone will blow you away."

Eve only watches my lips move and then makes a few grunts. She looks so human out of her large, black eyes. She only grunts, not an intelligent sound, not something a human can understand. However, it sounds like she wants me to follow. Before she gets all excited, I follow behind her while she walks the trail a little ways down the river. She is watching the male. Did he get mother's permission to leave?

CHAPTER 21

Tying a rope to the cat's hind legs, Jim strings the black beauty up on a large oak tree, so sad for such a magnificent animal. Grasping his hunting knife on his hip, he removes it from its sheath. He then grasps his knife's antler handle with his strong, stout hand. He then holds the sharp blade up in front of his face. He wants me see it. Yes, it is big and nasty.

"We will have to hurry, Jack. Soon, it will be dark."

He used his knife with the skill of a surgeon. Soon, bloody remains mingle with the snow-covered ground. I stand there with the cold wind to my back, watching the cat's pelt separate from its carcass. Then, with a dead thump, it falls to the ground, unlike the sound the enraged cat made when it thundered toward Jim.

"Now that that's taken care of, let's get moving." He removes the naked cat from the tree and throws its body to the earth.

"I remember its beauty. I remember its freedom, but it no longer roams the earth. I can no longer let it die in vain, now for vanity's sake and my admiration, its pelt will lie on my cabin floor. What have I become?"

"Suck it up, Jack! Better him than you. It is the law of jungle, in this case, the river. Jack, we must hurry. It is starting to get dark. I do not want to be on this trail after dark. Wait a moment. So no animal can reach it, I need to stretch out the pelt farther up a tree. By the time we come back this way, it should be dry."

It reminds me of a drum skin, but this skin says, "Stay away from Darkman, the great black hunter who shows no mercy."

"Come, Jack. Let us find a place to camp away from the trail." He takes charge and hurries farther up the trail. "What about that turn in the river? It looks like a good sandbar. We can see all around us. Also a perimeter we can defend."

Like a cloud coming into view, the closer we got to the bend in the river, a long sandbar becomes visible.

"Jack, when we get to the campsite, I need you to start gathering firewood. We do not have much time. Before long, darkness will fall on us, making our task difficult to see. I will get more fish for supper."

I hate it when a plan does not come together. That overgrown housecat made things more difficult for us. We are here just in time—only a few minutes to get things done. Good. Firewood is everywhere. There is enough close by to last all night.

"Some of the wood is wet. I'll stack it next to the fire so it will dry out."

"Make the fire high, Jack. We need to keep a high profile tonight. If we have visitors, we can see them!" Jim shouts while standing in the river.

I shout back at him, "I don't see how you can do that as cold as the water is!"

"I try not to think about it, but you are right. It is cold enough to kill, but I won't be in it long."

I am glad I do not know much about what he is doing. I did not say I do not know how. I hate the cold water. Maybe if I brag on him he will not ask me out there.

"You are a true fisherman, Jim!"

Grabbling, he calls it, reaching his hands under submerged rocks.

"Aren't you afraid of getting bit by something?"

"No. I reach and feel ever so gently."

His shy self shed his clothes up there somewhere in the dark, out of sight but on my side of the river. He has been in the forest all his life, but there is still a glimmer of humility left in him. Jim gave up a lot to become an old pro at what he does. Taking chances like that, I wonder if cottonmouths like him. Even though the current is swift, he manages to keep standing. I cannot see him well, but I hear him talking to himself.

"Come here, you slippery devil. Let me get my hand on you!"

Nice and hot now, my fire spreads light across the water, and flames leaps ever so higher.

Even though Jim blends in with the night, I can now see him clearly, removing his hands from the icy water. Another one is flopping about in his hands. It's a large channel cat. Its whiskers are almost as big as his mustache. He then throws it to the sandbar.

"Jim, you going to be out there all night?"

"No. I'm coming in. My feet are freezing."

He said it with a shiver in his voice. Jim fights his way across the swiftly flowing river. He is cold, grunting, and mumbling as he stands at the end of the sandbar. Light flickers off his naked body and makes him look like what we are tracking but with no hair.

"Jack, you have a nice fire going there. Soon, I will pull their thick hide off. And then they will be ready to cook."

I have never heard it said quite that way, but Jim is not the eloquent type.

"Come over here and get warm. Put your clothes on first! Bread, coffee, and some potatoes will taste fine with what you have in your hand. Not quite such a meager meal."

After supper, I crawl into my sleeping bag and lie there, looking up at the moon, wondering if Ina is gazing up at it too. I think of James's and Ina's state of mind, what they must be going through. I turn my head and look at Jim. I felt reassurance, having Jim Darkman with me. Feeling the day's end, I lie on my sleeping bag contemplating the events of the day and thinking how fortunate I am to have a family.

CHAPTER 22

"The sun has gone down, and the big male is still gone."

What are they going to give me to eat tonight? More fish, no doubt. I have had raw fish for the past two days now. They need to discover fire. If I get a chance, I am going to show them what Dad taught me: how to make a fire with sticks. Sticks and stones should not be too difficult for them to learn. They look somewhat human. Perhaps they can learn how to make and use fire.

We stop where the river is shallow, and a field gives way to tall trees in the foreground. The ape-looking creatures now give me more freedom to move about. Still, so not to escape, the female keeps a close eye on me. I use this new freedom to gather firewood. As I gather, the two walk around in the river, catching fish. The female watches my every move with a look of curiosity. I am sure she thinks it a human thing to do. Before long, they are back on land. With enough wood gathered, I take some grass and dry wood. Then I begin to spin a stick into a hole in a softer part of the wood. Soon, smoke begins to appear. The female begins to mimic me by rolling a small piece of wood between her hands.

After seeing the smoke, she reaches for my arm and pulls me away. Not understanding what I have done, her instinct is to pull me away. Being with them also gives me a chance to understand and mimic some of their passive sounds. I try to reassure her that fire is good, but she never lets go of me. However, she does watch with curiosity. Soon, smoke turns to fire. Her patience turns to grunts of fear. Although Eve pulls me back from the fire, I manage to reassure her that I am in control. Finally, flames rush higher. *Dad, you would be proud of me,* I think. They scamper away.

"Fire is good!" I shout so they can hear me.

Suddenly, they turn their heads to see my loud scream.

"Come back," I shout while I turn my head and look toward them.

Next to me is a willow tree. I rise and then back away from the fire. Eve stops her retreat and then watches me walk to the tree and break a living branch from it. I see a look from her, eyes wide open, almost looks like a smile, never on her face before: witty curiosity. She wants to know what I am doing and watches my every move.

I murmur to myself, "Hunger is a good enticer."

Still, catfish flop around on the wet, sandy ground, trying to find the river. I reach for a large one, making sure she sees what I am doing, hoping that somewhere in her primitive brain is a spark of light. I hold the fish and the willow branch high over my head. I turn toward Eve while pushing the branch through the fish.

I shout at her, "This is food, Mom! All of you beasts need to learn how to do this!"

Still standing on the flat river rock, one creature behind the other, they look somewhat human, gravely watching me.

Like any other animal, hunger brought them back. Now they focus on me, all of them looking at the fire and then looking into my eyes. There must be something about the eyes. They express emotion with their eyes, so humanlike. I place the fish over the flames, and soon it starts to sizzle. The smell of food excites their taste buds, and they start jousting about like dancing bears. With the fish still smoking from the fire, I hold it out to her.

"Look, Eve. You will like this. It is hot."

Reluctantly, she slowly reaches her hairy hand out to me and takes it.

"How do you like that?"

Now I hope to encourage a love for cooked fish. How better to be accepted than to act like them. Loud, happy creature sounds start emanating from my vocal cords while acting like a monkey in a new-found coconut tree.

"Mom, what do you think? Wasn't that good?"

Eve and the lesser male park themselves opposite me on a tree washed up by the river. I do not see the big male. He is not as eager as these two.

I reach for another—a large catfish. Once again, I push a willow through it. After it thoroughly cooks, I give it to Eve. To my surprise, she gives it to the lesser male. He must be her child. Before long, only one fish remains. It was enough for me. I take a bite. They watch me devour it. "What do you think, Eve? Will anyone believe me?"

I now have a wonderful story to tell Mom and Dad.

CHAPTER 23

The sleek black cat met its demise just two hours ago. Now nailed to a tree, its carcass signals other cats to stay away. All of a sudden, a concerning thought enters my mind.

What if he has a mate? What will she do?

How will she take the death of her mate? I lie there beside the fire in my sleeping bag, pondering those possibilities.

"Keep the fires going tonight, Jack? We have had too many peaceful nights."

Lying in my sleeping bag, I look toward Jim. He is still standing, looking around the forest perimeter, listening for sounds, sounds from the great creature that moves around in the forest ever so silently.

"Jim, the moon will set early tonight." Pulling his sleeping bag up around his shoulders, he looks over at me, saying, "Most males would have entered our camp by now."

He sounds concerned. I get the impression our luck is running out.

"Perhaps it is the brightness of snow and a full moon that keeps then away from us."

"Perhaps, but conditions are now favorable for a visit. He does not want to kill us, only see our weakness. Unlike our cat, afraid of fire, the ape-looking creatures are somewhat intelligent, probably not fearful of fire, but still cautious of us."

When Jim speaks about them, for some reason I get a strange feeling. He is keeping something to himself. It is more than just being one with nature.

"Surely they have come in contact with fire from lightening strikes. They should make the jump soon," I said, wiping dust from the Belgium.

"When they do discover fire, what will become of our apelike creature? And what will be mankind's roll?" Jim asks, as if I had the answers.

"I don't know. Perhaps conflict."

I do not see it happening, us fighting with them, clubs and guns.

"Can James make a fire?"

"Yes. James is a very capable twelve-year-old. You are not suggesting! That cannot be so!"

I waited for him to speak again. I have an idea where this is going.

"Jack, we will find out soon."

"How do you mean?"

"A fire tells all."

Jim twisted about in his bag, trying to make himself comfortable. I lie there, listening to the stillness of the night. I could not help but think about what he said. It would answer the question why they took James. Jim is now fast asleep. Planning to wake up, every so often, so I can keep the fire burning, I set my inner clock and settle into my bag. Later into the night, like a butterfly crawling out of its cocoon, I can shed the sleeping bag and feed the fire so wild animals will stay away.

Late night, I wake from a disturbance in the tree above me. Something is jumping from limb to limb, shaking loose pine needles to the ground. It is not one of the creatures but something else. Now out of my bag, I walk around the dwindling fire, looking up into a high pine. Jim is now out of his bag, also looking up. At the same time, his hand reaches for his weapon, but he does not take his eyes off the ruckus in the tree. Glancing at him and then back to the tree, I ask, "What do you think it is?"

"Don't know. Whatever it is wants to come down from there."

Then, jumping from limb to limb, a yellow-and black-spotted bobcat screams as it leaps to the ground and turns, pointed ears tucked in toward its head and screams at us again.

"Whoa, what's bothering him?"

"I believe he does not want us here," said Jim.

Stepping out of its way, standing still, Jim does not want to aggravate the thing. We watch the sleek, long-legged, muscular cat as it disappears into the forest.

Jim then says, "It must have been up there all this time, wanting to come down."

I think about what he said. If that cat can be silent enough to hide so very close above our heads, one of the creatures can easily be out there at this moment, watching.

Now out of my warm sleeping bag, the wet wood I piled close to the fire is no longer steaming. With wood in hand, I pile several more pieces onto the fire. It suddenly comes to mind that Ina might be running out of coal. It doesn't matter. The old man has plenty of coal at his house. All Ina has to do is fill a wheelbarrow and roll it to the cabin.

What will become of Mr. Valentine's estate? Did he leave a will? While up, I walk across the sand, place more wood on the fire, and settle the coffee pot into hot coals. Soon it is steaming hot. After removing the kettle from its hot spot, I pour myself a cup and sit by the warm fire. I ask myself, *What will tomorrow hold for us? Will there be any evidence of a quest for fire?* This was hard to comprehend. I could hardly believe it. *If this is true, why now and why did they take James?* I take my cup in hand and walk to the sandy riverside. There is a log lying next to me, so I sit down on it. Down river, the moon slowly sinks into the water, casting a wavy, eerie reflection across the water. I sit there. A twig snaps somewhere up the riverbank from me. Is it one of the creatures watching us? If he is there, he makes little noise, but I did hear something. I am sure he has no difficulty seeing me. Do they know I am James's father?

CHAPTER 24

I wake to a sound of what must be some kind of bird. Jim leaps to his feet, swinging left and right like a wild man, it frightens him from his bag.

"I was dreaming about panthers. They had me cornered."

Jim quickly looks behind himself.

"What was that?" I ask him. "It made chills run up my spine," I say to him as he stumbles around in the sand.

"Don't know, Jack...Sounds like it's somewhere upriver. No matter. The sun will be coming up soon. I will cook something for us to eat."

It does not take long for Jim to recoup himself. After rolling my bag up, I stand up, yawn, and stretch out my arms. Jim fools around in the dark. I hear pots and pans rattling. He cannot see what he is doing. If anything is close by, Jim has run it off. I then speak so he can hear me.

"Sure do feel stiff this morning. I have slept in better places."

I don't hear any reply from him. Then he comes out of the dark with a coffee pot in one hand and a skillet in the other. He places the skillet next to the fire and then fills the coffee pot where a stream of water pours from a rocky cliff.

"You are too soft, Jack...spent most of my life on the ground. I hardly ever sleep in a warm bed anymore."

Shivering with that thought, I am glad I do not have to make that claim.

"Just the same, I can hardly wait 'til I get back to Ina. I need so much to snuggle up to her, safe at home, away from this wild, frozen place."

"I know how you feel, Jack."

I am sure he does. Most likely, she is very hairy. While Jim fixes our breakfast, I reach for a pile of wood now dry from the fire. Piece by piece, it makes the flames burn hot and higher.

Jim rustles around the fire, trying not to let it burn him, working hard at making breakfast. I try to show my appreciation with a few kind words.

"Coffee tastes good on a cold morning."

"Yes. The bacon, eggs, and fried bread are not half bad either."

Before long, a bright morning star gives way to soft rays of light shining through tall, thick, curly barked hickory trees. Sitting on a fallen log with my blue tin plate lying in my lap, warming my cold legs, I fill my empty stomach.

"Today might be the day of reasoning. If we find out our suspicions are true, a completely new meaning can be placed on why they took James and why they went to the old man's house."

I look back at Jim. He sits facing me on the other side of the fire.

"Jack, I still find it hard to believe he was killed by them."

"If you had been there, you would have seen things different."

Jim seems confident in knowing the creature's behavior. Sometimes he acts as if protecting them.

"Why they did it is still a mystery to me." Jim speaks with his back to me.

It has been more than two days since we started this hunt. We are no closer to understanding what the creatures are than when we started. I want answers, but I do not quite know the questions to ask. Breakfast is over.

"Drink up, Jack. Now that we have light, we need to get moving."

CHAPTER 25

We sit opposite each other at the table, reminiscing about yester-day. Joni misses her sister. It had to be a hard life watching her die, confined to a bed. I miss Jack and James and wonder if I will ever see them again, a horrible thought. What would I do without Jack's strength and James's playfulness? I do not see how the old man with-stood the years of loneliness after the river took his wife. Joni's sis-ter has been dead for ten years now, and she never gathered enough courage to tell him of her secret love. Now that Roy is gone, she feels she will not be here on earth much longer. I want to be with Jack for the rest of my life.

Joni stares wistfully out at the cold winter day.

"I am eighty-five now and have lived a full life."

"Do you have any family left, Joni?"

"None that I know, perhaps I have a long-lost cousin somewhere in Florida. Perhaps I will leave all I have to your family, Ina. What would you think of that?"

I think you have been living alone too long. "Joni, I have not done anything to deserve your property. Let us talk about this another time."

She makes me feel awkward. Still sitting at the table, I rise from my chair, open the door to her refrigerator, and remove a carton of milk. I do not know why I did it. I never used milk in my coffee before. Anyway, it has been in there so long it turned solid.

"I do not have much time left, Ina. You have shown me kindness. That means a lot to me."

"I enjoy being with you, Joni. But you hardly know me."

"Roy loved your family enough to leave everything he owns to you."

She is speaking of something I know nothing about. For all I know, she is losing her wits or just trying to be nice.

"I have not heard anything about that, Joni. How do you know that?"

I take the ancient carton of milk then place it on the table and wonder how she managed to live so long without dying from food poisoning.

"Last time I saw him, he said everything will be left to Jack—this house, savings, I think around six hundred acres."

Jack is my husband. Wonder why the old man put it that way, to Jack. He did see much more of Jack than I did. Maybe it has something to do with living alone, no woman around the house. Still, I thought the world of the old man.

"Joni, he was a very good man. I don't know what to say. Here lately, my life has been changing in bad ways—and now something wonderful. I feel so overwhelmed but thankful."

Joni takes my hand. "Ina, there is some good in everything."

It's nice to know she is so optimistic.

Right now, my life is in shambles. I fear if James vanishes, forever it will become unbearable. I need to escape this kind of thinking and concentrate on something more positive.

"I need to start thinking about supper. No, I don't either; I keep forgetting Jack and James are not here. Joni, would you like to spend more time with me? We can go back to the store and see other faces and have supper there if you like?"

Been a long time since Joni has been around anyone this long; probably likes her own company more than that of others. Nevertheless, I do not want to spend another moment alone.

"I enjoy being with you. It has been a long time since anyone has shown any interest in me. Most people don't like being around old people."

My face feels warm.

"Joni, I don't think like that. A person such as you has a wealth of knowledge. Are you ready to go?"

"Give me a moment. I need to clean these dishes."

Joni removes dishes from the table and places them in her kitchen sink. After rinsing them gently, she then places them in a cupboard. We talk in the car for a time and then leave. When we arrive at the store, we sit at a table in the back of the room, close to the heater so Joni can stay warm. There are other people waiting for Anna to serve them dinner. The heater is nice and toasty. Joni draws near and warms her cold hands as Anna comes over to our table. Anna has a bright smile on her face. We have taken the best table in the house, next to the heater—Fatso's warm spot.

"I don't see you getting up for him, Ina."

Anna's eyes grow large.

"No. I'm not likely to do that."

To see if he is in sight, her beautiful, black face tensely stares at the door. She knows he is making his way inside.

"What do you ladies want to drink?" Anna asks as she turns her head back toward Joni.

"I would like a cup of hot tea, Anna," says Joni, smiling at Anna.

"On a cold day like this, Joni likes her tea nice and hot."

"Okay, Ina. I will make sure it is still steaming when I bring it out."

I can see that Anna is nervous as she waits for her morning encounter with Fatso, but he will not say anything with me in here.

"What will you have, Ina?"

"I'll have some coffee."

After a while, she comes back with our drinks.

"What will you girls like to eat?"

I glanced at Joni. She is always famished. "What are you hungry for, Joni?"

"A chicken sandwich will be nice."

Anna nervously looks toward the door before asking "How about you, Ina?" "Bring me the same thing, please."

Glancing toward Fatso, I reassure Anna, "You don't have to worry about him. I will stop Fatso before he gets nasty."

Anna sighs deeply. "There will always be that hatred toward us blacks. However, I don't see why they hate me, Ina!"

It makes tears come to my eyes. I hate what he does to her!

"Anna, will you be caught up soon?"

She looks around the store. "I think so. Why?"

"Sit down and talk with us."

Mr. White is in the back room, talking to Robert. Most of the time, when Anna needs help, both of them are somewhere out of sight.

"How did your day go, Anna?"

"This morning I started the day out all wrong."

Joni looks at her with anticipation.

"Do you remember where we keep the cheese, in the lower part of the cooler?"

Anna sheepishly smiles as if she did something wrong. I remember the place well cannot help but know. Every time I pay for a slice off the big, round wheel, I should be getting more for my money.

"Yes. I know where it is, in the back of the store next to the meat department."

"I put my foot through the glass door this morning."

"How did you do that?" asks Joni.

"Miss Joni, I was in a hurry, not watching what I was doing. I closed it a little too hard with my heel."

"What did Mr. White say about that?"

"At first I was afraid to tell him. But I did anyway."

Gentle Anna, how can anyone be hurtful to her?

"Did he understand about it?"

"He said he would take one off the old freezer from around back."

Now that sounds like him. Mr. White always has a backup plan waiting somewhere. He will never toss anything. I look at Anna and praise her.

"If that had been me, Anna, I would have cut myself or something much worse."

"The sheriff came by the store today, looking for Darby Baker. You know him, Ina. He always has a pretty girl with him."

"Yes. I know him. Wild as he can be. He sometimes works with Jack at the shop."

"Darby was in the restroom when the sheriff came in looking for him. Mr. White always told me not to make that wild one angry with me, so I just looked at the bathroom door and pointed. I am sure the sheriff thought me odd, not saying anything back to him. He then said, 'I will take it from here.'"

Anna then turns toward the front door as a traveler passing through asks for directions to Ware Shoals.

She sounds disappointed as the handsome man turns to leave. Anna continues her story.

"As I said, the sheriff wanted to know the whereabouts of Baker. After I silently point toward the restroom, the sheriff calmly walks toward the door. The two of them are back there for a while and then come out. The sheriff said, 'Darby test-drove a new car for three days and did not bring it back. So now I have to arrest him for joy riding.' Baker held his head high and waved at other customers without any shame." Anna spoke again. "I told him to leave alcohol alone. Every time that boy drinks, he gets into trouble and his dad always gets him out of it."

We sat there at the table, listening to Anna. She loves to talk about things that happen in the store. Most of the time, people only tell her what to do.

"One other thing happened today," adds Anna. "You know these boys, Joni, the family that lives across the bridge down from you. You know who I am talking about."

"Yes. I know the two young boys. They live with their grandmother. She has a hard time controlling them. I see them in my barn sometimes or walking up the road."

"Well, now Mr. White will not let them in the store by themselves anymore," said Anna, leaning on the table with both hands palm down.

She completely had our attention.

"Those young boys are no more than nine or ten. Nevertheless, if I am not around, they steal candy. When they came back in the store with their grandmother, Mr. White told her he could not allow them alone in the store anymore. That's just fine, though. When I am here, they are welcome."

People are so different. James would never think of stealing from anyone.

Joni says, "I did know her well. However, that was a long time ago." A ray of light fills Joni's widening eyes. She then calls out, "Emily! That is her name! What did she say to Mr. White, Anna?"

"Their grandmother asks, 'Why the children could not come in anymore?' He said, 'For stealing candy.' Lo and behold, she pulled her belt off right there in front of everyone and tanned their little hides. I felt so helpless unable to defend them."

I do not know what I would do if James did such a thing.

"She made them tell Mr. White, 'Sorry.' Then she ordered them to the car with their heads hung low."

The poor little darlings, probably never get anything for themselves, must not be one of those times Anna gives candy away.

"The day was full of events." Anna laughs about the boys. "I give them candy every time they come in the store."

My stomach rumbles, and just in time, the cook rings the bell for our meals, and Anna scurries toward the kitchen.

Anna stands at the door and then watches us drive away. I cannot help but believe how wonderful a person Anna Marie is and how she came to these parts. I sit with eyes fixed on the road but can see Joni looking at me. She wants to say something but keeps holding it back.

"Can you stay at my house tonight, Ina?"

I try not to show my dismay. Nevertheless, what can I say?

"Yes. Sure. If you like, I can do that. I will have to stop by the house and get some night clothes to sleep in."

Joni quickly responds, "No need for that, Ina. I have a gown for you to sleep in."

Well, if she can sleep there after what has happened, I can also. We pass the cabin and head straight toward Joni's house.

Her place is an ancient two-story house. Longer than it is wide, the structure is surrounded by a porch. Wooden planks curl painfully away from nails pulled loose with time. Abandoned bird nests litter the eves with loose spider webs collecting dust. The evening sunset casts scary shadows over it. I pull up to the kitchen door.

"There is no place like home," I hear her mumble to herself.

I hurry out of the car, making my way to her door, saying, "Be careful not to bump your head while getting out of the car, Joni."

Carefully lowering her head as she inches out of the car, Joni hoarsely whispers, "Come, Ina. We can go in the kitchen door." Beckoning to me, Joni takes hold of my arm and slowly steps up to the kitchen door. "Come in, Ina, and make yourself at home."

She reaches up with her left hand and holds the screen door open. With her right hand on the glass doorknob, she opens the door.

We walk into the kitchen and place our handbags on a wooden table scarred with numerous rough cuts and several round, dark spots.

"Have a seat Ina. I will turn the heater up some."

Old and falling to pieces, the last request of this old house is not to burn down. Knowing what the house needs, Joni only heats the lower rooms and her bedroom. Dusty boxes full of what she wants to keep line the floors. Every visible spot is full of old furniture, but the kitchen is clean and tidy.

"I have not seen the upstairs of your house, Joni."

She shuffles around in the kitchen for a moment and then speaks. "When we go upstairs, I will show everything to you. Now that I have gotten old, it is hard for me to make extra trips up there."

"Ina, would you like a cup of coffee?"

"This time of the day, a cup of coffee does sounds good, Joni."

I notice she is a different person at home, but everyone is. In the corner of the kitchen is a white, ceramic, electric stove. Joni moves about the kitchen with confidence while making coffee.

"Now all I have to do is get it good and hot. I made some pineapple cake earlier," she says, sliding a plate of cake across the table. "Would you like some with your coffee?"

She sits down at the table and begins to talk. There is no way I am going to turn someone else's pineapple cake down.

"Ina, I need to get rid of some of my furniture. My sister collected most of it, and I have no use for it anymore. I would like your family to have it if you want it. You can use it or sell it. If you sell the older antiques, there will be enough money to put James through college."

What she said surprises me.

"Joni, are you sure about that?"

"Yes, I am. I don't need it or the money. I want to show my gratitude for your kindness toward me."

For a moment, words did not come to my mouth. I cannot find the right words. Joni might not remember our conversation. I will feel like a fool.

"You see this place? It is like me: almost gone. I cannot take care of this big house anymore. I am too old. Soon, I will not be around. In addition, my house and land will belong to your family. With my land and Roy's land, your family will not have to live in poverty anymore."

"I know that Roy left a sizeable amount of money to Jack, and I will leave mine to you. This land has at least a thousand acres in rich, fertile land, all of it fenced in with two barns. My barn is falling apart, but Roy has taken good care of his."

She smiles at me when she says it. Jack and James are coming back to a new life. There is something wonderful rising from these flames. Joni has a big heart. She is up there in years, but she is not losing her mind. I have no reason not to believe her.

"Ina, I have lived a long time and have nothing to show for it, so this will be my legacy, me pleasing the Lord."

"I promise I will do well with it, Joni, turn this land into something never forgotten."

Strange how all this came about. One moment, I am worrying about electricity in the house. This horrible thing happens to James. I get to know Joni. Then we become rich. What is going to happen next?

Joni stands frail and small before me. She then looks into my eyes as if she can see something I cannot.

Then says, "Sweetie, look at the past. Starting from the time Roy built your little cabin, everything has been falling into place for you. God blessed the land when Roy put his heart into it. He will bless it again. Do not worry about Jack and James. Something beyond belief will become of their journey to the Great Smoky Mountains."

Astounded by the suddenness of Joni's expressions, she feels something I do not. The Great Smokies, can they really be going that far away? Joni stops what she is doing and goes to the stove.

"The coffee has been boiling for a while. I hope it isn't too strong."

"I will pour it for us. Where do you keep your cups?"

While I fill the cups, Joni's head nods to her chest.

Suddenly, my thoughts go back to Jack and James. I feel lonely. Talking can no longer distract me from them. I ask myself, *how close are they to the Shoals Junction Bridge? Surly they have not reached it yet.* I need to know what is going on with Jack. There, I can be with him before he disappears back into the wilderness.

Joni and I finish off our coffee while sitting in quiet thought.

"Would you like another cup of coffee, Ina? It is still hot."

"No thanks, I am ready to sleep now. It has been a long day."

"Good! I am worn out."

"Yes, Joni. My mind and body tires faster these days."

"Watch your step. I need to put more light in here. The stairs are a long way."

Yes. I have been thinking about them for quite some time now, wondering how you manage to not fall and break your slender neck. "You should not be climbing these long stairs. They are awful. You are not the young girl you used to be."

"Yes, darling.

I know, but I have been climbing them for many years. I have to take my time so as not to fall."

"Is that the bed I am sleeping in tonight?"

"Yes. It is."

I walk back to the bedroom to see the bed—big and massive.

"What do you think? My grandmother gave it to me when I was eighteen."

Eighteen? A parent would give this to a daughter who wants to marry. I do not believe Joni's mother gave it to her for that reason. I like the bed, but someone needs to move it out of this house before it falls through the floor.

"It has a beautiful canopy on it, Joni. It looks fit for a king or queen. It must be a very heavy bed. How did you get it up these stairs?"

"I had help. It comes apart easy. It's not so heavy that way."

"It looks like it is made from cherry."

Everything in her house is old. I see why she cannot part with the past. Everything around her is always closing in on her.

"I know there is not much room in your cabin, but it will fit in Roy's house."

Another gift, staring at the bed, I wipe a tear from my cheek. Mr. Valentine is dead. James is gone, taken by the creatures. This is all happening horribly fast for me. Take it all back. All I want is the way things were, nothing else.

The old house pops and then crackles as if commanding, "You don't want to leave Ina."

I reassure myself—Jack and James will find their way back home. Blinking back tears, I look to Joni for the strength to distract myself.

I hope people do not believe I am taking advantage of her.

"It still looks new, Joni. It has been with you for a long time. Are you sure you want to give this beautiful bed away?"

"Yes. Everything in the house will be yours, Ina. You will have to build a new house for your furniture. You and Jack will have to decide where to put it!"

I wonder how she will respond if I get rid of all of it. In truth, Joni needs to let go of the past. Some people might look at it different. The past is all she has.

What can I say? Here lately, there has been a lot of change.

"If you want, I will go tomorrow and have a will drawn up. Can you take me?"

"You know I will do anything for you, Joni."

The old grandfather clock in the corner of the bedroom, it just struck ten times. Joni goes to bed much earlier. I must remember she tires much earlier than I do. She is too fragile a woman not to get enough rest.

CHAPTER 26

Jim and I leave our campsite and then return to the river trail, eventually turning north. Jim believes the creatures are going home, back to high ground, where clouds cover great, snowy mountaintops. Deer and other animals now beat down the deeply trodden trail. Lonely howls woke me several times during the night. They must have known the fire was down to red embers, needing to be rekindled. Wolves are majestic animals but rarely seen. We also came across some bear tracks. In the midst of a grove of elms, we come upon fallen trees lying across our path.

"Come here, Jack."

Jim stands over a dead tree.

Trailing from behind, I approach and then stand beside him. Effortlessly, he points his rifle to the ground.

"Look...the creature's muddy footprints."

Hat in hand, he speaks with a raspy voice, clears his throat, and spits on the ground. He then stares up the river in the direction of the creatures. While pushing with his foot, he rolls a log away, revealing several tracks. After a quick look around, his foot still propped on the log, he quietly speaks again.

"What do you make of that? The big male paid us a visit last night."

Why is he so cautious? They are long gone.

"I had a feeling we were not alone last night. When I was nearly asleep, I heard a twig snap but did not pay it much attention. It was one of them sneaking around out there. Glad he didn't come into camp."

"He does not want us close to them. So he came to see where we are," he says as he takes the smelly cigar out of his mouth and then thumps ashes on the ground. I have a bad feeling about our situation.

"Jim, evidently, because we are downwind from them, they cannot smell us. That must be why he came so close last night."

Morning sunlight now breaks through scattered clouds, casting long shadows over the ground, reflecting sunlight off rushing water. I watch fish jump out of the water for low flying insects, but all I can do is watch as we pass by. My stomach rumbles with hunger.

"No time for that, Jack. There won't be any fishing until late evening."

When we get hungry, cannot go any farther, I think to myself. Trying our best not to crowd the creatures but still making good time, snow still covers the ground. The stuff still lies heavy on the ground from a winter still having its grip on our situation.

"A fine day to be hunting.

What will happen if we catch up with them? Will we have to kill them to free James?" I put the question to Jim bluntly.

"That does not go with the norm of things," said Jim.

"What do you mean?" I do not see us negotiating for him.

"Under normal conditions, they will not risk us catching up with them. Like I said earlyer, when this close to them, they always free their captive."

They know we are behind them. Still, they keep James. Something strange is going on.

"This must be something different than your past experiences with them."

"Perhaps they do need the boy for something."

"Better be something good. If they hurt him in any way, they will become an extinct species." To make sure Jim understands me, I say it loudly. "Do you know how far we are from the next bridge?" I ask as his smelly cigar smoke drifts my way.

"Judging how far we have come, we still have about five miles to go. The closer we get to the Shoals Junction bridge, the more worn the trail will become."

Jim speaks without breaking his stride. Still five miles away, it seems we should be closer than that. If humans are there, I hope they do not spot James and his captors. No telling what might happen if they believe James is a captive. I am sure they will not know what to think. Most humans do not see farther than their noses and do not bother to ask questions, as if it will do any good.

"When we near the bridge, we need to be aware of people on the river. People might be fishing, and hunters can be anywhere up or down the river."

Jim takes what is left of his cigar, thumps it into the river, and speaks.

"Like any wild animal, they dislike man. If people are present, the creatures will either pull back or slip through. We will see when we approach the bridge." Sometimes I wonder whose side Jim is on. He never tries to overtake them.

"I don't know them as well as you, but they must be capable, slipping through anything without being seen."

"On the other hand, if humans see them, they might want to take shots at them. Farther up the river, we should start seeing rapids," Jim predicts as he turns his head back toward me.

"How far does the white water run?"

"It's bad for about two miles, a lot of rocks in the water."

That means a lot of noise. We will not be able to see or hear them. The creatures might be close to us. They will need a lot of control over James for that to happen. Maybe I have been out here to long. It's starting to get to me. My toes are numb with cold, and I worry about Ina.

"Shoals are a good place to grabble for channel cats. People mean trouble."

"Yes. The creatures will not like them being there. If we approach the bridge as night falls, we will have to keep vigilance."

Vigilance.

Did not know he knew such words. I wonder if he taught that word to them. They are vigilant, sneaking around in the woods at night while we are sleeping. They watch us most likely all the time.

"Hopefully we should reach the area a little before sundown," I say to Jim, but he says nothing.

The thought of them passing by with James raises my fury and the thought of this going on and on bewilders me to no end.

Jim removes his hat and scratches his head then remarks. In past years, their behavior has been predictable. But this is turning out to be an unusual experience."

Sometimes, Jim sounds a little unsure of himself.

"We have not reached their next campsite yet." Jim speaks as he pulls his hat down over his head.

We have seen only one place they have stayed the night.

"No matter, Jack. If we quicken the pace, it will be hard on the boy. The best thing for us to do is to track them to their cave."

"Wait."

I stop then point to tracks in the snow, a place where they must have stood and pondered before passing to the other side of the river. Oversized prints lead to the waters edge. I can see that even though sunlight has melted around the outer edge of the prints, the creature's feet are enormous. It appears as if a group of several creatures followed a leader to the crossing. Again, Jim stops, takes his hat off, scratches his head, and then looks around the area. We have another hunter on the trail. He sees other tracks on a sandbar. A black bear comes out of its den, looking for food. I stay alert. We do not want to startle him. I hate needless killing.

"I want no more encounters with black bears," he says as he pulls up his shirt.

He has scars from the top of his back to his beltline.

"What happened to you?" I ask him as he tucks his shirt back into his jeans.

"Two springs ago, one tried her best to kill me."

I know this will be a good story, so I press him to tell it. "Jim, tell me what took place." His stories are good for killing time.

"I was in Colorado, about fifty miles west of Denver, on a hunting trip with a man named Dan Redroot, a Native American from Arizona. We came across a brown bear, and I lost a wrestling match."

Arizona? I do not know much about the place. It's hot as hell in the summer, and there's not much of a winter. I would not want to live there.

"What kind of Native American is Redroot?"

Looking at the angry expression on Jims face, I don't know if he will tell me.

"Lakota Sioux," he says passionately as if grieving the great loss of land taken from his friends. Jim asks, "Remember Manifest Destiny? The white man is like Caesar. They come, they see, and they conquer. It is clear to the Native American who lost."

I walk behind Jim, following wherever he leads me, trusting him as his native friends trusted the newcomers to their lands long ago. However, with Jim, I feel no deceit.

"We spent two weeks in the mountains, mostly enjoying ourselves, sitting up camp here and there."

"Was the weather like it is here?" I ask.

This is the freakiest winter in many years, so I hear.

"No, a little cool, but the weather was not hot, yet. Something about me likes a place where a trail twists and winds as it snakes down a river over a great distance. It is a place where hunters call bears pets. They look for one with a lot of ferocity—one of those Native American traditions."

Sounds more like one of those crazy hunter things—not the one that got away but the one eaten by a bear and he was never heard of again.

"Jim, you were in those hills and did no trout fishing!"

"I fished for trout, but we were after bear. We did see some bears while fishing, but they kept their distance. One Sunday evening, we found a cave that went through to the other side of a cliff. It looked too big to be a den. After looking around the cave, we found a dry spot and set up camp just inside the cave. A good draft made building a fire perfect."

Following behind Jim is not the place to hear everything he says, and I miss some of his story. Rather than ask him to repeat himself, I let him carry on.

"We packed in food on the back of a burro, clumsy oaf. More trouble than he was worth. To keep the food out of the weather, we tied him just inside the cave, open to the river. Knowing that bears were in the area we kept the fire going all night, hoping to keep them away. Nevertheless, things do not always work out the way we plan. Dan and I were up late at night, talking about the day's events."

Sounds much like what you and I do. I guess the more things change the more they stay the same.

"Like other nights, supper was fine. There is nothing like fish cooking over hot embers. Well, as I was saying, we turned in around midnight. I was nearly asleep, had no idea something was coming through the cave. It must have been very hungry. It smelled the food, the burro, or maybe the fish odor left from cooking. Early morning, a mother bear with two cubs came through the cave, looking for food, and underweight, very hungry."

After the mention of food, I find a powerful hunger in the pit of my stomach. All this hiking is wearing me out. I am accustomed to Ina's cooking. Man, I want to be home!

"Our pack animal was still at the mouth of the cave. He wanted nothing to do with her and ran into the river. Dan, more asleep than awake, was unable to focus, was probably having flashbacks from days gone by. He came out of his bag, screaming, 'Where is my rifle?' Everything happened so fast. I did not want Dan killing the mother and then leaving the cubs orphaned. Crazy as it sounds, I intercepted him in flight toward his weapon, grabbed the rifle away from him, and then screamed, 'Don't kill her!' That is not me, Jim. If it comes down to little, four-footed killers not having a mother to raise them or me still standing upright, I will take the latter. When I did, I must have startled the bear. Right away, she protected her cubs. Then she came at me with her mouth open, baring her long, pointed teeth, not smiling but lips turned upward, which means that if you can get away, you had better do it now. She was now in killing mode. She could have left, but then she turned her head back toward the cubs to see where they were. I know how bad these things can get."

I hope that is not a bad omen: how bad things can get. Things can get bad for us also. Maybe it is not such a good idea to tell this story. It's too late to stop Jim now.

"Suddenly, she turned back toward me, mauling me in my head and then biting me in my hip, throwing me against the cave wall. I was almost unconscious, in terrible pain. Just the same, I tried to lie still, stay motionless. While I lay there, Dan was at the front of the cave, looking for our fortunate pack animal. He was still in the water."

See there. They are not so stupid an animal as people say. It ran for the water while the bear ripped you to pieces.

"Dan, wondering if I was still alive, shouts at me. However, I dared not make a sound. She was still in a state of frenzy, protecting her cubs. For a moment, I thought she would leave me alone. I uncovered my head to see if she was still around. She made several swipes at me with her paws. She ripped my back open like spring-cut ham. I thought I was going to die, almost gave up when, as fast as it began, it ended. She and her cubs turned away and went out the same way they came in. When it was happening, I thought it would never end. Still, I did not want to kill her. She was only doing what bears do. I lay there in bad shape. If not for Dan, I would not have made it out alive. In spite of all the pain, Dan took fishing line, a fishhook, and then unbelievably sewed my torn body back together."

It sounds horrible. That is what happens when a person gets reckless. I know that. I am still alive. Many of my army friends are dead. Fighting for what, I do not know. Still, I would not want to go through a bear attack, such a terrible ordeal for you, and your friend to go through.

"Being out there in the deep wilderness, one begins to feel immortal and then becomes careless. I made that mistake, Jack. Now, in my dreams, it haunts me. Now I never let my guard down. It is too great a price to pay. We went there to relax and have a good time. It ends up being a fight to survive. When I see bear tracks now, the first thing that comes to mind is that terrible morning I almost lost my life. The second is, 'Stay away from bears.' In light of that, never let a bear of any kind sneak up on you," says Jim.

Jim's vivid tale of terror gives credence to the creatures that live silently among us, the apelike creatures we pursue cross the river to the south side. Over the years, beaten down deep into the earth, many wild animals have made their way up the river from here. Usually, this means there is a better way to go around an obstacle, such as a bridge. It is a good sign. Now the creatures can pass by without human conflict.

Softly, Jim speaks. "Jack, look to your left into the ravine, see the bed in the trees? Did they stay here last night? Look around. Can this be the moment? Do you see them anywhere?"

"Not yet, Jim."

"Let me know if you do."

I walk away from the area to a willow tree, and then I see it: a campfire with hot embers still among white ash. My curiosity runs high.

"Darkman, I need you over here."

Jim is looking around for their tracks. He hears me, stops what he is doing, and then comes to see what the excitement is.

"What?"

Looking down, he sees the ash and fish bones lying around the fire. Like an archeologist searching for bones, Jim pushes the ash back with his shoe.

"James didn't eat all this fish."

Jim is seeing. There are more than fish bones here. Does he see the big picture?

"Jim, we are seeing history made here!"

I believe it is coming to him.

"Jack, will anyone understand what is going on? Do you think James knows what is happening?"

We look at each other with amazement, wondering what the following days will hold for all of us. Jim leans his rifle against a tree and then speaks.

"This changes everything. No longer is James a captive person but has become a teacher."

"This is something wonderful, Darkman. No longer will they be creatures but reasoning beings wanting to evolve."

Like ancient discoverers, we stand there, looking at each other in preponderance of the evidence we discovered.

"All kinds of thoughts are running through my mind, Jim. Where will this lead?" No more will they be shy and elusive. Will it lead to their demise? Jim Darkman, all along, I was wrong. They did not come down from the mountains looking for food. They also came for a captive."

"Well, Jack, in a way, this is good. Now they will risk their lives protecting him."

"On the other hand, they might not let him go without a fight. When we catch up with them, can we reason with them?"

"I cannot say, Jack. We need to get moving while we still have light."

Hoping to close the distance, we quicken the pace; but it does no good. The big male was keeping an eye on us at night, letting the female know where we are. A distance up the river, I can hear his loud, thundering screams.

"Hear that, Jim?"

"Yes. I know! He is calling to his mate, letting her know how close we are, watching us like a soldier, scouting for the enemy."

What Jim says takes me back to the jungle. If a sentry had been on duty that night, men might not have died. I wonder if these creatures are anything like what entered our camp that night. I can still hear its screams as it ran through our camp, killing men while in their sleeping bags, bashing their heads in. There was no way to trace it down and kill it. Everything looked the same. Glad to get out of that place.

"Does that mean their stronghold will have soldiers guarding it?"

We advance farther upriver. The shoals are getting louder. Soon, our ears will fill with sounds of rushing water.

"The roar of the rapids can be to our disadvantage," said Jim. He reiterates. "Remember, we can only hear the rush of running water. Keep your eyes open for movement. Not for our captives but from big cats and bears."

"Are you saying one might want to get even?"

"I am saying, if a cat or bear is smart, they will keep out of sight while they lurk behind us. Just the same, don't take them for granted!"

Not me. I am the one bring up the rear. I came to the age of reasoning a long time ago, promising never to let it happen to me.

No overgrown housecat is sneaking up on me. "Jim, I know they are very smart animals. A bear comes rushing in from out of sight, while a big cat is a stalker—and then strikes."

Off at a distance, I can hear a clattering sound, a car passing over an old, wood-slated bridge. The closer we get, the louder the sound.

"We are getting close," I say to Jim. "The trail is branching off into two parts. A while back, you said this would happen. Which trail should we take?" One path veers off to the left, through thick overgrowth, toward the foot of the bridge. The other more travelled trail follows the course of the rivers edge. Off in the distance, the small township of Shoals Junction sits at the end of the road too quietly to be noticed.

Jim is not too far up ahead. I try to shout just loud enough for him to hear me. I am starting to feel like a rat in a maze. If we take this one, will it be the right one? I will have to wait for big Jim to pass the word back this way.

"Jack, we need to take the fork away from the river. If we see anyone along the way, do not say anything about what we are doing. If everything goes all right, we will see the bridge in about an hour. Our feline friend is following us, and I hope the scent of other humans will confuse our stalker and keep it away.

"We must be getting close, Jim."

I look up to make sure Jim heard me. Trash is starting to litter the area. When will man learn to cherish the earth? It disheartens my soul to know that man is his own worst enemy.

"Jim, do you think man will ever learn to cherish the earth?"

To think that back there in the wilderness, very little human encroachment exists. However, the closer we get to what humans call civilization, I see the creatures wanting to be like us. I hope they do not follow our example. Jim finally answers me with resignation.

"Almost certainly man will never learn, but I still have hope. However, I know where there is no civilization, nature is always flourishing."

Jim has spent most of his life with nature and not us.

"I hate to come back to civilization. I envy the apelike creatures and their state of nature. They are better off than we are."

Jim says it proudly. I hate to admit it, but he is right. Humans are forever at war. What can we possibly teach the creatures? Maybe it is our chance to do something right.

"Jim, someday they will remember the way they were, when they were better off, lost in their obscurity."

Ina knows that Jack will soon be approaching the Shoals Junction Bridge. If the creatures came from the mountains down the river, surely Jack will follow the river north. In Jacks prior hunting and fishing trips, the bridge has always been the arranged meeting place. Patiently, Ina peers into the woods for any sign of her husband.

At last! Now our bridge is in sight. I see that someone is watching us. From a distance, a tall, slim woman leans forward on a handrail, watching us approach. Time passes. Now I can see who she is. My heart fills with joy. It's Ina. Seeing me and knowing I am still alive, she jumps for joy, dancing around in a circle, filled with excitement. After arriving, we then climb a path to the bridge's surface. Wanting to be close, Ina runs, throwing her arms around me, holding me tight. I do not want her to let go.

"Jack, I didn't know if you were still alive. Where is James?"

"He is farther up the river, with the creatures, but he is fine. They will not harm him. We have made a great discovery, something strange and wonderful about James and the creatures."

"What, Jack?"

She takes a step back and then places her arms akimbo, the posture she gives when she is suspicious about something.

"What are they doing to him?"

"Darling, they are not doing anything to him. He is doing something for them!"

"Jack, they killed Mr. Valentine, took James away from us! Have you forgotten what they did to us?"

"No, Ina. I have not. I am starting to wonder if they did kill Roy. What is happening now is what is happening in the creature's evolution. You know what I mean. They want to be like us. We have seen signs of them coalescing around James's campfires."

I know Ina is seeing from a mother's point of view. It's hard to explain what is going on with James and the creatures. I would be skeptical myself.

Stern with her questioning, she says, "Jack, will you please put it in plain words. What do you mean by, James and the creatures?"

Every now and then, I hear it said, "Never separate a mother from her child." Ina is usually quite timid. However, concerning James, she can display extreme confidence. She speaks in a firm voice.

"Are you suggesting they want James to teach them how to be human, about fire, that sort of thing?" An astonishing look washes across her face as her eyes widen. "Jack! Man has always been at the top. I have strange and mixed feelings about that plan."

"Yes, Ina. I feel the same way. Of all the animals in the world, nature selects this elusive creature to come out of obscurity into a light filled with knowledge."

The town of Shoals Junction is not for away. Here, the Saluda River is a fine place to fish and hunt for deer. Perhaps the little town is not adventurous enough. The population never goes deep enough into the wilderness to know what is there. Glancing my way, Jim tries to discourage people from asking questions. I am sure he wants to get underway.

"Jack, I brought supplies for two people to last two weeks."

"Ina, no way can we carry that much food. Spectators are starting to gather. You brought along a crowd as well."

"I know that. I guess people were listening at the store where I met Mr. Amos. They followed me here after I met Mr. Amos and picked up the trailer. He let me borrow one of his burros to pack all these supplies. You know who I am talking about, the goat man." Ina looks toward the rusty trailer nearby. "The smelly beast is all packed and ready to go. Do you have any idea how long you will be on the river?"

We have been gone too long all ready. How can I say, we do not know when James will be back with us again? I take Ina by the shoulders and look into her questioning eyes.

"Everything is different now. Though still concerned for James, unless something goes ballistic, I do not believe they are going to harm him. Ina, what can I say? This is not a common occurrence. We cannot overtake them and start shooting. James might get in the way."

Ina's shoulders slump in disappointment. I do not want to leave her. However, just to the side of us, curious people are watching. Murmurs are starting to grow.

Because of the crowd gathering, we need to hurry.

"Jim, can you unload the burro?"

"Jack, his name is Abe."

She is determined to give him a name.

"Did you hear that, Jim? His name is Abe."

Jim, tugging on the animal's line, pulls him out of the trailer.

"Okay. Whatever you say, Jack. Abe it is."

I sense some urgency from Jim. He is becoming leery of so many onlookers.

"Jack, we need to get underway. People will start asking questions."

"Okay, Jim."

Jim takes his chance to speak with Ina. With a final handshake of good-bye, his large, dark hand swallows Ina's pale, small fingers.

"Thanks for the supplies. I hate to take you away from Jack, but we need to get underway."

"Yes. I hear you. I hate to let you go, Jack."

I pull her close to me and hold her tight. I do not want to let go of her.

"I'm sorry, Ina. I don't want to let go of you either. Parting is terrible. You know Jim is right. This is not a good place to be. All these people mean trouble. Remember, James will be fine. They do not intend to harm him. In fact, he is important to them. I might be gone for a long time, Ina. Are you ready for that?"

A stupid question to ask. I am not ready to be gone a long time. I hate to think the rest of my life will be in pursuit of James. If so, I will not have a home anymore.

"Do I have any choice? Do not worry about me, Jack. Everything is fine. I made friends with Joni, have been spending a lot of time with her. She is turning out to be a fine friend, the mother I never had. I found out through her that Roy left everything to us. Joni is also doing the same thing. It is all a shock to me."

Ina is uncomfortable with what she does not earn.

"It's a lot of change in such little time, Ina. I feel great joy. But for good reason, I don't feel like celebrating."

I glance over at Jim as he quickly loads more onto Abe's growing burden. There is no time to discuss this now. I know Ina needs to talk. I too miss her very much, but the more she stays here, the harder it is for me to leave. Ina looks toward Jim as he silently stands by the heavily laden burro.

Ina releases me, saying, "I understand perfectly."

Always the logical one in the family, she makes the right choices. I do not see how she can be so calm.

"Jack, if you have a chance to write, even if you have to give the letter to someone you meet, let me know what is going on. I will pray for all of you. Soon, people here will ask questions. I should leave for home.

Take good care of yourself, Jack. You too, Jim."

"I miss you, Ina."

"I miss you too, Jack."

I hug and kiss her. Resting my hand on the trailer gate, I test the latch, tugging firmly against the lock. It releases the gate. Reluctantly, I take one more look at Ina's smiling face as she waves good-bye. With a sigh, I turn away and follow Jim as he hurries, leading our pack animal by the reigns toward the river.

As I leave, I overhear a man with a rifle ask Ina what we are doing.

"They are on a hunting trip," she explains.

Darkman crosses the river with Abe, heavy footed, following behind him. His load gently sways side to side with each step. As we make our way, more people gather at the bridge, watching our progress and asking questions.

"Jack, I hope none of them decide to follow us." Jim clutches his weapon tightly as he turns to me. "If they do, I will persuade them to turn back. Before long, the sun will be setting. We need to put some distance between them and us."

Nodding my head, I agree with him. "We cannot let anyone interfere with what we are doing, Jim. We might as well call this a scientific expedition."

Jim makes a lot of sense about hunting and tracking. I really do not know if he fully appreciates the severity of our situation.

"Of course, our main priority is to set James free."

Jim speaks proudly and confidently, like a great hunter. After that statement, I wonder what will happen to us and where this will lead.

Thinking back to the beginning of this misadventure, thoughts of horror frequently entered my mind about losing James into the clutches of the creatures. Now our pursuit has new meaning in the discovery of these animals, which seem more like humans with each step we take. I feel James is safer than he was. Nonetheless, time moves on, and we must do the same. More than ever, I now play a defining part while hoping for the best. Because of today's busy pace, I am so tired from hiking through the snow, worn out. So is Jim.

He is a distance up the river, trying to find a campsite before sundown. Our stubborn new partner slows us down every chance he gets. Now it probably does not matter if he does. I feel comfortable knowing that James is not going to die by the creatures' hands. Now I wonder if taking him away from them will be a fair thing to do. Will

I be able to reason with them? Jim interrupts my thoughts and hands me Abe's reigns.

"Jack, finding Ina at the bridge, did she surprise you?"

"Having seen her, I do feel better now. I think because of Joni, Ina is also feeling better. An old woman trapped in a falling down house on a hill, and Ina spending her life without her mother, they are now better off together."

Holding our pack animal's tether, I lead him along beside me.

"Abe, the magnificent animal that you are—we are stuck with each other. Keep those big ears of yours open. Stay alert. You need to help guard the rear."

Giving the impression of being in pain, Abe lifts his left back hoof off the rough terrain and grinds his molars against the bit defiantly. As if telling me off, he lets a steady stream loose, and steam rises from the yellow snow. When he wants to go, he lets me know.

"Go ahead. Do what your kind needs to do."

Moreover, he does whenever he wants.

Looking at Abe with disgust, I say, "You need to stop drinking so much water."

I look back over my shoulder toward the bridge. No evidence of civilization remains anywhere.

"We left those humans far behind in a hurry, Jim. It is not long before sundown." I kick around at loose rocks and can almost feel a blazing campfire warming my frozen toes. "These rocks sure would build a great fire ring. Are we far enough away from the bridge yet? I can't hear voices behind us anymore, not the voice I would like to hear anyway!"

"We will find him still in good health. I am sure he will have a lot to say to you."

Knowing he has little daylight left, Jim says very little and then gets about his business.

"The trail is still wide from human wear. Soon we will reach that place where few have gone. We need to get there fast."

Jim foretells the future. Soon we come upon a place where a man and young girl are fishing. Jim peers through the falling light into the river's haze.

A loud voice calls out from around the bend, "Where are you two going?" A short man stands up from the riverbank, demanding an answer. He suspiciously stares at our pack animal, but he says nothing about him.

"Toward the mountains," replies Jim.

"What's up there?" asks the man as he brushes dirt from his trousers.

"Wonderful things."

Jim, a man who loves to tell a good story, speaks with few words, trying not to involve the man or the girl, who seems to be his daughter. As always, when Jim feels a need, he takes his rifle by the shoulder strap and then removes it from his shoulder. He grips it tight.

"Shoot. Then ask questions later," Jim once told me.

Truly, there are other reasons people call him Darkman, because once a foe has come out of the dark, it is usually too late for reckoning. I worry about what Jim might do when we catch up to our foe. Jim, not wanting to give up any information, angrily looks dead into the man's eyes.

"Why so many questions? If you have something to say, say it!"

The girl, taller than the man, sheepishly stands next to him. She finally speaks. "Long way to go for a hunt. Things out here can kill you."

Immediately, a thought comes to mind. Exactly what does she mean by that?

"We know what you are looking for. We also hear them calling to one another, but we never see them. Is it right to kill one of them?"

Darkman looks at him calmly. "Why would I kill one of them?"

Hands across her chest, the girl boldly accuses, "I don't know why, but I know who you are, Darkman. You wouldn't be here unless it was serious."

Jim quickly turns his head to me, commanding, "Jack, we need to get going before the cat climbs out of the bag."

That must mean if we stay here too long they might know too much. I nod in agreement before Jim gets hostile. The man tries to invite him and the girl along.

"Let us go with you. We can help!"

Jim speaks frankly. "You will add tension to our effort!" Now Darkman, realizing this is a dead-end conversation, takes a step toward him. "Take the young lady home! It is no longer safe for children here! Do not follow us! There is much more at stake here than you can imagine!"

Jim stalks off, leaving me to follow.

Tightening my hand around Abe's reign, I lead him up the river until we are out of sight.

"Jim, I hope they don't follow us. We need as few people involved as possible. As long as we can, we need to protect the creature's anonymity."

That is all we need: another child disappearing, more people on the trail encountering the creatures and James. Humans will die and creatures killed.

"The world will find out about them soon enough, Jack."

As before, Jim is in the lead while I bring up the rear. Back there, for a time, we lost our focus and our mission to keep pace with them. It does not matter. Our distant relatives are smart enough to realize we are still following them. Jim turns his gaze toward the forest.

"However, once we follow them to where they are going, I do not know what to expect from them."

Jim points toward a large oak tree wrapped in wild grape vines. He searches the ground for signs of passing.

"Jack, I can see their tracks from here. James is walking beside them. He must trust them."

"Do you think he knows what is going on?"

I have asked the question more than once, looking for reassurance. He turns around, biting the cigar between his front teeth.

"If he knows, he should feel safe with them. At least he should believe they would not kill him. I do not know. You know more about how James thinks than I do. What do you think? James is in a better position to know the threat of danger than us."

Jim has a point.

"We will know if we find a fire built by them and not James."

"That is a long stretch. We do not know just how smart they are. When James built the fire for them, everything changed. Unless time permits, I do not believe we will see them reason on their own in such a short period. Your son is not out of danger until he has returned home. This is uncharted territory, and there is no telling what is yet to come for James. "

"Do you see any cat tracks?"

Jim whisks around, facing me, rifle on shoulder. "No, Jack. You know how things are. That doesn't mean they are not somewhere back there. We still need to keep a lookout for them. The big cats spend a lot of time on the river, looking for game. The closer we get to the mountains the more frequently we will encounter them." Jim glances at Abe. "Now that we have this smelly animal, we can expect to see them more often."

There is a better side to having the burro. If a feline friend visits, Abe will let us know before the thing pounces on us. With his reigns in hand, I look at the heavily burdened animal thoughtfully.

"Jim, what can we expect from the creatures when we get to their lair?"

"I hope your son has softened them enough to accept us."

I stop and then listen for sounds behind us.

"I don't see any sign of the two annoying fisherman anymore. I hope they take your advice and turn back so that no one else dies. The creatures might not like the girl being nearby but will not kill her."

Jim removes the thing from his mouth, spitting on the ground. "Some other creatures in the clan might be less willing to accept another intruder," he says, biting the end off his wet cigar and then taking a long puff.

"Then fighting within the clan might escalate into final conflict. I am amazed at what you are saying. They sound like humans, Jim."

Sometimes he works hard, keeping it lit with fire; other times biting and spitting.

"Speaking of humans, Jack, I have to come clean with you about the anglers we met back a ways."

I listen quietly for him to speak.

"They didn't really want to go with us."

Jim sheepishly takes off his hat, rubbing his hand across his head. Facing into the wind, Jim discards the thing and then lights another cigar. Between puffs, he explains.

"The old geezer wants information for his paper. He is right. He does know me from a few years back."

"Who is he?"

I sense Jim is not so proud of something. Perhaps it's a good time for him to get it off his chest. Everybody has a skeleton in his or her closet.

Instead, Jim disappoints my curiosity and says, "He is so far away from his home. Fancy meeting him here on the river. He has no fishing gear. We assumed he was fishing."

Now I do wonder what is going on.

"It's a long story. Nevertheless, I suppose they all are. This one does not have a successful conclusion. About twenty years ago, his older sister approached me. She said an insurance company gave my name to her. At the time, they did not know of my whereabouts. Someone always knows my whereabouts. If she asked someone around the Devils Blowhole area, a little village on the Oregon coast, someone would know how to find me."

A gust of cold air pushes against my chest, nearly knocking me over. Jim stops speaking and then listens for a moment.

"Hear that?"

Jim takes his hat off and looks all around, even in the trees.

"I don't hear anything."

He speaks all of a sudden. "You are not listening!"

Abe does not run away. I pull tighter on the animal's lead. Then I hear it. A long, low-pitched moan echoes up the river.

"Hear that?" Jim asks again.

Nodding my head, my eyes widen. "Yes. I do."

"What is it?"

I have my own ideas of what it is. "A panther calling for its mate. Doesn't it know what has happened to him?"

I look off in the distance behind us. I see nothing silhouetted against the snow-covered ground. However, this thing is here for revenge. There are probably not many of them around, and then Jim kills its mate. How tragic when I think about it.

"Sounds like a female. She must be a quarter mile back."

Jim's story must have tainted his mood. He sounds like an unwilling executioner.

"What do you think we should do?" I ask him cautiously.

"We cannot do anything until we see her. Unless I have to, I don't want to kill her."

He sounds like a man tired of killing. The idea of always having to aim and destroy; eventually, the hunter becomes his own amoral victim. Nonetheless, at this moment it is survival of the fittest. Perhaps in a million years or more, our feline friend will need our help.

"Remember what happened the last time. You said that about the bear. It almost cost your life."

"No, it will not come to that. We can scare the cat away. She will avoid us when possible. Let us wait and see what she is doing. She might be on the prowl for food and hopefully not us. If she means us any harm, she will keep coming."

I still wonder about Jim's story. He seems unwilling to reenter. Well, if he mentions it again, I will listen. Looking at Jim's stony glare, I can tell this is not one of those times to poke my nose.

"What should we do, fire off a few rounds in the cat's direction, and see if it runs away?"

I feel I am playing cat and mouse with this elegant creature of the forest. If I do not stay alert, it will rip me to pieces.

"Foolish things.

They don't know when they have it made, living in the forest off nature with no care but to stay away from humans. God didn't give them enough sense to do that."

I know how you feel, Jim. I would hate to kill another one also. "You know, Jim, if we kill every one of those black devils we come across, none will be left in nature to admire. Most of the large cats are gone."

We walk a while, lift our ears to the wind, then stop and listen. It's a scary feeling knowing the stalking feline is somewhere back there, doing the same thing. Before pouncing upon us, it wants to get as close as it can.

"Let's go down to the riverbank in the bend of the trail and wait on her," suggests Jim.

Jim is the leader of this expedition. He makes the call when to kill and when not to.

She smells our tracks, knows we are up here. Scaring her off might make her forget for a while, but she will be back."

The cat forgetting and then coming back reminds me of a bull I once had. Mean and ornery, he always met me at the pasture gate at feeding time. I had to be careful not to turn my back to him. If I did, he would put his head between my legs and throw me into the air. I was at my wit's end wondering what to do about him. Hoping to teach him a lesson, while slowly sneaking up to him, I hid a shovel behind my back. I knew he had a thick skull. Wanting to leave a lasting memory, I hit him between his eyes. It drove him to his knees.

Slowly, he rose to his feet. He was smart enough to know what happened. Wanting to get away from me, he walked away. As soon as what happened left his memory, he was back doing it again. He wanted me to know he still ruled the pasture just like our cat wants to rule the forest. Suddenly, a ray of hope crosses my mind.

"Abe has a foul odor, Jim. Maybe she is after him and not us."

"You might be right, Jack, but I don't want to lose him either, unless you want to help carry his load."

I don't think so, Jim. Me trailing behind you, and I have a rope around my neck. "Don't look at me that way, Jim. If it's the cat or the smelly animal, it's thumbs down on the cat. When it comes to Abe carrying the food, I am all for the little pleasures in life."

Holding up his hand, Jim commands me, "Quiet, Jack. I believe she comes in sight."

Anticipating Jim's next move, I wait for her to show herself. What is it this time? Once again, another predator missing from the jungle is after us.

Jim fires a round at her. Sand explodes at her paws, making her leap high into the air. Falling back to her feet, she disappears into the forest. In the aftermath, I stand, stunned.

"You missed the target!"

Jim turns away, smugly reloading his 30/30. "Yes. I know."

I cannot tell if his aim is off by watching him. Either way, it is a wonderful shot.

"Jim, I hope she stays away from us so you don't have to put a bullet in her."

Perhaps I should have phrased that differently. I do not want to burden him with death. He must not have taken me seriously.

"Jack, let's leave here, move farther up the river, find a place to camp for the night. Standing there, all I can hear is the rush of river water. A moment ago, this was a completely different scene. A sleek, black cat with a long tail came running up the trail with designs on Abe, maybe all of us. In the event of a prowler, we need to find an open spot so we can see them before they get to us. I want plenty of room in case she comes back for Abe's ribs. You know what I mean, Jack."

He keeps reminding me of that cursed cow. Jim stamps his feet to warm them.

"Unfortunately, we don't have a lot of time to look for a campsite. We have a tree line over there and a sandbar that goes a long way up to the bend of the river. This is a good place to camp. Don't you think so, Jim?"

He says very little, yet he is involved in everything. I might as well not be here. Jim leans his weapon against a large oak tree and then walks toward the end of the sandbar. He is never without his weapon.

He hollers back at me, "Like always, Jack, you pile up the firewood for tonight. I will get what we need off Abe's back. We also need to keep him close by tonight so he does not become a casualty. I don't know what your Ina packed. But before it gets too late, I will cook something."

Jim must need some time alone. For some reason, he is standing at the end of the sandbar. Earlier, he mentioned getting supplies from Abe's pack. Perhaps I should tell him how late it is getting.

It does not take much darkness for Jim to disappear. I cannot hear or see any movement. Before he returns, I had better get a blazing fire going. I search the underbrush for dry kindling and firewood. A nice, hot fire will make settling in easy for both of us. If we wait any later, I will be stumbling around in the dark, falling into snow. Making my way back with a load of dry wood, I find Jim back in camp, starting the fire. He wordlessly prepares our meal. Jim's face tells no tales in the glow of the flames. Fire now leaps into the air, casting creepy shadows high into the trees. The aroma of our meal makes my stomach growl. Not good, this would be a fine time for visitors. Standing off by myself leaves me very uneasy. For that reason, I keep vigilance and step closer to the warm campfire.

None too soon, heavy footsteps are coming from behind me. Involuntarily, my head jerks around to see what it is. I am relieved. I must not have tied him tight enough. Abe comes into sight. It must have been a personal moment for him. Jim removes his pack and then fumbles around with our food.

"What about corned beef hash and eggs tonight?"

Never argue with the cook.

"That sounds good to me, Jim."

I watch him dig in the pack that now lies on the ground beside our smelly beast.

"The fire is going good now. Is it done yet?"

"Very funny, Jack. Next time, you can do the cooking and I will drink coffee and sit by the fire."

Jim is not a jokester. Sometimes I believe he should lighten up. He is so serious about everything.

"Now wait a minute. I don't mind cooking! I can, you know."

"About this time tomorrow, we will find out," proclaims Jim.

Oh, joy. Now I must hope for the best. Cooking I don't mind. However, if he expects me to wade out into icy water, fishing with my hands under murky river rocks, I will just smoothly tell him, "No."

"I tell you what, Jim. Tonight, I will make both of us some coffee. I will even pour it for you."

"Sounds good to me, Jack.

When we get through eating and cleaning up, I will finish the story I started."

"First, before we bed down, I need to hang Abe's pack high off the ground. We will not lose our supplies if some starving animal wanders into camp."

The oil is hot in the pan, ready for the hash and potatoes, some fried beans, and bread nearly done. The smell of food permeates my nostrils and excites my taste buds. It has been a long day and a long time since breakfast. *Bring on the food,* I think to myself. After a passage of time, we sit down and eat.

"Jim, you have a lot of experience camp cooking. I hope you find mine tasty."

"As long as it is not burnt to a crisp, I can eat almost anything."

I feel a little uneasy.

"Jim, do you think the cat will pay us another visit tonight?"

"I don't think so. They don't come around fires at night or around fires anytime, as far as that goes. Just the same, I will keep an eye open."

Abe will be the first to let us know if anything is around. Feeling more relaxed, I offer praise and rub my stomach.

"Jim, supper was good. Do you want another cup of coffee?"

"Yes. I will have another cup."

I look over toward Jim as he holds his hot cup. This is the best time of day, sitting by the fire, listening to night sounds. A hoot owl calls to its prey.

"Before long, we will be fast asleep."

Jim looks at me as he speaks.

"Yes. Fast asleep."

It sounds as if Jim is taunting me just a little. I don't like this. He always falls into a dead sleep. It takes both of us to listen for the creeping sounds of our stalker. A big cat could be upon us, and we would never know it. I doubt if I get any sleep all night. Jim lazily yawns and puts his back to the fire.

"Jack, tomorrow will be another long day. We need to start early. I will see you tomorrow."

Jim is almost too big for his sleeping bag. Without as much as a grunt, he tugs and then pulls as he slips slowly into his bed, away from home. There is very little small talk out of him. A matter-of-fact kind of person does what he needs to do to get by in life. I sit next to a fire full of hot embers, watching Jim fall asleep without any concern for what is out there. Like him, I too should let whatever happens happen. However, I am not a drifter.

Ina and James are waiting on me. Thinking of them helps me focus on the task. Soon, another day will dawn. This one is nearly spent. Effortlessly, I settle down to a cup of hot coffee. The day ends with me contemplating the day's events to the music of evening sounds, sounds of Abe moving about in the sand, fish jumping and trying to escape a busy raccoon, and then the sound of me sipping my coffee.

"Abe, you can stomp around all night, but you had better let me know if ferocious animals come a-calling."

Knowing the forest is unforgiving to intruders, I pile wood on the fire and then plead for mercy. I drift off to sleep, thinking about my family, and how desperate I am to get James safely home again. A sense of unease will not let me truly rest until that day comes.

CHAPTER 27

It's Sunday morning in the wilderness. The sun is already up. Birds sing. They fly around the river, looking for food, doing what birds do. I am only twelve years old. Some Christmas this is turning out to be. I want to be at home with my mother and father. *Why won't they let me go?*

She swings her long arms around and then looks down at me. Because they kept moving up the river, I got nothing to eat last night. I look down at the trail leading up to a cave and conclude they have used this cave many times for sanctuary. *Are they gathering wood for a fire?* They are learning! That is why they took me! I motion for them to bring the wood to me. Then they pile it close to the mouth of the small cave. She is such an unsightly beast with a large, hairy body and long arms extending far past her waist. She is tall with big feet and a massive head, somewhat cone-shaped, but they have a beautiful, reddish brown coat. Mom would not go for the color. She would say it reminds her to much of Owl's long, stringy, red hair. She makes me feel uncomfortable. Her eyes glare down at me. I'm sure she finds me just as unattractive. She watches me, an odd, peculiar stare out of her eyes. I wonder what she is thinking. So as not to startle her, I reach slowly, taking her large, hairy hand in mine, I then try to have a conversation with her.

"You are not like the large males. You have smaller hands." A smile spreads across her mouth.

"I believe you are smiling at me, Eve."

With the sound of my voice, her head jests toward her right shoulder.

"Here. Take this piece of wood, Eve."

She closes her hand. It disappears. I place another piece of wood in my hand.

"Eve, place the wood on the pile."

I show her how. She places it on a stack of firewood. Afterward, I ask her to do it once again. Before long, the stack of wood grows larger. She stops what she is doing and grunts and looks at me with intelligent eyes. At the same time, she moves her hands around in a circle as if to suggest, "What should I do now?" The next step will be much harder.

I look into her humanlike face and then say, "Eve, this will be the true test of your kind."

She looks back at me.

Does Eve understand what I am saying? She cannot be that intelligent. How should I teach her? "Come with me, Eve."

I lead her outside the cave and then walk with her over the flat rocks to a large cedar tree.

"To start a fire, Eve, you will need to strip the shaggy bark from this tree."

For some reason, she starts eating the bark.

"No, Eve. Don't eat it."

She puts her fingers in her mouth, removes wet strings of hairy bark, and places it in my hand.

"Eve, I do believe you are a fast learner."

Before leaving the tree, Eve pulls several strips of stringy, brown cedar bark from the tree. Leaving the tree behind, we go back into the cave and kneel down over our waiting firewood. Kneeling as if I should be praying, I look up at her.

"Come, Eve. Watch my hands."

Not so much with her eyes, but moving her head about, she watches curiously at what I am doing.

"Eve, take your fire stick and roll it between your hands like this."

I repeat my words more than once, watching her to make sure she understands. She has a hard time rolling it between her hands, but soon, she gets better at this primitive technique. To make sure she knows I am as smart as she is, I place the fire starter between my hands and start to spin it against a depression within a large piece of wood.

Facing her, wanting her to catch on, I ask, "Eve can you do this?"

She cumbersomely tries it herself.

"Don't give up."

She needs a lot of encouragement.

"This is your day, Eve!"

She watches the spinning fire-starter bring forth smoke. Suddenly, fire begins to rise up from a dry log where there was none. Eve is in an excited state. She understands. Furiously, she begins to make exciting sounds. I understand as if she could say it herself. Eve piles cedar bark onto the fire. I now understand my role in their evolution and feel much safer.

Watching her makes me talk aloud to myself. Eve notices. Every now and then, her large, black eyes look my way.

"Eve, you've done this before, haven't you. Keeping a fire burning is not new to you. You only need to know how to bring your creation to life. You know I am talking to you. Am I not right?"

Listening to every word I say, her happy, black eyes peer into my eyes. Eve and I are alone in the cave, but now the two males come from the river with fish and some kind of grass in hand. It looks like watercress. We cook fish wrapped in the green stuff. It gives the fish a delightful taste. The males must have been very hungry. They eat most of their catch. I now believe Eve can make fire and follow up by keeping the fire going.

"Eve."

She turns from the fire, facing me.

"Eve, you learn so much in such a small period of time."

She turns her head sideways and grunts, no serious expression on her face but one that casts a smile.

"I no longer fear you or your kind."

Eve and the other two males look my way. They are learning my inflections, much like a harsh, "No," and a friendly, "Yes."

I feel like Robinson Crusoe, not on an island but on a river.

CHAPTER 28

The big cat did not come back last night. If it did, Abe would have made warning sounds. Jim is standing beside him, packing supplies away.

"Jack, so that we do not burn the forest down, be sure to take some water from the river and make sure the fire is out."

He should have also been a Boy Scout leader.

"Before we move farther up the river, I need to make sure Abe is ready to go. I am almost through with what I am doing. We will leave when you are ready to go."

"Jim, while you are scouting ahead for signs of the creatures, I will bring up Abe."

Jim still has his hands in Abe's backpack with his back toward me. After speaking to him, it seems like I am giving him orders. Sometimes I catch myself doing that. Jim's eyes shift my way, but he disregards me. He then speaks.

"Jack, keep a visual, especially behind us. Don't let your guard down. Be ready for the unexpected."

Here I go, bringing up the rear again.

The unexpected? What does he mean by that? I look to the rear. There's no sound but the river running downhill.

"Jim, how far back is the bridge?"

"Not that far away, Jack. I don't believe we'll see anyone this far up river. The tracks I see must be James's. He is now by himself a lot."

You do not have to be a mind reader to know what Jim is thinking. James trusts them now. Our theory of them must be real.

"How much farther is it to the mountains?" I ask Jim, wanting a hint of how much longer it will take to overtake them or perhaps a final destination.

"We still have a lot of distance to go yet. The river will start to narrow before long."

Suddenly the reigns pull taunt as the burro digs his feet into the path. I tug hard on the reigns to coax him on, but he stubbornly holds his ground.

"What is wrong with you, Abe? Come on. Don't act like that."

Watching Jim, I stop dead in my tracks. *What's wrong?*

He does not say anything but holds his rifle up, ready to fire. He's behind me, pacing slowly, with deliberant intent; it reminds me of a bad nightmare. Almost unseen, a black spot with four legs among snow becomes a panther. Jim holds his rifle ready and then discharges a shell. Watching and frozen in time, I feel the force of a concussion. Then a bullet passes by me. Like slow motion, her body crashes to the ground. Thank God for Abe and, of course, watchful Jim.

"I didn't see her, Jim. Where did she come from?"

"She must have known we were coming and lay waiting on us. We will have to keep a watchful eye. We are now more in their domain."

Jungle animals this far north. What else is hiding here? That is a crazy question. In this modern world, anything can happen: A-bombs, aliens from outer space, the Three Stooges.

"They don't like human encroachment anyway." It is Jim's justification. "I hope this is not frequent, Jack. Killing them is not something I want to do. We do not have time to skin them. I cannot let it die in vain, not to mention our time lost. We need to get him strung up fast so we can get moving."

Before long, another dead animal hangs beneath an oak tree. It almost reminds me of an ancient ritual. Before long, the big cat's pelt packs away on Abe's back. However, Abe is uncomfortable with the cat's dead remains. Finally, we are on the river trail, heading north.

"Well, Jim, that makes two now. What next, a bear?"

"I hope not. I hate cleaning those smelly things, but we can use the meat. From here on, Jack, we start using leg muscles. The terrain will start moving uphill, and the river will flow faster. Soon, we will come to a waterfall."

"Is it a high one?" I ask him.

"You will like it. It's a hundred feet tall with a large basin. The hole is large and deep. You might see black bears there, fishing. Maybe if you are lucky. Why they migrate so for south, I do not know the reason. Does not matter anyway; most people don't believe panthers are here until they come face-to-face with one."

Jim speaks the truth. Life does change people. I am a firm believer.

"At one time, I didn't believe, but now I think I will believe anything. I do not live in my father's world. What kind of world are you and I going to find?" I ask Jim, knowing a lot of responsibility comes with the discovery of these strange creatures living so close to us.

Just think. Not long ago, life was different.

"Jack, at the moment, we can take only one step at a time. We still have a way to go before we reach the waterfall. There is no runoff from snow yet. But when the river is up, the falls are spectacular and dangerous."

I love waterfalls, a place to sit and rid myself of bad thoughts. Do not know about this place, though. So far, there has only been pain and sorrow. Something is either taking what I love, or something is trying to kill me.

"Jim, because we are not hunting bears, if any are there, I don't want you to kill any of them."

"Whatever you say, Jack. Do you want to go there? If you do, you will have to say so. The trail splits a ways up the river. One goes to the falls, and the other takes a side trail over the falls."

Just in case they are at the falls, perhaps I should close the gap between Jim and me. He has one encounter in his memory. I am sure he remembers it well. I would hate to be between him and his target.

"Considering how late it is, by the time we arrive at the falls, we will need a place to camp. I would like to know I have been there. I love waterfalls anyway."

"I thought you might say that, Jack."

"I just don't want any more encounters with wild beasts."

"Do not trouble yourself, Jack. If they are any bears there, they will be too busy to notice us. Just stay away from the cubs if they are any."

You need not tell me to stay away. They should stay away from me. This forest looks the same as my forest back home. One moment, I am home. Then I blink my eyes and I am in another world where beasts and burdens rule. When I get back home, the only thing I want to do is sit on the front porch, stare at the woods, and contemplate how to cope with my surroundings.

"What do you think the falls will look like during this time of year?"

"The best time to come up here is in springtime. The basin is alive with flowers, feather moss, wild iris, and different birds. Dogwood trees surround the basin. But nevertheless, it will still impress you."

"Do many people know about the place?" I ask Jim.

"Not many people come here because of the distance. Twenty miles is a long hike for most people. I think most people are afraid of the deep woods here. You know why. I come here sometimes with a female friend, a tall, lanky, backwoods woman who calls herself Jasmine. Pretty as a flower and mean as a snake. She's the only woman I know who can wear my trousers and fight like a man. We spent several days fishing some trout and some bass and doing other things. She loves the place. She didn't want to return to her other life," Jim reminisces.

She does not sound like Ina, although sometimes she does wear my pants. I would like to see her in my pants right now—her beautiful face, graceful body. Lord, I wish this would hurry up and end.

"Under the right conditions, I would not leave the falls either."

However, I know that will not happen at this time. I have to keep pushing on, or James might think I am lost, or worse, dead.

"Also, there is a deep cave behind the falls. Because of the heat, she and I slept in it on hot days." Jim speaks as he kneels down by a clear spring for a drink of water.

"Sounds very nice, Jim. Staying for a while would be relaxing. But tomorrow early, we need to push on."

I wait on him to move away from the spring so I too can quench my thirst.

"We are coming up on the trail that goes around the waterfall. Are you sure you want to see it?" Jim sounds excited.

"Yes, Jim. I do. If I don't, I will always wish I had."

Jim's eyes squint as his attention turns to me.

"Jack, do you think the world is ready to see what we are about to discover? When we get there, you will understand why it looks the way it does."

"What do you mean?" I ask him.

"So far, this waterfall is undiscovered territory. It is unspoiled. The beauty of the place will be lost because of man's intrusion."

Jim makes sense. However, I do not have a need to tell everyone about our utopia away from home. I only want Ina to see where I have been.

"Take it easy, Jim. I will keep it in the family. I do not want anyone else to know about this place. No one will ever know the whereabouts of our apelike friends, not by me. People who see the proof of their existence will never know where they are. Jim, I promise you this."

I now hear the sounds of falling water. It drowns out all other sounds in the forest.

"Jim, these are unusual circumstances."

I stop suddenly and then look around. Even though the thickness of a wooded forest lies a reasonable echo away, still, will we be able to hear a predators advance toward us?

"What do you mean, Jack?" Jim removes his hat and then runs his black, white palmed hands through his hair.

"If we are attacked by a predator, which also means the creatures, we cannot hear them coming. We will have only our sight to rely on."

Jim did not say anything. I thought maybe this time I had the last word. He just stood there, staring in the direction of the spillway.

It's unlike him not to say anything. Now this is a real moment. However, it did not last long.

"That's true, Jack. But the creatures could have already killed us. With luck on our side, we will make it to the spillway. Once we get there, there is only one way in."

He speaks as if he expects them or others to drop by like guests at a party, one way in, and one way out for us.

"Our only protection is to keep vigilant, ready for anything. Jim, when we catch up with the creatures, we cannot let anything happen to them. We cannot afford to let anything go wrong in this time of their progress. People's involvement will destroy them."

CHAPTER 29

I put it directly to Joni, all the reasons she should not live isolated in this relic of a house. I understand Joni is old and feeble, but she is not without her wits.

"Joni, is there anything you want to do today? You know, today is Sunday."

After a night of sleep, Joni's eyes are half-open, still very tired. Patiently, I wait for her to speak. After rubbing her eyes, she responds.

"Not today. I try to keep the Sabbath. But we must do what needs to be done."

It is not that I do not listen. I have a problem hearing her if there is any background noise. Most people do not like to repeat themselves, so I listen closely to hear Joni's quiet voice.

She asks, "Ina, is there something you need to do? Don't let me hold you back."

Maybe that is why she spent years alone, thinking she gets in the way.

"You are doing no such thing. However, because of all that has been happening, I have been putting off something. I need to check on Jack's mother, Edna. It has been a couple of weeks now. I need to see how she is. The snow has been so deep, the roads very bad. If I do not make sure she is all right, Jack will be furious." Silently, I take a deep breath, pondering my thoughts. So much is happening at once. I'm lost in my thoughts, mumbling to myself. Joni watches me curiously.

"When Jack is home, we visit Edna every weekend. Now that he is looking for James, you and I can go see about her. You will like Edna. She is a good Christian woman."

I know the kind of woman Joni is: warm and thoughtful, perhaps one foot still planted in the past, the other now touching down on new ground. She will enjoy being around Edna. Like Joni, Edna has seen desperate times: Jack's father dead by the age of forty, Jack and Owl growing up without a father. It gave way to Owl's nonchalant attitude, his reason for taking nothing serious. They were hard times, the Depression days. We are all lucky to be alive, not starved to death.

"How old is she?"

Joni hopes for someone near her age. Joni is twenty-five years her senior.

"Sixty. She lives in Ware Shoals, next to the regal textile mill, in one of the mill hill homes."

Nicely built brick homes, all of them look alike. To keep everyone close to the mill, Old Man Regal built towns much like a labor camp. It's a good thing Joni did not live here then, working for a dollar a day.

"Edna lives by herself just like you. But you don't have to anymore."

I've been around this sweet old woman for a short time now. Once, I thought her to be a crazy old coot with a cane. I feel so ashamed of myself.

"Like you, Joni, she spends a lot of time alone. However, Owl still sleeps there. Nevertheless, most of the time, he is gone. God only knows where! Her husband died from drinking alcohol and left her to raise two children."

Joni slides her chair back from the table. "Will she mind me dropping in?"

"She won't mind. Most of the time there is no one with her. Owl gets impatient with her and then stays gone all weekend or longer. His name is Albert, but everyone calls him Owl because he is a night owl and does not give a hoot."

Joni sits across from me, feet planted flat on this old house's scarred, wooden floor. Her face expresses a need to talk.

"Edna and I will get along fine. I know how it is to be alone. She and I should have a lot to talk about." Joni perks up with a smile on her face.

"If you don't mind, after breakfast we can ride over there and see if she is well. It will do you good to get away from this old house."

After breakfast, I clean the kitchen. Then we leave for Edna's house. Joni is not familiar with riding in a car. So as not to frighten her, I drive slowly.

"Joni, do you go to town often?"

"Before Merry got sick, we went every Sunday to the First Baptist Church. When she got worse, we had to stay at home. Through the week, some people from church would visit. Sometimes the pastor would drop by in the evening, but after coming by a few times they stopped visiting. I miss Merry so much!"

Tears well up in her eyes; it breaks my heart to see her this way Before long, we approach Jack's work place. I lift my foot then gently step on the brakes. A squeaky sound comes from the rear wheels, and then we start slowing down, not too sudden, though. Ice is still on the road. Joni looks out her window to see what I am looking at. God forbid. Jack might be gone for a long time. No one knows when he will return to work, if he does at all. I do not know what George will do without Jack. He'll probably go out of business. I look toward Joni.

"Joni, before we return home, I need to tell George something. He's Jack's boss. Jack will not be coming back for a long time, if ever. See all those cars with snow heaped up around them? They need fixing. George is going to be disappointed. He is going to be very disappointed!"

I hate driving when this stuff is on the road. I have been watching that white line mix with snow for about fifteen minutes.

Soon, we will cross the dam on the Saluda River. Every time I cross it, I think about what my grandfather told me when I was a child. I was very young then, about twelve. Granddad was a tall, slim man, his hair white and thinning. He hardly ever combed it. He let it blow in the wind. He always held my hand wherever we went to keep me safe.

Then, Granddad would look down and whisper, "Stay close to me, Ina. Don't get out of my sight."

He always made eye contact with me when he spoke. One day, he took me fishing at the dam.

After a long hike through the woods to the backside of the dam, we entered a cove with high cliffs. It was a hidden place where few people went. There was no wind. The water was deep and calm. It was his favorite fishing hole. We sat near the water's edge and unraveled line from his cane pole. I watched him put a night crawler on the hook and then slowly lower it into the water. He would say, "Still water runs deep."

We sat there for a while, watching the bobber drift slowly out into the quiet water. Distracted by geese landing on the other side of the lake, he raised his hand and pointed the way he always did. With all fingers on his hand pointing at the geese, he loved to talk about the river's history.

He told me one day, "A small distance up the river from the dam, the water is shallow enough to wade across the river." He said, "When I was a child, herds of deer crossed the river there." He also said, "Long ago, many Indians crossed the sandy shallows during their travels."

We then stood up and watched a log float toward the face of the dam. It crashed onto the rocks below. There behind the dam, the water is deep and wide. After flowing downhill a distance, water surges through large turbines. When forcing water through the turbines, they make a loud, defining scream. They make electricity to power the mill.

Joni sits quietly while I ramble through my past. We pull up to the stop sign near Edna's house, and I notice Joni has fallen asleep. Her head rolls to the side, waking her from a light slumber. "Ina, are you and Jack from Ware Shoals?" she asks.

"Been here all my life, Miss Joni. It's hard to believe that if not for this river, the town would not be here. I am one of those people who never went anywhere else to live. I would not know where to go. Like others looking for work, my family came here in the twenties. Jack's family came here around the turn of the century. Do not be surprised, Joni. You will not see much change around here."

The mill is the only thing that keeps this town alive, and the river is the only recreation for people who work in the mill. We are almost there. I hope we do not catch Edna at the wrong time, like at work. Sometimes she works many hours to make ends meet. Like many others around the mill hill, she does not have a car. To see if she is at home, we have to stop. Most of the time, she works in the bleachery; it is the large building behind the mill, next to the river. On the other hand, sometimes she works in the spinning room, doffing bobbins, you know, little spindles that gather yarn as they spin.

What is going on? I see a fire truck and several people around the bleachery. Something must have happened. I drive next to a man directing traffic.

"What is going on?"

"Move on, lady."

Waving his arms franticly, he does not take time to look at me in the face.

"My mother-in-law works in there!"

I pass by him and then slow to a stop. I am worried, and I open my door and then stand close by. Cars began to back up behind my blue Ford. They are desperate to know about friends and relatives. Determined to gain someone's attention, my shaking hand grabs the freezing cold door. I lean forward and then shout, "What happened here?"

Standing by himself, a man holding a fire ax holds his left hand high in the air. It protrudes through a tattered, detached sleeve. He is doing what most people run from. His clothes are still smoldering with an odor of chlorine. He knows how unsafe life is here.

"Been an explosion!

Five people are dead! You need to get back to your car and get out of here!"

As the man said, I get back into the car then drive away.

Trying not to panic, those four words keep running through my mind: "Five people are dead." If my actions match the grimacing deformity of my troubled face, then Joni might be overwhelmed with grief and then begin to cry. If that happens, I will surely have a mental breakdown. Reassurance is what we need. I gather my thoughts. Before I can say anything to Joni, she speaks in a reassuring tone of voice.

"Things are never as bad as we think they are. Remember that, Ina."

Perplexed by what I hear coming from Joni, amazed by her countenance, I stare at her with a blank expression. Can it be she just does not know what is going on? My head rests in my trembling hands, running my fingers through my smoky, dirty hair. I think aloud, mumbling unrecognizable words to myself.

"More horror.

What should I do now? Joni, I hope Edna is not one of them. I am going back to find out where they are taking people. You stay here. I need to find out if she is one of the victims."

I hold back the tears. Still, I feel worry welling up inside me.

"Ina." Joni places her hand on my head and then speaks softly. "Don't go there full of fear, sweetie!"

I try to be calm and collective. With all her wisdom, Joni tries to confront me. Rolling down Mill Hill Road but not fast, I lift my trembling leg and press the soft brake pedal. It does not let me down. Jack keeps Old Blue in mint condition. Effortlessly, we come to a screeching stop. My car is not so big, but dark blue does stand out. I am no stranger in town, but no one asks about Jack or James. I can see why. Too much unpleasantness is going on. After stopping, I make a hasty approach to a sheriff's deputy.

"Is Edna Palmer all right? Can you tell me anything?"

"Don't know her, is she some kin to you?"

All kinds of thoughts run through my mind. I hardly know what to ask. Finally, I speak. "She is my mother-in-law."

Already, the deputy has turned away. He has no time for me.

I shout after him, "I know what area she works in!"

After pulling the car to the side, I open the car door, swinging my feet around to the ground. I turn toward the burning building. Smoke and heat surround my face. This part of the mill is five stories high with brick walls still towering high in the sky.

"You can't go in there, lady! That wall is going to crumble anytime! Stay out of there! Let the firemen do their job!"

The deputy still stands in the middle of the road, directing traffic. I go back to the car and sit helplessly there for a moment. My hands grip the steering wheel. My head leans forward, resting on my hands. "What now, Lord?" I whisper to myself, holding back tears.

"Are you all right, Ina? Before you start thinking that Edna is dead, we need to see if she is at home."

"You are right, Joni. I need to get my head together before I start thinking horrible thoughts. Her house is not far from here."

I start the engine and then back out into the road. Heading toward Edna's, we drive away from the crumbling building. Joni sits quietly. She is probably afraid she will say the wrong thing. Jack's car—I think of it as his, and it is—it makes its way up the steep hills, the mill hills, without any effort, only a small shake in the steering and a squeak here and there. Finally, I pull into Edna's driveway. As soon as the car stops, I get out then run to her door. My hand pounds on the door.

"Edna!" I shout.

Her door, old and marked up, needs a new coat of paint. I pound harder. It makes a loud, solid sound enough for the neighbors to hear. Nevertheless, no one comes to his or her door.

"Are you in there, Edna?"

There is still no answer. Suddenly, a feeling of panic comes creeping like a dark cloud approaching from the north. Jack and his mother are very close. What awful news to come home to: his mother dead. I go back to the accident, where the man is directing traffic. He watches me come to a stop and then get out of my car. My legs feel weak. I try to stay calm.

This deputy is unknown to me; so much for everyone knowing each other in a small town. Still directing traffic, he watches me.

"Where are the casualties taken?"

So that passing cars do not hit me, I stand next to him in the middle of the road.

"They are at the mill clinic!"

The deputy manages to get his words out as his hand points to the top of the hill. I know where the place is: on the south side of the mill at the top of the hill. We are not far from there. Most of the rubberneckers are gone. Traffic should not hinder us from getting there. On the way back to the car, I picture the place in my head. I have been here only once. Other people are here from the mill. There must be more people hurt than they are telling. Confident, walking like nothing is wrong, I push the double doors open and then walk inside. An old, gray-headed man sits at a table in the middle of the room. He is holding a yellow pencil in his left hand, scratching his head with it. He is a familiar face.

"Mr. Green, what are you doing here?"

"They need help. I'm the only person they can reach."

"Is Jack's mother among the dead?"

He looks at me with a wrinkly blank face. Mr. Green is a tall, slender man. He looks a little like the photos of my father. He is doing what most would not.

"Mr. Green, are you all right?"

"Yes. I didn't know what to say to you."

It's okay, sir. We have been through a lot lately.

He rises from his chair, disappears into the back room for a while, and then returns.

"No. She is not dead but in a bad way. They are taking good care of her."

Finally, Doctor Ames comes out. Before speaking, he stands erect with his hands hanging heavy beside his body. His glasses are low on his nose. He then lowers his head and looks over the top of his glasses. Everyone is silent, waiting on him to speak. His years working on the mill hill are wearing him down. I know he wants to be at home in bed. Most of us do. He turns toward me.

"Ina, Mrs. Palmer is injured. She inhaled a lot of smoke and chlorine." Placing his hand on my shoulder, he reassures me. "Nevertheless, she is a tough old girl with a strong will to live. We should know more by morning."

The doctor has a fine bedside manner. There is not much more I can ask him. People are sitting stiffly in chairs, hoping for as good a report. Others are pacing around, about to go out of their minds. Rubbing my tired eyes, I wonder why everything is falling upon me at once. Glancing at the treatment area doors, I decide to stay with Edna all night. Can I do that? Peering into the long hallway, I search for Dr. Ames in his long, white coat. Nervously, I fold my arms across my chest. Perhaps he will not mind my staying. His hands are full. On the other hand, I am not one of his nurses following him room to room. He might not like me slowing him down. If I stand in the hall, in-between rooms, I will catch him when he comes out. It is not like me, but I can be deliberate.

As soon as opportunity presents itself, I will take hold of his arm. Tired, leaning forward to keep moving, he walks toward me, eyes nearly shut.

"Pardon me, doctor."

He looks down at me, standing gauntly. He waits for me to speak. With a deep breath, I throw away my caution. "So much is happening at once, Dr Ames. Will I get in the way? Edna needs me with her all night."

Dr. Ames smiles and then nods his head. He knows my question before I ask it. "You will do her a lot of good." He turns his back to me and then disappears into a vacant, silent, dark room where no one enters unless led in by a compassionate, embracing arm.

Is this where dead people end up? Dr. Ames moves about in a dark room. He must know where everything is. I hear a deep sigh, his breath raspy. The smell of tobacco fills my nostrils.

"Come with me. I'll get you a cot to sleep on."

Dr Ames leads me into a cool, lightly lit room and then quickly strides away. Mom lies silently, resting with shallow, labored breathing. By this time, Joni is in the room, standing beside me. I turn to her with tears in my eyes.

"Look at her. How could this happen?"

"Ina, she'll be fine."

She said it smiling, with great confidence, as if she knows more than I do.

"How can you be so sure, Joni?"

My eyes clear long enough to see her looking in my direction.

"A little voice told me."

I try to focus, my mind dazed by horrible thoughts. I look at her. *Joni, you need to be at home, resting.* "Are you tired, Joni?"

"Yes, but I'm fine." After placing her soft, warm hands on my face, she softly speaks. "Don't worry about Edna, Ina. Put her in His hands, and give it no more thought. It works that way. She will be fine in the morning. Cry for the dead, not the living."

What does that mean? I ask myself as I walk with her out the door, her tiny hand in mine. After helping Joni to the car, I then go back to the tired Dr. Ames and tell him not to bother with the cot. I need to take Joni home and stay with her tonight. I know Edna will be safe.

"Come, Joni. Let's go home. We will come back tomorrow and see how Edna is doing. We can also take care of your will then."

God must have paired us up for a reason. She must be very close to God. How else is she so sure about finding James? Now she says Edna will live. She must know something I do not. We climb back into the car. Slowly, I back out of the driveway and then head home.

"Joni, how do you know these things?"

Her brow crinkles up. She is amused by my question.

"What things?" she asks so naively.

"When you speak about James, you sound so confident. Are you so right with God that you know His mind?"

Joni looks at me through her gentle, blue eyes.

"At my age, Ina, I want to be with Him. He takes care of me and answers my prayers. He sometimes whispers in my head things that I need to hear. I am old enough to see your future, your families. When events take place I can see the rest unfold."

"What does God show you about me and mine?"

Joni tells me, "I can see you, Jack, and James living in your own home, a beautiful place with many acres and people who love you. The world will seek you out, but be silent as long as you can."

"What does that mean, Joni?"

Now I turn my focus to the road. Patches of snow and black ice cover the blacktop, making our travels treacherous. The ice sparkles from my headlights. I must be cautious and drive slowly. Glancing over at Joni, I think about what she said to me. *Who am I?* It comes to mind a leaping unknown, caught between a rock and a very hard spot, not even average intelligence. Nothing good happens. It's all bad. Joni leans across the middle of the seat, smoothing away a loose hair from my face.

"Ina, all these things will pass. But now we might as well head home, unless there is something else you need to do."

There is something I need to do—something I have been without for a long time—a hole left in my life where Jack and James are gone perhaps forever. Church, at one time, my little family went every time the doors opened.

"Joni, would you like to go to church with me tonight? It's now too late to go this morning."

"Sure, Ina. I have not been in a long time. Anytime is a good time to start back."

Back in church, things will never be the same. Now I feel a horrible emptiness, fear of what everything means, me starting a new life in church without Jack, God giving me hope that things will get better for us.

"There is so much going on in my life now. I do not know which way to turn. Joni, I have always meant to start back but never did. Perhaps this is the way God brings me back!"

I try not to lay my head on the steering wheel and sob. It will do no good.

CHAPTER 30

Now I can see misty falls. A great spray of water splatters on reddish cliff rocks. Because I hate having to repeat myself, I shout loudly so Jim can hear me over the roar of the strange-looking falls.

"The basin is big, and its water is a deep blue. It took a long time for ice to build up on its shore."

This place looks so peaceful. Abe must like it here. He seems to be more compliant.

Shouting at Jim, I ask, "Just how deep is it?"

"It's not that deep. About forty feet, give or take a few."

Approaching the falls makes me think of Ina. This is a romantic place for lovers. We will come back during summer, not in this frigid cold. Shaking my head, I think, *How can I entertain such thoughts with the looming task ahead of me?* Finally, I walk up behind Jim with Abe still in tow. Jim does not say anything.

I whisper to myself, "I am unaccustomed to this kind of beauty. No wonder you want to keep this place a secret. People will destroy everything here. The falls look to be an acre in size. The water is so blue."

Jim looks up at the frozen face of the falls, staring at the accumulation of hanging ice, like great, otherworld icicles. Ice gathers around what is still a flowing river, something from a fairy tale. Nearly everything is frozen, but still, water makes its way through hanging ice.

Jim looks like a shivering porcupine as ice gathers on his whiskers. Even though victory still waits, his tattered red scarf blows about in the gusting wind.

There is no celebration, yet Jim says, "Looks like the stuff is still freezing fast, Jack. I suppose when everything melts, this place will be like Niagara Falls. We have to be out of here before that happens. You do not want to be around then, do you?"

Jim asks a foolish question.

"No, I do not! I would like to bring Ina up here. But after what brought us here, she might not like this place."

"After the river swells, becoming a torrent of water, this place will not look the same after it pushes trees, ice, and everything else downstream. I have never seen anything like this. The whole thing is starting to look like a great iceberg."

Jim keeps talking while I stare at the frozen spillway, mesmerized by the swirling currents as they churn about floating mounds of ice in a continuous cycle.

Jim scouts for a way over the falls. I ask, "Have you ever dived to the bottom?" "No, Jack, but you can jump in and see how deep it is. When you look up at the ice, tell me what you think of it."

Looking at Jim's smirk, I laugh and then come back with a retort. "Some people do just that, take off all their clothes and then plunge into the icy Potomac. Initiation they call it. The idea of it makes me shiver. It's bad enough to be here, must less act like a fool."

A cold gust of wind plunges down from the frozen mound of ice. It brings me back to why we are here.

I brace myself against the wind and then declare, "I will make a pact with you, Jim. When we come back this way and James is with us, I will be the happiest man alive. I will take that plunge into the spillway. Afterward, you can chip the icicles away."

Jim points to a small, spindly dogwood tree. "If you think it's a sight now, see it in the spring. Tie Abe to that dogwood, and then follow me."

Obediently I trudge through the crunchy snow with Abe peacefully trailing behind. While I tie him to the dogwood tree, I hear Jim's voice echo around the basin.

"If you hug the wall, you won't get wet when you slip behind the falls!"

I hear him, but he is out of sight.

Glancing around the cave, dazed, a little confused, I then call out, "Where are you?"

Jim sticks his head out from behind a wall of ice. He seems hidden, not like him at all. He is one of those trailblazer trackers not afraid of anything. His voice sounds barely audible behind the ice and falling water. "Not all of the water is frozen."

"I can see that for myself!" I shout it loud enough for Jim and any creature to hear.

"I am not blind," I want to say aloud, but I keep it to myself. Looking past the entrance into the cave, the inside is cold and wet. Possibly a few feet in, the floor looks less wet.

His voice resonates in my direction. I look through the entrance to a watery cave.

"Bring your rifle with you. There might be animals. They will not like our company. Take care. Keep your eyes open."

Cautiously, I follow Jim's lead, slipping past the watery entrance hidden away behind the falls. Ready for anything, my grip is firm on the cold iron of my double-barreled ten-gauge. I do not want to see any more ferocious animals. Unlike me, Jim takes it all in a day's work. However, I had my fill of jungle life years ago, never believing I would see another one of those creatures again. I hope they are friendly this time. I hate to think how things might turn out when we finally do catch up with James.

Jim holds onto the lantern's thin wire handle, holding it before him as he advances farther into the cave. The cave glistens like sparkling diamonds in the lantern's dim glow. Now close enough to count the hairs on his head, I thrust my heavy gun into his hands.

"Here! Take it from me. You are a better shot. I am glad James is not here to hear me say that. Let me carry the lantern. I will hold it up high enough to see."

Something glitters. Jim is watching me. I know he is going to say something.

"It's not gold or diamonds. It is mica. I did not bring you in here to show you a goldmine." He snickers as he says it.

Just so Jim does not forget, I say, "Remember, only kill if you have to!"

Jim suddenly turns his head toward me, a moment's stare, his face noncompliant. He forms not even a glimmer of a smile. He must know I am becoming a bit weary of the situation and him. James and Ina are heavy on my mind. It's just a chance to vent some frustration without me being hurtful.

I remember the cat, the black beauty, his discard of past trash, its carcass thrown aside. I said little back then. Just the same, I think about it a lot. My mind drifts back to a not-so-distant time, but my body is still here in the present. Jim stops his attack on the cave, turns around, and then faces me.

"Come on up here with that light."

Like the creatures, his eyes glow red.

"Hold the light up a little higher, please. I do not want the day-light scared out of me. This cave goes a long way back and then turns into a cavern. Bring the lantern up here. I see something in the sand. Some deer tracks, some bare feet, but these are not human track, do you know what that means?"

So that I can see Jim, I lift the lantern toward the ceiling and then speak softly, hoping Jim hears me.

"I don't see any so-called human tracks leading out the entrance."

I come closer into his view. Jim stops mumbling to himself and then speaks.

"That means they already heard us. Usually they don't take chances. These are inexperienced juveniles." Jim speaks as if they are children.

"Watch your back, because they will most likely run like scared rabbits."

"Jim, you better let them get away. Don't shoot at them."

"Do not tell me that," Jim barks at me as he pulls the hammer back on his rifle. He then says, "Just stay out of their way. If they want to leave, they can do just that!"

Perhaps the cave is too small for all of us. Jim seems to be a little perturbed with me. Sometimes I think he responds too quickly—shoots and then asks questions later. I see no reason to kill unless we are threatened.

"Why would they be here in the dark?" I ask Jim.

"You know that answer! They are more animal than human is why! These did not take James, but they might be going where he is. Watch now. When the light strikes those eyes, they will glow red."

Now that brings back a nearly forgotten memory that makes me a little uneasy: that deadly night in the jungle. It makes shivers run down my spine. Red eyes are what I remember, those things running through my camp, screaming, hammering the men with clubs. They reeked of a bad odor. The smell was enough to kill. It happened so fast. I am still not sure how many entered the camp.

"Spooky," I say, thinking aloud.

"You haven't seen anything!" Jim's voice echoes through a narrowing opening. He continues. "Come up on them on a full moon. They look like large, red fireflies."

My sentiments exactly.

I stumble around in the darkness. I do not feel too safe right now.

"Bring the light closer. Hold it as high as you can."

The lantern's wiry handle digs into my sore fingers. Still, I do as he asks. Holding the lantern high, I see nothing, only damp, wet walls of moss. Some of it looks creepy hanging from the ceiling. Disturbing sensations tingle down my spine. I look up, expecting the stuff to fall down my back—it and all the little creatures that dwell in it. They will not find safe haven on my not-so-warm body.

At last, I catch up with Jim. He turns himself around without moving out of his tracks.

"What kept you?"

"You know I am doing the best I can, Jim."

Jim stands patiently, waiting on something to happen, as if a long-lost friend is about to pass by. Sometimes I wonder about him. How is it that he knows so much about them, these apelike creatures living in the woods? It's strange how he happened to be at the store, showing up at the bridge as he did. I never hear him say anything about who his parents are. Jim's voice interrupts my thoughts.

"I see them coming."

One of them screams as he passes by Jim.

"Watch out, Jack. He's coming your way."

Jim shouts as if I am a mile away. Then one of them crashes into me, knocking me to the ground.

"What a foul smell. You know, Jim, I've smelt that odor before. Just think. I was that close and didn't even know it."

I lie there for a moment and then scramble back to my feet.

"Jack, are you all right?"

I am a little bruised. I should have seen it coming. Reaching for the lantern, I lift myself off the wet, grimy floor.

"I'm fine. It felt like being hit by a smelly rug. All I saw was large, red eyes darting about. He walked over me as if I wasn't there. I did not slow him down at all."

Hoping Jim might see things my way, I say, "Let's get out of here. I can't see anything but darkness in here."

"What do you think, Jack, now that you have been up front and personal with one of them?"

More like hit by a ton of bricks, I said to myself. "One thing I know for sure: I don't want to tangle with one of those carpets ever. He had long, shaggy hair and stunk like a wet dog. Now I smell like him. Why are they so afraid of us?" I ask, brushing all the wet crap off my jeans.

"Like other animals, they fear us. And these know what guns can do."

Seeing the light at the entrance to the cave, I stumble about—do not even care. I do not like dreary, wet places anyway. Jim seems not to care.

"They know what guns can do and still want to be like us."

"Not like us, Jack. They do not want to be killed by us."

Jim is right. I do not believe they want to be like us, not really. "Not wanting to be killed. Yes. I suppose that is the truth of it all."

I am first to leave the cave. For some reason, Jim is still back there.

"Frightened by the sound it makes, they scream when they hear a big bang. I heard one of them off in the distance when I killed the cat. Sometimes, humans are bad about shooting haphazardly at anything that moves. Sometimes it makes me sad to be human."

I watch Jim's face as he speaks. He has a certain love for them and their survival.

"Don't get wet, Jack."

I am already wet. We slide against the wall while leaving the cave. Now out in open sight, Abe is still in sight, but he is not where we left him.

"Have you seen enough?"

"Yes. I'm still a little shaken, but we can move on uphill to higher land if you are ready for that."

The closer we get to the mountains, I suppose we will start seeing the river began to narrow. Jim interrupts my thoughts.

"Jack, we have to go back to the trail, back down the river so we can start the climb. When we reach the top terrain, the land will start to level out."

"What do you think? How long will it take for those two to tell the others where we are?"

He knows more about them now than when we began. Jim crotches down to tie his worn, leather shoes.

"Not long. It does not matter anyway. They know we are trailing them. Soon, they will reach where they are going. They cannot run forever." Jim continues. "The cave we were in is one of many in these mountains they can reside in before making the climb over the falls. We are much closer now. Before long, we will arrive at their location."

Standing at the base of the falls, looking up, I am amazed by the grasp of winter on so much water. Even though frozen, I do not cherish the thought of coaching Abe to risk a climb over the falls. This place is wet and noisy. Just the same, I'm still able to catch sight of my fearless leader.

"Jim, the two in the cave, they are juveniles? How they do stray far from home!"

The three of them far from home, the reality of it now dawns on me. James was playing in the woods. I should have been watching him, of all places for him to be after seeing that ape-looking thing at the river. What was I thinking?

"Jack, you know the old saying, a nut doesn't fall far from the tree. These nuts are not far from home."

Just because one crashed into me, I would not go as far as saying *nuts.*

"I have a feeling we will see them sooner than later."

Then Jim has a recollection, something from his past. "I know where there is a large cavern about five miles from here, about two miles off the river trail."

"How do you know so much about these woods?" I ask him. "Don't you have a life like everyone else?"

He turns around and looks intently into my eyes. I must have struck a sensitive place. "What? You don't like the way I live my life?"

If I were his nemesis, I believe he would have taken a swing at me. Just in case he has second thoughts, I say, "I didn't say that. You spend so much time away from home, wherever that is. Don't you have a wife, family, that sort of life?"

"Not anymore. As you say, I spend too much time in the woods, tracking here and there. I come home one day, and she and my son are gone. I haven't seen them since then." He grows suddenly silent.

"Sorry, Jim, I didn't know. Sometimes I run my mouth too much."

His back is usually to me, but not this time. Facing me, he drops his contentiousness.

"It's not your fault. I chose this kind of life, living in the forest, helping people."

"You were talking about the cavern." It's one of these rare times I feel I should change the subject.

"Yes. A while back Dan Redroot told me about it. Several bears made it their home. He came upon it years back, tracking a bear after it killed a hiker."

"So you think they might be there?"

I want to know. Then again, the reality of catching up with them I dread to no end. What if worse has come to my son?

"I have a sneaking hunch these two are headed that way."

I need to know what we are facing.

"How many openings are there to this ape city?"

Jim recollects what Dan said. "Hidden from sight, it has a small opening. After descending down to a lower level, it opens to a large cavern."

CHAPTER 31

Meanwhile, James and his kidnappers have reached the cavern, the city of creatures. By teaching them about a new world, he is gaining their trust. The leaders of the creature clan are waiting for his arrival. James is about to enter a world unknown to man. Finally, he enters an area only known to apelike creatures that have eluded man for centuries, creatures capable of seeing in the dark. Now getting closer, a knobby hill slowly rises up from a rock-faced, shattered earth where prehistoric tree trunks now reside like great monoliths.

"Eve, where are we going?"

Her reddish, hairy body turns around, staring at me as if understanding my words. She then points ahead with her hand tightly closed. Not animal, but perhaps more human than not, she is trying to get her point across. Then Eve makes a loud grunting sound. Showing her pearly white teeth, nonstop, she repeats it again.

"Are we close to the rest of them?"

She becomes quiet. Her face looks a little sad. I hope it's not a bad sign. Her pace quickens as we enter a long, flat, rocky area. I look to the east. Another creature stands majestically as he hides in plain sight. He must be standing guard. Following behind her, Eve leads me to an enormous flat rock. I stand poised, looking around the rocky hill. This place looks devastated by upheaval, perhaps a not so ancient earthquake.

Standing beside me, Eve looks hard into my eyes. I look straight ahead. "It leads down into the earth, Eve."

I say it aloud for her to hear as I look into the dark hole.

"What is beneath the earth for me, Eve?"

She shows me a mouth full of teeth. It must be her way of being friendly or bravely telling me I have no choice. She then takes me by the hand, leading me down to a place that must be deep into the earth. I can no longer see before me. I fall to the ground, hurting myself. Eve picks me up and then places me on her shoulders the rest of the way down. I can hear a noise down below, a language I have never heard. I cannot determine how many are around me.

"Where are we?" I shout out loudly.

Silence recedes away from me like a great wave. Finally, all I hear is a sound here and there. Not knowing why, one of the males with us makes a chuckling sound. Something is happening. Eve places me on the floor in front of her. I still cannot see them, but I know they are there, pressing in close to me, touching, smelling, and pulling on my clothes. One is forceful and seems to be angry. Eve shoves me behind her. My bodyguards, the males, throw him to the floor. I want to see them and see where I am. A feeling of fear is welling up in me. We move forward. Then I fall over a pile of brush.

"This is what I need!" I say it loud. "Not even a glimmer of light! Move back!"

I say it in a commanding voice as I kneel down on the cave floor. Using my hands to search on the ground, I feel around for dry wood, something to bring forth fire. Finally, I find what I need. I sit on the base of a large rock. It helps. With a stick between my hands, I set in motion a most important need that will eventually change them just as it did us. I smell smoke. More of it begins to climb. It goes through my nostrils, taking away the cave's pungent odor. Soon sparks and then a small flame start to grow, lighting an emerging cavern. First, red eyes dart through the blackness of stale odor, flames leaping higher. The apelike creatures rush back. They believe the flames reach for them.

Dancing flames horrify them.

"Eve, what do you think? Will they ever trust themselves with fire?"

She looks at me. I look back at her. I believe Eve knows what I am saying. She trusts me. Eve stays put while the others run for cover. Keeping their distance, two males move away from us.

"Eve, you must trust me." I then say to her, "At least on the way here, you help build fires. So please, show them you are not afraid. The others will see you and then come closer."

She removes herself from the rock, reaches down, and then wraps her hands around a tree branch. It is much too large for me. She tosses it onto the fire. Finally, light reveals secrets of the cavern and then the creatures within. Red, glowing eyes appear everywhere, revealing a great number of them. As the flames grow higher, a massive ceiling appears. Smoke lifts up and makes its way to the rear of the cavern and then out through a hole.

"A natural chimney," I say to myself aloud. "Eve! What am I doing here?"

I dare not raise my voice to her. She gestures her head sideways at me with a smile breaking across her face.

"You have something in store for me, do you?"

I look around the cave. They are all looking at me, still afraid of the fire.

"Eve," I say to her in a calm voice.

She twists her body around toward me, making a sound she seems to love, a sound unlike the other grunts. I catch on. "Don't bother me," I think it means. She now stands in the doorway with a group of males. They all face Eve.

"Stay with me," I say to her.

She looks back at me. Some of the males are leaving through the entrance.

They come back soon with more wood. Seeing Eve close to me, the fire gave a lot of them courage. Soon, they come close into the light for warmth. "Eve."

She gives me her attention.

"Do you see what I see?" I talk to her face-to-face. "Some of your friends, I don't think they like me being here. There seems to be a division among your clan."

I think she likes to hear me talk. Attentive, she watches me carefully.

"Eve, I know you can talk a little. Do not be afraid to talk. Yes. You know what I am saying."

"James!"

She gets it out. I cannot believe my ears. She speaks my name! With a very serious attempt, she points to a creature some distance away.

"I understand, Eve!" I glance back to the rear of the cavern, where they are. "You don't even need that many words to get that thought across."

I place her hand in mine and then my other hand on top of hers. She smiles at me as she places her other hand on top of mine.

"Good girl, Eve."

I say it reassuringly.

Smiling back at her, I say, "You catch on fast."

I need to teach Eve more English. I hope in time she will pick up enough to teach others. If there is a division in the clan, I need to discover it before they split. I know my father is close behind. I wonder how they will accept him and if someone else with him is carrying guns.

CHAPTER 32

Joni and I are now on our way back home.

"Joni, I am getting hungry. Are you?"

"Yes. All the running around made me hungry too. We can stop by the general store and get something to eat before returning home."

After about thirty minutes, we pull into the store's parking lot. I then see Owl drive in. After seeing him, I ask myself, *Does he know about his mother? Is he looking for me?* I get out of the car and help Joni so she does not fall.

"Joni, I see Owl. I hope he knows about his mother and her condition. He should be there with her."

"He might not know anything yet, Ina."

"Watch your step, Joni. Don't fall and hurt yourself."

We walk onto the porch. Joni goes inside and then makes her way to a table in the back of the store.

"Sit where you want, Joni. I need to go to the restroom."

"This is a good place to sit, next to the heater."

Joni slides her chair next to the heater.

By the time I rejoin Joni, Anna and she are deep in conversation. I interrupt and ask Anna a question. "I saw Owl drive up. Do you know where he is?"

"He is outside, helping Mr. White with his car."

I am not going out there in the cold to fetch him. When Leon gets tired of his nonsense, both of them will come inside.

"Is something wrong, Ina?" asks Anna. "You must not have heard yet, Anna. There was an explosion in the bleachery. Five people are dead."

"Not Mrs. Palmer?"

Anna's dark eyes are wide open, about to break down in tears.

"No, Anna. She is in bad shape, but she will be fine."

"Oh my God," she says, placing her hands over her mouth.

Out the door she goes.

Owl appears on the porch and then comes inside.

"Owl, do you know what has happened to your mother?" I try not to raise my voice to him.

"Yes, Ina. When I first heard about the explosion, I knew right away. It has to be where Mom works. I left Mom to go to your house so you will know what is going on. After knocking on your door, I left and went to the store. So here I am."

Owl grins at me while shrugging his shoulders. "Leon's hood was up on his car. He's helpless with cars, you know. I went over to see what he was doing. He said, 'It sounds like it needs a tune-up.'"

"Your mom is in bad shape. Don't you think you should be with her?"

"Ina, I am going there. She is my mother. Do you think I would just leave her there and not be with her?"

He places his greasy hand on the backrest of a chair as he slides it across the floor and then plops himself down in it next to me.

"No, Owl. I suppose not. I am sorry. I know you love Mom."

Owl's voice trembles as he speaks. I see worry in his eyes.

"She will be fine, Owl. Joni said so. She has the right words."

Lifting his head to her, I can see he believes me. Anna is still standing next to us, astonished by what she is hearing.

"I would ask you to go to church with us today, Owl, but I know you want to be with Mom."

I see a side of Owl he seldom shows to anyone. Holding his face down, he rises from his chair and turns his face toward the door.

"See you later. Lunch is on me. I will take mine with me. See you later. Enjoy your lunch."

"Owl, I will come by to see how she is after church. So believe she will be fine. We have authority on that."

When Owl leaves, he seems to be distant. I watch him drive away.

"Joni, how is your sandwich? Can you help me eat these fries? I can't eat all of them by myself. After we eat, I need to go by the cabin and check on things, make sure everything is still there so Jack does not have something else to worry him. His mother will be enough."

CHAPTER 33

Jim and I backtrack to where a narrow river trail diverts over a blue, icy, frozen monstrosity. To look at its frozen mass, one would not believe seeing a waterfall. I dread this climb. My hand holds dangerously to my insipid, smelly beast. But then again, I do not know why I should be so temperamental. This is supposed to be second nature to his ability to climb towering distant places.

"Abe, remember, I'm your friend."

He only plucks a tender shoot from a trailside bush, looks back at me, and then continues. Jim, now some distance up the trail and now over the falls, I have a suspicion he is quickening his pace. It reminds me of what Owl says. The closer he gets to home, easier it is for him to make mistakes. Hearing him, it is not him close to home but polluted.

Pulling, breathing heavy while tugging on Abe, I shout, "Jim, do you see anything yet?"

Breathing heavy from the climb, he shouts back at me. "Just a little farther, thirty minutes or so. Keep your eyes open. Do not let your guard down. Don't want them sneaking up on us."

Not long after, we come upon a huge, flat rock where the mantel of the Earth protrudes outward. Soon, Jack walks up behind me. Standing high above the surrounding area, I look behind me to see the Saluda River wind its way southward, leaving the Great Smokies behind. What a moment, tired from the chase, now discovering where James is and what a glorious view, makes it all worthwhile.

Huffing and puffing on a newly lit cigar, he says, "This is an ancient place where many a creature has stood." Jim says it proudly, like a general after a great battle. "Dan never mentioned this to me. Great erosion has uncovered most of the hill down to nothing but naked rock."

"Jim, let us move to the other side of the rock and see if there is an opening somewhere that goes down into the earth."

Not sure if it is my head pounding or something I am hearing, I say to Jim, "Do you hear a pounding sound? It seems to be coming from everywhere. On the other hand, is it in my head? I'm holding my hands over my ears. Can you hear or see anything?"

"Not yet, Jack. No. Wait. Over there. One of them is pounding on the ground with a club!" Jim scrambles closer to the creature. "Watch him! Tell me if he leaves."

I am not there long before the hairy club bearer disappears into the crevice of a rock. I tie Abe to a pine tree and scramble over to where Jim is standing.

"We will make camp here," Jim says, staring at the dark, cold hole where the creature vanished deep into the earth.

"Why make camp?" I ask him.

"We cannot go into the cave now. If we do, there's no telling what will happen. Maybe panic will wreak havoc on James and us."

Jim thoughtfully considers the gaping entrance in the hillside. Turning toward me, Jim comes to a decision.

"Let them become accustomed to our presence. Maybe James will come out. What do you think?"

Jim begins to unload his pack, laying out his bedroll. Glancing up at me, he impatiently points toward Abe.

"You know the drill. Get what you need from the pack. I will build a fire this time. They should appear sometime after dark."

I think over what Jim said. Some of it makes sense. Some does not. Why would the kidnappers invite themselves to our campsite? I place my hand to my hollow stomach. As I listen to the hungry growling of my stomach, Jim interrupts my thoughts.

"Jack, what is for supper?"

First, Jim, you have to build our campfire high enough to reach heaven. Then I will think about the menu.

Looking at the rations lovingly packed by Ina's hands, I wish I were home, eating dinner with her.

Shaking my head, I grumble, "It always comes down to your stomach."

As I open a package of salty bacon, I wonder why Jim did not let me rush in to get James back tonight. If I did not know better, I would believe he does not want to fight while hungry. I hope to God it does not come to that. I do not know what or how many there are in the earth, but I am sure they outnumber us by many.

"What about a breakfast for supper? How about that? Does that sound good to you, Jim?"

Jim is in a hurry as he stacks a pile of firewood in an open area. Finally, he speaks.

"One of us will have to stand guard tonight so we do not get our heads bashed in. I will take the first watch."

I know what he will do, out there somewhere, asleep. If he is out of sight, perhaps they won't get the drop on him.

"No. Let me. I won't get much sleep anyway. I do not feel safe with those things sneaking around in the dark. With Abe out there, they might decide to eat him. How will I explain that to his owner, Amos? He would be minus one burro. Jim, I will be glad when this is all over. I miss Ina and James. So life can be better for her when I get back, I am going to wire the house, get some light in the place."

"Food smells good, Jack. I am starving. It's just what I need to help keep me awake tonight. Coffee smells good. Do you want me to pour you a cup?"

"Yes, please. I could use a cup about now."

"Come on over, Jim, and have a seat before I eat everything. Here you go...Your coffee, three eggs, three pieces of bacon, grits, and fried bread. Eat up."

"This time tomorrow, something will be good or something will be bad. One way or another, we need to see what is going on in that opening in the ground." Jim speaks as he warms his back close to the flames.

Once more, I need to remind him. However, as usual, I know he will do whatever he wants.

"Jim, I do not want anything happening to the creatures. We should leave the guns out here, where we can get to them fast if we have to."

Standing on a high point on this rock, I see all around for miles. This is a good vantage point to make a stand. Why did the creatures choose this particular place to inhabit? Can the facts be it is a center location and a high point?

"Jim, I see smoke coming out about five hundred feet away. Jim, did you hear me?"

He suddenly looks my way.

"Come over here." I point across the rocky hilltop to a place west of us. "There it is, Jim: proof! James is inside!"

Jim turns toward the rising smoke. "We still cannot storm in and take James back, as much as you want him back. We don't know how badly they want to keep your son."

In my heart, I know Jim is right. "Jim, I hope we can count on them being much friendlier. Not long from now, the sun will be going down. Spectators will be coming out."

As the shadows grow long, the entrance to the cave becomes a black hole against the white blanket of snow surrounding it.

The menacing cavern beckons with the unknown.

"Jim, I hope they will be friendly."

I feel the tension of the showdown that is coming soon. In the changing light, Jim's silhouette transforms into that of a giant. With a large club in his grip, Jim looks much like the creatures we follow.

"Jack, keep the fires burning so we can see them clearly. I am going to lie down and try to get some sleep before they come out. You should really do the same. Abe will let us know if they start sneaking around."

Sipping on my coffee, I smirk. "Maybe you can, but I do not have the instincts you have. As for me going to sleep, I don't think so, Jim."

It has been a rewarding day. We found their living place. The sun is starting to go down. I can hardly hold my eyes open. Nevertheless, I am not letting them sneak up on me, even if I have to drink several pots of coffee.

CHAPTER 34

Inside the cavern, I try to convince Eve to come outside with me. My little hand can only grip two of her large, dark fingers. Pulling on her gently, she resists lightly, making her way slowly to the exit.

"Eve, come. Come with me."

She wants to go. Then again, she does not want to leave the sanctum of such a stronghold, but she is willing. On the way out, she motions for two other males to follow. Two large, reddish-brown creatures swing their long, hairy arms in unison as their bodies oscillate from side to side. What else can they be but guards? No guns, no wooden clubs, the appearance of them is enough to intimidate. Not able to help myself, I watch them but dare not look at them in their eyes. I can hear them talking to themselves. It must be talk, a discussion of what they expect to find outside where humans wait. Finally, we emerge above the crevice, out of the hold, on top the great mound of snow-covered rock.

I gaze toward the rising smoke from Dad's blazing campfire.

Taking Eve with me, I comfort her with soothing tones while encouraging her to be peaceful. Not far away, my dad waits for me. Soon, adventure will be over. I will be a twelve-year-old boy again, but for now, I must be a peacemaker. I say a prayer before leading Eve over to my father's campfire. My dad sleeps with deep and even snores. I pull my protector close to me. Eve, see the fire. Come with me."

In a final move, she follows me to the fire. She is still my trusting creature mother. I point to my father and then speak to Eve.

"Dad!" Afterward, I lay hands on myself. "James!" Then back to her. I bury my hands into her hairy shoulder, saying, "Eve."

After a moment of puzzling, she finally understands and points across the campfire, saying, "Dead!"

"Yes! Dad!" Patting her on the shoulder, I praise, "That is close enough, Eve!"

Watching us from a strategic place in the shadows, I see a tall, husky, black man. He says nothing. We lock eyes for an unsettling moment. I have to turn away from his gaze.

I begin my introductions first. I have to shake my dad in order to wake him up. He opens his eyes wide with alarm. "Dad, this is Eve." Recognition lights in Eve's eyes, and she places her hand to her hairy chest. "She is the first of her kind, a prodigy of nature, if you know what I mean."

Dad smiles eagerly. "I do, Son. I do indeed."

Eve peels back her lips, showing sharp rows of teeth in an attempt to smile. Dad turns toward me, keeping a close watch on Eve's dangerous-looking incisors exposed by her grin.

"James, do you know what is going on?"

"Yes, Dad. I believe I have figured out why they took me!"

Dad peers into the darkness surrounding our camp. "I told you, Jim! He is a smart boy."

Now that Eve is comfortable by the fire, the two males watching over her begin to come closer.

As the furry guards sneak near, Dad looks nervously over at me, asking, "Are we safe?"

Eve grunts and motions for the guards to sit with her. Without questioning, they quickly perch themselves on each side of Eve. Dad sits dwarfed by the three imposing figures. He nervously leans away from the giant beings and glances over to the pack animal. The donkey quietly chews some dried grass without any concern.

"Where is your gun, Dad?"

"So they don't get scared, Jim and I have them put away."

My eyes widen and dart nervously toward the cavern's entrance.

"I can see Eve is friendly, but what about the others? One of them did kill the old man."

James shakes his head. "I do not know if one did or not. I do not know how rational they are. What I do know is we have to give them a chance to go forward so they can survive. Dad, they need protection from humans. If we don't, they will be killed off."

"James, this is an admirable thing you want to do, such a large task, but it must happen before their whereabouts is discovered."

Looking at Eve I say, "It would be awful if she did kill Mr. Valentine."

"Of course, James. Humans will be hard on her if she did kill the old man."

Jim speaks as he conceals the large, knotty club behind himself. Eve lifts her head with innocent curiosity at the mention of her name. I look at her motherly face and cannot see her murdering the defenseless Mr. Valentine. If she did, we can do nothing about it. That was then. This is now.

"When do you think we should go inside?" ask Jim.

No longer at a distance, Jim cautiously inches forward, waiting for an answer.

"I don't think we should go in until morning, Mr. Darkman."

"Call me Jim."

Jim smiles, looking at James's surprised face. Jim then turns his head away as the rustling of pines distracts him.

Creatures make their way through a dense thicket of young saplings.

"Dad, it looks like they have been out hunting."

Silent but heavy footed, twenty males make their way into the clearing, carrying several deer. Heads flop around loosely, recent kills. The two male guards watch Dad as he slides closer to the fire.

I quickly ask James, "Have they been giving you raw flesh, James?"

Eve's eyes curiously watch my mouth as I speak. Perhaps she recognizes a few words.

"The first night, they gave me raw fish. But the next night, I built a fire and cooked what they caught from the river." James quickly adds, "They liked it."

"Perhaps this will be a good time to continue their education."

"James, this is a good time as any. Soon, daylight will break."

Jim pushes further. "Ask her to take us inside."

"I want to go see what they do to the deer."

I interrupt. "Do you think they skin it or rip it to pieces like they did Daisy?"

"Eve."

James takes her by the hand and then looks into the entrance of her home. She understands. The two brutes at Eve's side grunt disagreeably, watching us suspiciously.

"Lead her back to the cave's entrance," Jim says in a commanding voice.

With one large, hairy creature in front of Eve, the other behind her, we follow like ducks in a row, cautiously entering their world under the ground, invited into the cavern to see what they are doing with the game. The two males are now at the fire with the buck.

"Dad, they want me to cook it on the fire, but it needs to be dressed." James grimaces with fear of failure. "Dad, I have just recently learned to fire a twenty-gage, much less killed or dressed any game."

"I will do that," interjects Jim eagerly. "But I need a place to get it out of the dirt."

I look around the dark, smoky cave. "Jim, why don't we clear a place against the rock wall to tie it down?"

Jim nods his head with approval and turns toward the cave entrance. "Jack, can you go outside and get some rope from the pack?"

Leaving the cave for a moment, I return quickly with a roll of thick jute.

"Here you are, Jim."

With a coarse burlap rope in one hand, the deer's hind leg in the other, Jim wraps the rope around the deer's limp, now-profusely-bloody leg. Soon, the animal is on the wall with an audience in front of Jim. He holds the long, sharp hunting knife above his head.

"Knife!" he shouts.

Its shiny blade reflects in the cave fire's dancing light. Jim then plunges the knife into the deer's stomach and begins to cut until the entrails fall to the ground. The beasts gather around, chattering with pleasure and thrusting their hands into the warm, bloody pile of organs. They put them in their mouths and began to eat.

We all turn away from the disgusting spectacle. To our amazement, Eve rushes forward, screaming and waving her arms wildly above her head. She clearly does not like what they are doing. A path clears before Eve as she moves into the middle of the macabre mob. All with bloody hands turn away their gaze as Eve makes clear her disapproval.

A sudden realization lights up my face as I blurt out, "Jim, do you think...is she the matriarch?"

"Looks that way to me, Jack. No wonder she chose James."

"What do you mean?"

"Looks like she had her eyes on him a long time. She is smarter than what we give her credit for."

Turning back around to finish his work, cutting it away and revealing its flesh, he removes the hide from the animal.

"Look." He smacks his hand on the hindquarter of the deer. "What do you beasts think? Does this excite your taste buds?"

They like what he does. Grunts began to sound from the gathering multitude. Finally, the skin falls to the ground.

"James, take the hide and roll it up so we can show them how to tan it."

James frowns disapprovingly at this idea. "Pushing it, aren't you, Dad? Eve can barely speak my name. Take baby steps, Dad. That's what you always tell me."

"Jack, go outside and get what we need to cook the venison."

"I already did that when we needed the rope."

His voice is distant and disapproving as he hands the gear over. Jim smirks impatiently.

"We are ready to start." Jim growls loudly, "Bring it on. It is time for supper."

Jim cuts a hindquarter off the deer, pierces a metal shaft through it, and places it over the hot coals.

"Where did you get the roasting gear?" Jim eases closer to James, seeing he might have rustled some feathers.

"Ina must have thought I was going to need it." My voice softens with the thought of her. "God bless her big heart."

Jim smiles jokingly and elbows me in the ribs. "How did you end up with such a fine person as Ina?"

Turning toward Jim, I look directly into his eyes. "I don't know, Jim. You tell me."

In one small moment, the lightness in Jim's voice clouds with concern. Jim's brow furrows deeply, and his lips press thinly together.

"Jim, are you all right?"

Jim concentrates on the observant hairy beasts sitting around the fire. One of Eve's guards slowly turns the venison over the flames with the skewer.

"I suppose so. This is not how I remember these guys. They seem more human than before, more like hairy men. This is all too fast for me. This is history in the making, Jack!"

I look at Jim, wondering what his past with the creatures was like. I think better of it, agreeing instead, "I believe we are making history, Jim."

Jim lifts his head high into the air, sniffing and wrinkling his nose. "This place reeks of a foul odor. This is ancient man. Just think. Long ago, the evolutionists say we lived like this."

Jim glances around the fire-lit cave, mesmerized by four shadowy figures that dance along the ascending wall.

"See those four shadows over there, next to the wall. They're beating each other over the head to see who gets the deer's heart. If they are intelligent enough to evolve, they have a long way to go."

"Have you had a chance to check out the cavern, James?"

"No, Jim. Eve will not let me out of her sight. Strange things are happening. It's too soon for complete trust. Perhaps when I find my courage I will go amongst them and check the place out."

Big Jim, as big as he is, he can afford to take chances. Big Jim manages to carry that big stick around, keeps it by his side all the time.

"See those over there." James points to an inner cave some distance away. "They don't look too friendly! Big Jim!" James takes a few steps away from the fire. "There are so many. How have they kept this place a secret for so long? I'm still wondering why people don't see them more often."

"Dad, what are we going to do tomorrow? We cannot stay here very much longer. You have a job, and I go to school."

Jim speaks loud enough for me to hear him. "Jack, we don't know if they will let us leave."

"What do you think?" I ask.

"Perhaps we can appease them enough to let us go without a fight."

"Jim, there can be no killing. They are asking us for help. We must come to some kind of understanding with them."

"I understand, Jack! What if we teach them some civilized ideas, such as building fires, cooking meat, some English, that sort of thing before we leave?"

"Dad, we cannot do what we need to do in such a small period of time."

"We can come back more often in the future and teach them. Eve is learning English faster than I ever thought possible. What do you think about that, Son?"

"I don't believe that will work, Dad. We are forgetting why they took me."

"Yes. Of course. Point taken. We will have to come up with something more invasive. If we leave them for any length of time, there can be a disaster."

James asks, "Dad, what if we take Eve home with us?"

Dad runs his hands through his hair, deep in thought for a moment. "James, I think that is a good idea. Nevertheless, I am a bit concerned about that. I don't know if that will work. She is a wild animal. I need to give that a lot of thought. Your mom will have to spend a lot of time with her. What about other people? They will not accept her."

"She will stay only a few days, long enough to learn some of our language and ways."

"I cannot make a commitment without talking to your mom. Then again, what about the sheriff? We cannot keep secrets from the law. Because of the old man, the sheriff might take Eve's life. I know it will be good for her to be with us, but I am concerned for her life."

Once again, James is probably right. We need to take Eve back with us.

"Dad, I know I am right. They will take another child if we do not help them. Another family will not be so kind and understanding."

"I see your point, Son. That will not go over with the public very well."

Big Jim wants to say something. "If I can get a word in edgewise, please. Next, they will want to live in houses. What are we going to do, build houses for them? What you two are talking about will never come to an end. You do realize that, don't you?"

"I am only twelve. I leave that to you adults."

Big Jim is more than a hunter but also a visionary. I believe he is right. There's no time now to answer his question.

"Dad, when are we going home?"

"In a couple of days, Son."

I don't know exactly what to tell him. So much is happening. When James disappeared, I had no idea that any of this was going to happen. It all seems like a dream now.

"Can Eve build a fire? Can she cook anything?" I ask James.

"As soon as she can learn to spin a fire stick in her hand, she will be able to."

Eve is intelligent enough to know we are talking about her.

"You need to work on her doing just that, Son. She can teach others. We also need to build more than one fire in this cavern. It needs more light. Show Eve how to take fire from one place and move it to another."

"That takes some skill," said Jim.

"We are going to have a hard time protecting them from people and their guns."

James worries about Eve—not only Eve, but all of them.

"Jim, the land they are on, do you know who owns it?"

"No, Jack. At one time, it was a quarry. You can't tell it now. That was back during the Civil War days. It takes something catastrophic to cover up a great hole, something Earth changing."

Jim stands there, shaking his head in amazement. "Some years after the Civil War, a great earthquake shook the South. Storytellers say the Great Mississippi flowed backward. I believe the earth cracked open around the abandoned quarry and revealed a cavern home for these creatures."

It's as if time made a way for the creatures. Can that be? We are all playing a part.

"Jim, I feel that something wonderful is taking place. This is no coincidence. Can you feel it?" I stand in awe. Eve must know more than we are able to understand. This place is good for nothing else to anyone else.

"What do you have in mind, Jack?"

"I was thinking if we know who owns it, maybe we can buy the place and make a compound out of it. Then we can protect them from encroachment. What do you think, Jim?"

"I do not know, Jack. That will be a great idea. But if we do that, we will be totally in control of their evolution. How will they like being in a compound where they can no longer roam the countryside, hunting and whatever they do?"

We are making history. Then again, I cannot do all this without telling Ina. I am moving too fast.

"What about Ina, Jack? Will she go along with your ideas?"

I was already thinking of her.

"I believe she will do what is right. Ina is a humanitarian. Besides that, they are more human than animal. They could learn a lot on a ranch, raising cattle and growing their own food."

Now my brain is growing tired. This is moving much too fast for me, us.

"What about the cavern? To come out of the dark, into the light of progress, they will have to change. It does not come easy, and neither will it for them."

"I do not have all the answers, Jim. Small steps. What we need to do now is get Eve back to our home and start her training. We will build what we need to build, and then get them out of the ground as soon as possible. Are you with me?"

"You can count me in, Jack. The only way I see us being successful is to take James up on his idea of taking Eve home with us."

CHAPTER 35

"This beast is quite done. All I have to do now is carve it."

Jim moves about quickly in a ritual dance, a furious display around leaping flames as he thrusts his long, razor-sharp knife deep into the venison. Brutal creatures gather all around, watching the spectacle, not realizing that their history of living wild in the forest will slowly disappear. Black, scorched flesh fills large, wide nostrils as hundreds of big, ugly, hairy beasts jump up and down in a ritual chant.

Before long, push comes to shove. Then Eve pushes her way forward. Some see her coming and hurriedly move out of her way. She then takes control of what is becoming an out-of-control situation.

In the background, they are creatures still keeping themselves apart from enjoying what civilization is offering. Scenes of violent conflict flash through my mind's eye. *Raw flesh eaters,* I think to myself. *Are they the ones who will not change?* I foresee conflict between the classes, maybe even trouble for us.

"Jim, what do you think about Eve's progress? Do you think she will catch on?"

"Jack," he says, curiously watching those in the rear of the cave, "she is moving forward, but she gets frustrated with such a small thing as a stick while trying to make a fire. Too bad we can't just give them some matches," Jim says, curling his mustache with his finger.

Seriously, now that is like putting a gun in a child's hands.

"We will later on, but if we do now, they will set the world on fire."

"Big Jim, waiting on the spark and then waiting on the fire is enough for her. Look at her and then the others. She must be far ahead of them."

"I think so, little man. Do you believe the others will ever catch on?"

Big Jim knows more about them than Dad or me. For the sake of all of us, I hope so, or this will be an experiment in futility.

"I hope so, Big Jim, for their sake. It frightens me what might happen to them. We have a bad habit of civilizing what we don't understand."

Staring at Eve, pondering her importance among the creatures, I cannot help but speculate.

"When they took James, why do you think Eve came alone? She has to be the matriarch of the clan."

"It would fit, Jim, knowing how smart she is and what she wants to do for them."

I notice that some distance away, Eve is spending a lot of time with another female. The diminishing light makes it hard to see them clearly. James watches them carefully, finding importance in what they are doing. He keeps glancing over at me and then speaks.

"Dad, Eve is teaching another female on the other side of the cave how to craft sticks together for fire. She has been with her a long time. She is much younger than Eve."

Suspiciously, we watch them.

"Can she be Eve's daughter?"

Dad's face contours with amazement.

"If she is, I see her being in charge when she is gone. If her prog- ress is good and she learns the art of making fire, we can leave here tomorrow by noon."

Dad says it as if saying, "I am ready to get back to your mom, Son."

"Big Jim, we haven't been here long enough to teach them a lot. We don't know much about them. But the females seem to be smarter than the males."

Some have now satisfied their hunger. The dead animal carcass is bare to the bone, much like me when Ina leaves a mixing bowl around after making fudge.

"Dad, Eve is starting to pick up words from us, broken attempts but still intelligible. On our way home, she should pick up a lot more."

Hearing James talk about the creatures, I hope someday he can look back on all this and make sense of it all.

"Jack, I have a suspicion."

"What's up, Jim?"

"When we come back for the rest of them, there might be a division in the clan, everything in chaos, violence, and death."

This is a serious warning coming from Jim, so I give him my full attention.

"Remember the creature in the upper cave. Those that surround him look rebellious, noncompliant. I believe that if he has a chance, he will try to kill us. What are we going to do if some want to stay wild and free? Will it be all of them or none?"

A good question. I can only think of Eve, what she might say about that question. Perhaps time will tell. However, she is able to explain very little right now.

"Jim, the way things stand right now, I believe that when it comes down to it, I think they don't have any choice but to go along with what is best for them. It's not so much what they might do to each other but what humans will do to them."

Jim stops for moment, thinking to himself.

"What are you thinking about, Jim?"

"What you said. In our history, we have been bad to what we consider lesser species. I don't want this to go that way."

"I don't either, Jim. We must not let it get out of hand."

"Look what happened to my kind when we were exploited."

I look at him dead in the eye. "We will not repeat those failures again, Jim. If we keep them in a compound, we can keep humans away from them."

"Jack, do you realize what we are getting into and the responsibility we will have?"

"Yes, Jim. When I think about it, it scares me to death. But great progress does not happen by letting fear get in the way. We have a chance to do something good for a change."

Jim is right. It is a frightening proposition.

"Jack, another serious problem will arise."

"What is that?"

"Our government will take control over what we are doing."

Jim has concerns, so I listen to him.

"How will they have any control, Jim? These creatures are not game or considered an endangered species...not yet. Jim, where did James go? Have you seen him?"

"He was with Eve a few minutes ago. Do you see her? I don't see Eve either. Can you look for them? Never mind. I see him."

I do not want to make the same mistake twice.

"Take care, Jack. He is with us now."

Yes. Of course. "I know I will never let him out of my sight again."

"There he is, Jack. Eve is with him at the other fire. James must be looking in on how they are doing. Too bad Eve can't talk well. She might tell us what is going on in the minds of our possible foes."

CHAPTER 36

I woke up early this morning with a lot on my mind and plenty to do. Before Joni woke up for her morning coffee, I loaded up a great many gallon jars full of loose change and bills hidden away in Joni's cupboard. After much discussion about the safety of bank deposits last night, the old woman finally agreed to deposit her life savings into the local bank. Joni and I fixed our coffee and came to town to see how Edna did during the night. We found Owl fast asleep beside his mother. Edna looked much better and was breathing much easier, just as Joni had predicted. The two of us decide on an early breakfast at the General Store

"Joni, I took the liberty of ordering your breakfast. I hope you do not mind. The cook is not here yet. Anna did not ask, but she needs help with the tables until the cook arrives. We have a lot to do this morning, but I don't want to keep you out late anymore."

Before I can rise from the table, Fatso and his grandson sit. I put on Anna's apron and grudgingly approach their table.

Why does he come in here? I ask myself. I don't like this man. I don't want to, but I must wait on him.

"Good morning. What will you have this morning?"

Lifting his head, he says, "You work here now? That nigger girl, where is she? Did White finally come to his senses and gets rid of her, off his property?"

"No, Fatso. She is still here, cooking your food, unless you do not want her to. In which case you can leave for all I care."

"I don't want that nigger cooking my food. She might spit in it."

He makes me so angry! "You crazy old fool! You spend your whole life hating. Why Anna Marie, I don't know! Do you want to order or not?"

"Grandpa, I'm hungry. Let's order. She is probably a good cook." George is really a good person. It's not his fault. He too is a victim.

"Boy, you sure you don't want to leave and go somewhere else. George, you order for me too. I only want coffee. I don't trust her."

I manage to hold back my anger. I fail to see how Anna puts up with him.

"Well, he's driving up now, Fatso. Your cook is now here. Now tell me, what do you want to eat?"

In spite of it all, I take their orders and then give them to the cook.

"Joni, our breakfast is ready. I'll get it."

We sit down and eat.

"I heard you talking to Fatso," says Anna. "I have known him for a long time. He never changes. All blacks get the same treatment from him."

Someday someone will even the score with him. Sad thing is, it will be a celebration of release.

"Now and then he pays the piper. His mouth gets him in trouble."

Anna has a story she wants to tell me.

"A man almost beat him to death one morning in Ware Shoals."

Why? What happened? Don't tantalize me.

"Fatso pulled into a service station across from the YMCA when a black man pulled in front of him, cutting him off."

I can't help myself. Anna puts a big smile on my face.

"You know Fatso, one foul word after another. In so many unkind words, he told the man what he thought of him."

Anna tells me the man said, "Sorry, I will pay for your gas."

I then look to see how Joni is while I listen to Anna's story of Fatso.

She goes on, saying, "Stiff-necked Fatso would not let go."

Anna tells me more of what he said.

"I do not take money from niggers."

Down here, most of the blacks will take the abuse, but this man must be from the north. She tells more of her delightful story.

"By the time he got through with Fatso, the man's tank was full. He left, leaving him on the ground. He did not learn a thing. He is still the same person. How is your breakfast, Joni?" Anna asks her. "Do you need more coffee?"

"No thanks. I can't drink much of the stuff."

"I never seen so much money in my life," said a man paying for his gas. "What did someone do, rob a bank?"

I will be glad when it is in a bank so I don't have to worry about someone robbing us.

"Joni, my better judgment tells me to call Wells Fargo and let them take it to the bank so we don't get robbed or killed. People are starting to comment about it; people I do not know."

I stand at the window, watching the money.

"Ina, before something happens to you, I'd rather sit here all day, waiting. The car might stop running on the way there, getting us killed. It won't do you any good if you are dead."

Joni has a good point.

"If it is all the same to you, I want to take no chances hauling it to town. I am going to call Wells Fargo. They can take chances."

I leave the window and then go to the counter, asking Anna if she will call for us.

"Ina, the truck is coming by at noon, a big, red, armored truck."

That's good...men with guns.

"Do they require it to be counted?" asked Anna.

No. I see the bank doing that. "Most of the time, they do. In Joni's case, they will put it in bags and seal them with her name on them."

Anna stands behind the counter, clutching a damp drying cloth in her hand.

"What time is it now, Anna?"

"In five minutes, it will be ten o'clock, still early morning."

"Joni, we still have two hours before noon. I can take you home and come back later."

I am hoping she will go home and rest.

"We do not need to leave, Ina. Here we have friendly faces around a warm stove and us. Where are the children this morning, Anna?" asks Joni, wanting to see children's faces.

"I don't see any waiting on the bus," says Anna.

"Today is a teacher's day, Anna. I miss watching James look through the candy." I rub my forehead and think about Jack and James.

"Soon, they will be home," said Anna. "Ina, would you like something to do instead of waiting? Time will go by faster."

"Anna, since you put it like that, I would like to help you with your tasks. What can I do to help you?" I need something else to occupy my mind.

"You can help wash the dishes. The dishwasher is not in either."

To pass time, I make myself useful helping Anna keep this place running. Joni is comfortable sitting in her chair. She would do the same thing at home. Here, she has people she knows coming and going. Time runs slow, like sand through an hourglass. Finally, the armored truck pulls in front of the store.

"Ina, the money truck is here. A man will come in and ask for four cups of coffee. He will also ask about Joni's money."

"You talk like you know him." Most likely, she does.

"He's been coming in here a long time," says Anna.

The door on the passenger side opens. A heavyset man in uniform stands there, talking to the driver. Soon, a lanky man dressed in a uniform comes through the door. He has a weapon on his hip.

"Good afternoon, Anna. How are you today? I would like the usual."

"Pardon me. My name is Ina, and I have an unusual request."

He looks directly at me as if looking for a gun.

"No! Not your money. I have a car full of it, and I need help getting it to a bank in Ware Shoals. Can you carry it there?"

No odd look from him; not even a squint.

"I suppose I can. That is what we do. How do you have it stored?"

I hate to tell him. "Well, that might be a problem." I speak softly to him. "This woman here, it is her money. Her life savings is in jars."

"Fine. My men can bag it for her, seal, and name it. She will have to sign for it. Can she sign her name?"

No doubt they have experienced every fantasy story told.

"Yes. Of course she can!"

"There will be a bagging and courier fee."

"She will agree," I said to him."

"Where is the money?" He asks me.

"In that blue fifty Ford." I pointed to the yard. "Aren't you even a little shocked?"

"No. Not really. Not in my line of work. I see all sorts of things."

Before drinking their coffee, they wait until her money is in the truck.

While walking out the door, he turns and then faces me, saying, "This is not unusual, you know."

He turned away from me, got in his truck, and then pulled next to the Ford.

"Come on, men. We have another life savings to load!"

I go to the car and unlock the door.

"Your name is Ed. I see it on your shirt. Ed, there you are. It's her life savings."

"Oh no, lady.

You must witness everything. Well, here we are for a while. Do you know how much money is in there?"

What does he expect me to do, count it?

"No. I have no idea, but I want the jars back."

"Yes, of course, all your jars back."

Ed opens the door and gets inside the car. Not knowing what is going on, two men with machineguns precariously hesitate before exiting the truck.

"Men, we have to help this old lady with her money. Mike, you stay inside the truck. Nick and I will bag it and give it to you. Make sure you tag it."

It takes more than an hour to ready the money then place it in the truck.

"Mrs. Palmer, do you have any idea how much money there is?"

"Like I said, I have no idea, Ed." *I believe he asked me that already,* I think to myself.

"I have been carrying money for a long time. It would not surprise me if it is a million."

"A million?

Are you sure? I have never seen a million before!"

"How did one old lady collect so much money?" he asks me.

"I do not know. She had a sister who lived with her for many years."

"When I drop the money off at the bank, they will sign for it."

"Do not forget your coffee before you leave. Come inside, and it will be on me."

I walk back inside. Ed follows behind.

"Anna, they want their coffee now. Do you want something to eat too?"

After that ordeal with so much money, they deserve a free meal.

"Sure. Can I get hamburgers, three of them all the way...all of them to go? After loading all that cash they will be hungry."

"It is on me, Anna. Joni, we can go now and take care of our business. Now there are many empty jars in the car. First, we need to rid the car of all the jars. We can use them for canning."

Soon, we pull into her drive and go up the hill to her house. After a while, the jars are back in the pantry.

"Do you need anything from here before we leave again, Joni?"

"No. I have everything on my person I need to open an account at the bank. We can go."

Before long, we are driving back down the road to Ware Shoals. Driving down the road, a thought enters my mind. Jack and James are on their way back home. Soon, if all goes well, I will see them back at home. With a few miles behind us, I enter the town limits. Soon, the bank is in sight. Before I turn in, I stop and let cars pass.

"Joni, we are here. But you can see that for yourself."

I pull into a parking area, get out, and help Joni with her door.

"Come on, Joni. Let me help you before you fall and hurt yourself."

We make our way to the bank. A man dressed in his Sunday suit met us at the door. "May I help you ladies? I am Joe Miller, one of the officers here."

"I am Ina Palmer. This is Joni Hill. A lot of money has been delivered here for her."

"Mrs. Hill, we have been waiting to meet you. We will be through counting your money soon. Will you have a seat at my desk? It is the one over there. It won't be long. Would you like a cup of coffee or a soft drink?"

I only want this to hurry and finish.

"How about you, Joni? What will you have?"

"If it is not too much trouble, I would like an Orange Crush."

"An Orange Crush it is."

"A cup of coffee for me, please."

He is back in no time at all with our drinks.

"Here you are, ladies. If you need anything else, please let me know."

Soon a tall, slim man with a slip of paper in his hand comes from the vault and goes to Mr. Miller. Handing a slip of paper to Joni, he says, "Here it is, Mrs. Hill, a total for your deposit and rare coins."

"I have rare coins?"

"Yes ma'am. For many years, so it seems to me."

"I can't see it without my glasses, Ina. Will you read it to me?"

She passes the money receipt to me. After taking it in hand, my head drops. Usually nothing surprises me. My mouth gapes open with disbelief. Still wide eyed, I remember the money stuffed into jars.

Joni asks, "How much money is there?"

I take a deep breath and try to calm myself from shaking.

"One million, two hundred and fifty thousand dollars, and some cents."

Joni stores all her money in gallon jars. She is lucky thieves did not take it a long time ago.

"Mrs. Hill, what kind of an account do you want to open?"

"Ask Ina. It is her money to do with whatever she wishes. Now she can build her dream house and hopefully take me in."

"Joni, when I said you would never live alone again, I meant that. You are the mother I never had."

"Mrs. Palmer, you are the inheritor of a lot of money. Do you want to deposit it in a joint account with your husband?"

"Yes. One million in a savings account and the other in checking," I said to him. "Joni, I don't know how to thank you for what you have done for us."

I want her to understand how genuinely grateful I am.

"Mrs. Palmer, I will mail your checks to you in two weeks. I will need your signature and your husband's to keep on record."

Soon afterward, so we can get Mr. Valentine's death certificate, we leave the bank and then go to his lawyer, Mr. O'Dell.

"We are here to see Mr. O'Dell."

"Who shall I say is calling?"

"Tell him Joni Hill and Ina Palmer are here for the reading of Roy Valentine's will."

We settle into red leather armchairs facing a large oil painting of a Civil War battle with flags waving. Before long, a thin, gray-haired lawyer towers over us in his office doorway.

"Come on in and have a seat. Let me get Mr. Valentine's will."

He sits down at his long, leather-framed desk. After pushing reading glasses over his ears, the lawyer looks over the document.

"We need you to read it so Ina can find out what he left her."

"He must have thought a lot of your family, Mrs. Palmer. He left the entire estate to your family. That includes his home, one thousand and ten acres of land, and nearly seven hundred thousand dollars."

I don't know what to say.

"I can make all necessary arrangements to transfer all capital to whatever account you like. What bank do you have an account with, Mrs. Palmer?"

"The First National here in town. It is a new account just opened today." These are words I am not accustomed to saying.

"All I need is an account number, and all will be transferred."

"In addition, I need to will all my estate to Ina and her family. Do you remember how much land I have?"

"Yes I do, Joni it's fifteen hundred acres adjacent to Roy Valentine's land. What are you and your husband going to do with that much land, Mrs. Palmer?"

"I don't know. But if I know my husband, he will have something in mind." *Oh, Jack! You are in for a surprise when you get back.* "Now that we are through, Joni, I have gotten hungry, how about you?"

"I will make sure every transaction is taken care of. And Ina, do you want me to handle the Palmer estate for your family?"

"Yes I do, Richard. Do whatever you need to settle matters. Before the day gets any later, Joni, let's get something to eat and go home."

It has been a long day.

"Yes. Let's do that before the evening crowd comes in."

"Joni, do you feel any stronger today? I was worried about you yesterday. Come take my hand so you don't fall and hurt yourself."

We walk out the door, get in the car, and drive away toward the Mill Hill Café.

"This time, Joni, I will play some music for you."

"Ina, I am so glad you have come into my life and happy I can do something for your family."

"Joni, I have great love for you also."

CHAPTER 37

"Dad, tomorrow morning we must leave this place, begin the trek back home." James stares across into the vast forest.

"I know, James. I know the great task ahead. Still, I fear a great change. Taking them out of their world and then indoctrinating them into our world will be an unimaginable undertaking. I hope Eve has chosen a successor to placate them until we can resolve their place in this new world we make for them. When they discover we are gone, I expect chaos to break out."

I speak to James. His placid face portrays a minor excursion. His trip back will be much more difficult. I fear a war might break out, followings closely behind us as we flee. *If they do bring a war to us, how close to the cabin are they willing to take it?* All that commotion coming from the back of the cavern; there are many of them back there, carrying on like crazy fools. When Eve takes her leave, their leader will know why.

"Dad, Eve is with the younger female now. You remember. We saw her earlier with Eve. This can't be something Eve recently come up with. It's all about nature taking a giant leap forward. Eve is afraid of the one I call Dab. He seems to be a troublemaker. He is the leader of many rebellious creatures."

I listen to him. James has a deep understanding of Eve's importance. I know he is a fast learner and now a teacher.

"Dad, I know she wants us to leave early morning, try to sneak out without creating a disturbance. Her two bodyguards will accompany us on our return."

James stands before me as the official voice of Eve.

"James, wake up, Son!" I roust him from his sleeping bag the next morning. "When will Eve come out to join us?"

He unzips his bag and then sits up. After taking a deep breath, he yawns, stretches, and rises to his feet. James points to a stony hill some distance away.

"Dad, they are already out, ready to get underway."

"What? Where? How did they get there without me seeing them?" Not even a snap of a twig did I hear, and I was so watchful."

James hastily shoves his feet into his boots and then rolls his bag up.

"We need to hurry, Dad. We cannot take any chances. We should put some distance between us and the others."

Glancing toward the quiet cave, Jim speaks up.

"He's right, Jack. No time to kill. We should get underway now."

Once again, Jim takes the lead with three mammoth creatures, one behind Eve, the other in front of her. James and I follow behind the creatures with Abe in tow. Trying to sneak away, we descend a rocky trail with the river off at a distance. We unlikely creatures—-are in a race to put as much distance as possible behind us before the cave dwellers besiege us. The creatures have long legs and keep stepping on Jim's heels. I know he is tired, but he must stay out of their way.

Seeing Jim's frustration, James asks, "How much farther is it to the river, Jim?"

Afraid of being run over, Jim gasps for air and then speaks.

"The river is still some distance away. If I can keep from being trampled, we will reach it in about thirty minutes."

Abe pulls back against the reigns and digs his hooves in with a loud bray. I look ahead to my son and Eve as they scramble quickly behind Jim.

While holding Eve's hand, James shouts in a serious tone of voice back my way.

"Dad, that's okay. One of the gargantuan creatures will carry him."

Under ordinary circumstances, I would take that as one of James's entertaining moments. Not this time, considering how powerful they are in appearance. One of them could tear a tree from the ground and discard it.

"Thank you, James. If it comes to that, I will truly take you up on that."

The creature in front of Eve suddenly stops. Smelling the air, he gestures toward the river.

"I smell it too," says Jim. "The smell of water, it won't be long now."

Finally, the glistening river lies before us. Rushing water flows over rocks and swirls into eddies along the opposite bank. We have reached the river, and none too soon. Abe's ears flop flat against his skull from exhaustion. He drops to his knees and then plunges his nose deep into the river, taking a long, breathless draw of water. With trembling legs, Abe stands up again under his tremendous load. I am so glad he did not collapse, requiring Eve or her guards to carry him. They stand lazily to the side of our unlikely group. The towering creatures seem unaffected by our hasty retreat.

As I sit, panting for breath on a large, flat rock, one of the enormous creatures studies my every movement. His stare is uninterrupted and intimidating, causing me to look away. The giant grunts, and he stands to his full stature of eight feet. Thumping his left hand against his reddish brown, hairy chest, the beast rumbles with a resonant, deep, throaty growl. James comes to my rescue, crawling to my side. He holds his head down low and whispers for me to follow his lead. The two of us crouch near the ground and find a place on the perimeter of our hasty resting spot. James looks down and refrains from glancing toward the male guards.

"Dad, you have to read them well. Those males are protecting Eve. You have to pay attention to them when you move around camp. Don't look at them in the face. If they look at you, look away."

James smiles and hugs me around the neck tightly. We creep cautiously around the riverbank and ready Abe for our departure. I hold his reigns tightly in my hands and consider the path ahead of us.

With Abe in toe, I follow behind the smelly beasts that walk before me. Jim is in the lead. Trying to keep up, even Jim is forced to lengthen his stride to keep from being trampled. Even so, between breaths, I still have a moment to ponder the skies. It's a bit windy, and I sense a change in weather. The wind is slowly starting to come out of the north. It can only mean another northerner is making its way southward—more snow. It's a bad time of the year to be caught on the river, but providence has it that I should be here. Through these great strides, great change is taking place.

The idea of change takes me back to Ina. She wants me to change the way we live. Dread, I am a bit frightful of the change I am bringing her now. Eve is now with us. How will Ina take her presence? At least Ina will not have to endure the male beasts. Thank God, I don't expect the two of them to stay. As it is, it will be most difficult to keep Eve hidden from the world. What I am doing is all so crazy. Sometimes I feel as if I don't know what I am doing. But James is right. Without us, they will become an extinct species before their existence is well known. I can see there is only one direction to move in. That is forward.

We move farther down our river trail toward our next point of civilization: the bridge at Shoals Junction. I hope that we will reach that point around sundown tomorrow. I can see why we were never able to catch up with James and the creatures. They are most certainly our masters. If Jim cannot hold his position in our trek back home, the powerful males will surely replace him. It is all Jim can do to stay ahead of them. Abe is driving me crazy. He does not like our hairy group members and does not want to move at this pace.

While in pursuit of James and his captors, we were not as driven as we are now to get back. Jim takes a quick look back my way.

Speaking aloud, he says, "Jack, I know they might be back there somewhere. It's all we can do to keep this pace. We will have to slow down. The creatures are used to this frightful hurry through the wilderness, but not us humans."

Jim is right. He having said that, I am reminded how weak we humans have become.

"I understand, Jim. Can we last a little while longer? They are starting to tire as well. Abe can sense it." It's better that way. Abe can take the blame if he is wrong.

"Okay. If that dumb animal says so, it must be so!" Jim shouts back his disapproval.

"James, can you slow them down just a little?"

"I will try, Dad."

James pulls away from Eve's hand and then drifts back away from her. Eve slows and then turns to see what he is doing. She knows what he wants. Eve slows down. Then, like a chain reaction, our little caravan is back measuring to a lesser giant's step.

Not that Jim is a giant. Just the same, next to the creatures, he is the tallest of us. Perhaps our return trip will be more manageable now that Eve is setting the pace. Eve suddenly stops. Looking behind us, her eyes open wide. Her nostrils flare, sniffing the air. Following her lead, the two males turn themselves around in unison. A gust of wind rustles trees and grass along the river's edge. Behind us, a large buck appears at the woods' border. Two mature doe run gracefully to the water, leaving the more cautious buck behind. The male guards watch Eve for the okay to attack. Ready for any response, the males will do whatever Eve wills. She snorts and looks away downriver. The female deer retreat into the forest woods' border.

I watch the gentle, brown doe raise their heads for a moment, flip their white tails up, and then scramble into the forest behind us.

I smile at James and say, "I guess they aren't hungry."

James smirks as he plods forward toward Eve. She is the real boss of this convoy.

Eve leads us on, with Jim fighting for his place as leader. Jim lags slightly behind, but the long-legged creature manages to stay several steps behind him. We race nearer with each step to the end of our travels. We know the rest of the clan plans to war with us for Eve. Each step closer to home brings us to safety. As we near the bridge, the Shoals Junction Bridge gives us confidence. My stomach growls, thinking of home with Ina, and a three-course meal topped off with some peach pie.

We are so close now I can almost smell Ina's biscuits. My mouth fills with watery anticipation. Suddenly, I realize the fragrant biscuit smell is a real, human-cooked meal. Alarm fills the air with an unknown presence. Eve and her counterparts are strangely absent. In the distance, faint voices drift downriver, and smoke hangs low over the water. Clearly we are about to come upon civilization sooner than expected.

Jim takes the lead, cautiously creeping around the next bend of the river. Putting his hand to his lips, Jim points in warning. The three of us crawl forward, parting the bushes enough to view the campsite on the sandbar. A small woman with yellow braids stirs a steaming pot. She leans over and lifts a spoon to her lips for a taste. Unexpectedly, the fair-haired woman looks up, staring directly in our direction. For a moment, she scans the edge of the woods and then locks eyes with me. I had forgotten about women's intuition.

She cries out with a startled, "Oh! Dad, we have visitors!"

Beckoning to us, she invites us into the camp's circle.

In the back portion of camp, the girl's father stands up and shouts, "We've been expecting you! You are almost overdue!"

Jim mutters under his breath, "Pesky reporters."

Now there are more humans on the river. Jim trusts our creature friends will remain hidden somewhere out of the way. He leads us into camp with his rifle across his chest.

The short, stout man pulls off his fishing hat with dangling lures and regards the disgruntled leader of our party. "Jim."

Jim's face cracks with a smirk. "Donald."

The vested reporter holds out his hand to me, saying, "Donald Castle, fisherman and reporter at large."

A smile spreads across his face as if somebody told a great joke. Distrustful of friendly people, I am suspicious of Donald's grin. You never know what is behind a smile. I make direct eye contact with him.

"Why are you still here?" I ask him as I lean the ten-gage against a tree beside me.

Jim sits in the dirt, warming his back next to the campfire.

"That is a good question, Donald. It seems too cold for a fishing trip."

The smile falls from Donald's face. He strikes me as a man used to charming his way into juicy stories. Trusting in his ability to influence, Donald speaks.

"My daughter and I were about to have supper. We made plenty, so why don't you join us?"

James quickly steps closer to the fire and grabs a bowl from the top of the stack. Donald eyes James with a big smile.

"Essie, get this young man a spoon and a cup of hot coco." The young woman obediently grabs a spoon from her pack along with a tin cup. Leaning over the campfire, she ladles steaming water into the cup.

Setting the cup on flat rock, she pops open the canister of Bosco with a large spoon, measuring several healthy doses into the cup. After stirring the contents, the chocolate fragrance fills James's nostrils. Essie hands him the cup and a spoon with a smile.

James's face turns a deep shade of red, and he mumbles, "Thanks."

Donald regards the interchange between his daughter and James as a success. Turning to Jim and Jack, he holds out two more bowls. "Is anyone else game for some supper?"

We watch James take a large mouthful of rabbit stew. For the moment, our growling stomachs rule over the danger lurking behind. Jim hastily takes a bowl and spoon from Donald's outstretched hands. He calls a truce between them, fills a bowl of stew, and begins to devour Essie's delectable dinner. Puzzled by the turn of events, I take my turn at the black stew pot bubbling over the fire. After one bite, Eve, her guards, and the pursuing creatures are a distant memory.

Silence rules the camp until the scraping of spoons against the bottom of the tin bowls breaks the spell. James sits close to Essie's side, taking occasional glances in her direction in between sips of his hot chocolate. Donald looks over James's tattered, dirty clothing. Turning to Jim, he demands, "Where did you pick up your young traveler?"

Jim scowls disagreeably. "It is none of your business. We will have to be on our way, and so should you and your daughter. Soon, we will be joined by others bent on vengeance."

I am surprised when Donald quickly begins to pack their belongings.

"How much time do we have?"

Jim looks at Donald's pale, alarmed face. "Not long, so you had better head out of here. Plan to travel light and fast." Jim turns around before leaving camp and disappearing into the woods, shouting with urgency, "Donald, you don't have time. Get your coats and leave the rest behind. Trouble is on its way!"

Some distance away, danger takes the form of a cave dweller bent on claiming his position. Left behind by Eve, he struggles to cope with change. Awake from a past night of human intervention, loyal followers respect him at arm's length. Poking at him, Eve's followers hold allegiance to their missing leader, inciting his wrath and determination. They regard him with caution and distrust. The coals of the dwindling fire glow dimly, releasing a sliver of smoke. Drifting upward, it escapes in a tendril toward the natural chimney and sky. The entire clan is edgy with indecision, fists, and shoulders tense with the division of allegiance between Eve and Dab. Dab, disillusioned by Eve's disappearance, knows she left the clan for a purpose. She will lead them all into a new way of living together with humans. Setting his jaw tightly, Dab shakes his fist at the opposition. Living in the shadows, eluding the humans, has always worked. With a snarl, Dab faces each of the clan. He stares into their dark, black eyes defiant with all his being.

Inside the cavern, twenty-five of Dab's warriors line the still-bloodied wall where the previous night the dark man strung up and prepared each deer carcass. Arms raised high, furious screams are directed at the far side of a safe sanctuary. The deafening sound reverberates from the rock walls traveling deep into the system of smaller caves. Though numerous, the larger clan of Eve's subjects cower under this murderous sound. Never before has the clan experienced such a division. Unsure of the best reaction, the clan considers that Dab's disobedience is best dealt with by Eve. He is like a wayward adolescent in need of subtle direction.

With a war cry, Dab leads the murderous mob. Infuriated, they pour out the mouth of the cavern. Striding around the clearing, he stops to breathe deeply. The stink of human prey fills his nostrils. The hairy giant crinkles his wide nose with disgust. The scent will be easy to follow. With a sharp cry, Dab gives the familiar signal for a kill. Twenty-five gigantic creatures storm the trail toward their prey. With an army at hand, this relentless general will wipe all memory of his clan from the humans and remove Eve from her throne.

Parting the bushes, I follow Jim as he steps into a clearing. The tracker peers into the woods, looking for movement. Disappointed, Jim sighs and picks up Abe's reins. Handing the leather straps to me, Jim watches James step noiselessly to join him. Abruptly, Jim speaks his mind.

"Soon, Abe will have to go his own way. He leaves a strong scent behind and will soon lead a path straight to us."

The harness feels warm and familiar in my hand. He knows Abe will surely slow the following creatures down. A tasty morsel, the beasts will abandon pursuit long enough for a meal.

"It will be too bad to let Abe die that way. He deserves better than that."

I have held tightly to Abe's rein since we left the Shoals Junction Bridge. However, Jim is right. Loosening his cinch, I set the burdensome beast free to a predictable demise. I hope his death comes with a heavy blow, not slowly and painfully. Now, we have one objective in mind: our rendezvous with Eve at the bridge.

Eve is not far away from her weary human counterparts. James is important to her kind. He is not within eyesight. Just the same, her strong natural instincts sense where he is at all times. With her quiet, soft grunts, the powerful curves in her aggressive body language signal superiority over the pair of colossal giants to do as she bids. Eve will go to no end to protect James, even kill her kind.

Jim turns his face into the cold wind. Breathing deeply through his nostrils, he detects a familiar scent. Crinkling his brow, Jim frowns with obvious concern. Jack has followed the tracker long enough to read his face. Jim takes his cigar from his mouth and turns to face his two charges.

"Creatures lurk not far upwind, not sure if it's James's friend or not."

James's face takes on a look of confidence mixed with relief.

"That would be Eve. She likes to keep me close like my mother."
Jim smiles and chuckles.

"Can't get away from your mama, can you, boy?"

A gust of wind hits the band, blasting the group nearly off their feet. Jim's hat flies off in an upward spin. A strong, musky odor fills the clearing with a warning of danger impossible to ignore. It is the dangerous musk of more than one angry male beast.

Jim catches his hat before it hits the ground and gruffly growls, "Time to hit the trail hard, men."

The two beasts follow closely behind Eve. They plod lightly with hairy feet through the shale and river rocks along the water. She stops suddenly, turns upriver, and stands alert. Without moving, all her senses stand at attention. Even the hairs on her neck flare out. Without flinching, Eve stands in stillness for a length of time. Motherly instinct urges her to turn back. The soft, hairless, young man responsible for this adventure is vulnerable to Dab's rage. Dab's scent is getting stronger as he and his followers near.

Dab is some distance behind. Just the same, Eve knows how quickly the rebellious young creature can appear. Her instincts tell her to turn back and confront him. However, the humans are not far behind; and soon, they will rendezvous with her at the Shoals Junction Bridge. Dab has no interest with encountering humans at any location. Even he will like nothing better than passing by the bridge with no humans in sight.

Eve and her bodyguards plod ahead of the humans on their way to the first bridge. Driven by fear and anticipation, they drive forward over water-worn rocks. Silently, the three creatures stride toward their goal. Eve trusts the dark man will see to James's safety. The big man is not weak or soft. His scent is not only human, but Eve senses him to be part creature as well. For the time being, Eve leaves her young human to the protection of this dark man.

The humans pursue Eve, following her path to the rendezvous point. A three quarter moon glistens over the water and river rock.

Jim takes long, hurried steps along the river without concern for stealth. Brittle shale rock crunches under their feet as the river rushes over rocks. Jim concentrates on the immediate goal of passing the bridge without human or creature intervention. Glancing behind, the dark man turns his head to make sure James and Jack are keeping pace. They scramble behind without complaint, puffing moist breaths of vapor into the frigid night air.

Abe sits in the hedges bordering the small clearing. Only a campfire remains after the humans left. It smolders as the cooling embers release a small wisp of smoke toward the starry sky. Abe, unconcerned for his safety, chews a mouthful of dry grass contentedly. Thankful for a chance to rest at last, the brown donkey closes his eyes and slowly drifts into sleep. Suddenly, the sound of rustling bushes and crunching limbs in the distance startles Abe from his slumber. His ears turn forward with alarm as the danger nears the clearing. Surrounded, Abe trembles with fear. Animals grunt with the heat of pursuit and the power of numbers. Pouring into the clearing, the angry beasts are filled with the need to kill. Dab steps quickly between the creatures and Abe. However, the instinct to kill in the group of creatures is stronger than loyalty to their leader. Dab, perceiving the turn of events, roars murderously and paces along the ranks of his disobedient army. The powerful creatures lose their muster and look away from Dab's irate glare. Abe still shivers in the clearing as he watches the group continue their thundering pursuit through the forest.

Eve stops as she nears the bridge. A rage-filled scream drifts in the icy night breeze. She turns her ear upriver, gauging the distance between herself and Dab. The faction mob is nearing, but Eve sighs with relief. The boy should soon join her and leave enough time to escape Dab. Leading the guards into hiding, Eve climbs the rocky embankment of the bridge. Under the recess of the concrete overhang, Eve retreats into the dark shadows. The three of them sit closely together for warmth and lie in wait.

Jim slows down, gazing at the welcoming landmark ahead. Stepping cautiously toward the bridge, he peers nervously into the shadows. A faint animal musk draws Jim's attention. Relief floods his voice as he turns back to James and Jack. "Come on, men. We should rejoin the rest of our crew."

Surprised, James looks at his dad with a puzzled expression. "You think they are already here?"

Jim explains, "There is no mistaking that musky odor."

Peering into the shadows, James calls out softly to Eve. Slowly, she advances from the shadow of the bridge, waving shyly at James. The two male guards flank beside her; and together, they descend the embankment. A quiet human voice echoes from upstream. Eve flinches with dismay as two lone hikers step into the meeting area. Too late to hide, Eve remains standing close beside James.

Jim scowls and turns to Donald and his daughter. "I thought we agreed that you and Essie would go home."

Donald smiles. "Well, you know how curious reporters can be."

Furious, Jim retorts, "This is where you live. You are better off going home to Shoals Juction. If you don't care about yourself, at least think of Essie."

Donald's face remains stubbornly aloof. Not easily discouraged, he observes the three calm beasts. One of them absently scratches his shoulder while gazing at the iron bridge.

Essie is the kind of girl who hopes to assume her fathers roll. Ever the curious reporter, she stares at Eve and James with open amazement. If her dad listens to Jim, they will return home without the best scoop ever.

"Dad, I want to see this through."

She stands perfectly still and observes the tall, hair-covered creature flanked by two aggressive, bulky guards. Essie smiles and looks into the male's eyes. Taking the smile as a threat, they lunge forward with a throaty growl.

James warns her, "Don't look at them! Turn your head and sit down now!"

No longer smiling, Essie complies with the abrupt command. She turns her wide, fear-filled eyes toward Jim. Donald gasps with surprise. To frighten to speak, he stands quietly at attention to the side. Jim smiles wryly.

"What is it Donald? You don't have anything eloquent to say?"

Jim steps in close toward Essie once the creatures retreat back to Eve's side. Holding out his hand, he takes the small woman's soft hand and helps her to her feet. Escorting Essie back to Donald's side, Jim makes one more attempt to reason with her.

"Young lady, there is a good chance that if you continue to follow us, you and your dad will not make it to the end of the trail. Those two males over there are the friendly creatures. Close behind us are murderous giants hell-bent on killing us all. Your best chance is to make a quick getaway to Shoals Juction."

The young woman tersely responds, "Thank you, kind sir. But wherever Dad goes, I follow."

Donald steps in closer to Jim. "So, where are we headed?"

Angrily chewing on his cigar, Jim is unaccustomed to taking no for an answer.

"If you follow, I cannot be responsible for what might happen."

Donald nods with agreement. Jim notices a hungry look in the blue-eyed reporter as he roves across the three red-haired creatures accompanying James. Eve darts her eyes upriver and shuffles her feet impatiently, sniffing the wind. Taking her cue, Jim throws his rifle over his shoulder, turns to his crew, and calls out marching orders.

"Let's hit the trail hard, people, before our uninvited guests catch up with us."

Jim swiftly takes the trail downriver, away from the Shoals Junction Bridge. Donald and Essie lag behind, unaccustomed to the fast pace.

"Time is wasting away, people, and the Maddox Bridge is just five miles away."

James sighs with relief, picturing his cabin and a home-cooked meal. *Mom will throw together a welcome-home breakfast.* As they run along the path, evidence of civilization begins to show along the river. Old fishing nets, bait containers, and tin cans begin to litter the banks. In the distance, James hears a tractor chugging along the Maddox Bridge. James imagines a farmer up with the chickens, spreading hay for the cattle in the lowlands.

Essie has adjusted to the physical requirements of their flight and now glides effortlessly alongside James and the three creatures. The sky is beginning to lighten at the horizon. The moon lingers behind the group, barely illuminating the trail ahead. Not far ahead, the large, iron bridge looms with its sturdy, secure, iron supports. Donald struggles to gain speed and catch up with Jim.

Huffing with the effort, the reporter gasps, "What comes next after reaching the bridge?"

Jim grimaces with the mention of the word *we*.

"Donald, you will head to the General Store and we will head to the cabin."

Scoffing in response, Donald argues, "We can't separate now. There is strength in numbers, and you have to face the facts. Essie and I are here to stay. Besides, we would never make the store before the creatures kill Essie and me."

Eve suddenly halts in her approach to the bridge. Sniffing the air, she detects a strong, musky odor. Noticing Eve's alarm, Jim turns around to face the path behind. Peering into the shadowy woods, Jim perceives an enormous silhouette lurking in the darkness. The large, angry male steps into the cold moonlight with a fearsome grin showing his sharp incisors.

Jim calls out in alarm, "People, we are not alone. Be on alert. Keep moving toward the bridge. I will hold them off."

Soon, more enraged creatures join their leader in a massive, volatile horde. As the massive creatures swarm into the clearing, Jim knows that soon, no retreat will be possible. Resolute in his decision, Jim firmly lifts his rifle and a thunderous boom fills the valley as he fires his first warning shot. Some of the creatures retreat, scattering into the darkness. Eve screams with anguish toward Dab. Her scream is filled with a desperate plea of a leader not wanting to see any of her kind die. Dab only yells furiously back, beating his chest in defiance. More creatures pour out into the faint moonlight from their sudden retreat. Surging forward, the army begins to build again in threatening numbers. Once more, Eve pleads with them all in a disappointed wail. A small number of the undecided creatures turn back toward the mountains.

The still-great numbers that remain pursue the three creatures and James. Jim watches impatiently as the rest of the group scrambles toward the hillside leading up to the cabin. James pulls a reluctant Eve along the trail. The sun begins to light the horizon with a pink and yellow glow. The light illuminates a growing crowd of reddish brown creatures. They cluster together menacingly around Dab, who lead them in pursuit of Eve and James. Left without a choice, Jim fires one more time into the angry, pulsing mob.

Rocks splay into their faces as Jim calls out urgently, "Jack, I need a little help with your cannon."

At the top of the hill, Jack stops to retrieve two shells from his pocket. Loading both barrels with shaking hands, he turns, decisively aiming the Belgium. James turns briefly, placing his fingers firmly in his ears as a deafening thunder rumbles through the valley. Creatures scatter into the receding darkness.

Eve stares dispassionately into the coming dawn. Pungent, sulfurous smoke drifts from the barrel of Jack's gun. Eve slumps in resignation and follows her young man. James still holds Eve's hand as he turns toward the welcoming cabin. Ina spots her son from the front porch and takes a plunging jump into the deep snow. Without thought, she runs downhill toward James. The unlikely group slowly begins to hike up the remainder of the hillside. Eve pauses briefly at the edge of the flat pasture with rustling yellow grass.

Suddenly uncertain, Eve resists James as he pulls her onward. Ina stands with one hand over her mouth, gripping the porch banister with white knuckles. Joni opens the squeaky screen door to join the welcome. With frail hands, she straightens her collar.

"I told you they would be back soon. I have a way of knowing these things. Your James looks like he needs a good bath and a meal."

Eve's massive, hairy form overpowers James's small frame as the two companions step into the yard. Ina steps closer to James and kneels with outstretched arms. Releasing his creature mother, James runs to Ina, into her warm embrace. I approach my wife with trepidation, ready for her disapproval. Ina stands to her full stature, hands on hips and voice sharp with accusation. Ina is the protective matriarch of this family.

"Jack Palmer, what have you brought home with you?"

Too angry to feel fear, Ina looks into Eve's wide unblinking eyes. James is pleased when his mother's stare fails to produce the usual show of aggression.

Taking Ina by the hand, James pulls his mother close to the shy Eve.

"James, what on earth are you doing?"

Without heeding his mother's shrieks, James firmly takes Eve's hand.

"Mom, I want you to meet Eve. She is responsible for keeping me alive in the wilderness, and now she needs our help. Will you let us help her?"

I ponder James's innocent face. The lines on his thin face have taken an unfamiliar character. Suddenly, I feel that James is not the same boy I once mothered. Reflecting back to the summer before, I remember when James stood on the porch in that same spot with bare feet and a suntan. Cuddling a smelly, tick-infested, and half-starved puppy in his arms, James begged me to keep the animal.

"James, I think your creatures should go back to wherever they belong."

Looking at Eve, I cross my arms and consider the hulking animals with burr-matted hair. All I can think of right now is that dirty stray James carried home last summer.

"James, it would be just another thing for me to clean up after. Besides that, they look dangerous, and we have no place to keep them. How do you hope to help them? They appear to be doing okay." After hearing all the arguments, I know they are empty. With a deep sigh, I press my lips together in resignation. "Okay, Jack. What are we going to do with them?"

Now it is safe to approach my wife. Placing my arms around her thin waist, I look into her face.

"We are going to keep them secret, give them a refuge from the world. Are you with us on this, Ina? I can't do it alone."

Ina's brow furrows with uncertainty.

"Why don't you lock the creatures in Mr. Valentine's barn?"

Turning to Jim, Ina holds out her hand.

"Thanks for bringing back my son and husband. Come inside for a meal and tell me all about your adventure."

The sun breaks out over the house as the bedraggled group stomps dirt from their feet and enters the warm cabin; an adventure ended and a new one begun.

G. D. Parham